Face Off

TEAGAN HUNTER

For Pam, Melinda, Jeff, Laurie, and T. Estes.
You know why.

Chapter 1

LAWSON

Me: I have to tell you guys something big…

Fox: Oh fuck. What'd you do?

Locke: Please tell me this isn't something we're going to get a brief about.

Hutch: Is this something your captain should know before the rest of the group?

Me: *CLUB

Me: You meant the rest of the club.

Me: And you're not the captain yet, Not Captain. Not until the new year.

Locke: He might not have debuted the C yet, but it's happening, and we all know it. He's captain.

Hutch: Yeah, what Locke said. And while we're clarifying things, we are not a fucking club.

Hayes: I was told we were a club.

Keller: You don't count, new guy.

Hayes: Not true. Lawson made me prick my finger with a needle for my blood and everything.

Fox: We were supposed to do that? Because I never did. Does that mean I'm not really part of the club?

Hutch: Fucking hell.

Hutch: For the last time…THAT IS NOT A THING WE DO, AND WE ARE NOT A CLUB.

Locke: Unsanctioned blood oaths aside, we really have to face the facts: it's starting to look like a club, Hutch.

Hutch: Not. A. Club.

Hayes: Buzz. Kill.

Me: I'm with Hayes on that. Hutchy is a buzzkill, and we are totally a club.

Hutch: Don't make me pull the captain card on you…

Me: Oooh, I'm terrified.

Keller: Are you two going to keep arguing, or are you going to get to your point soon, Lawson? Some of us have shit to do.

Me: Oh, I'm sorry. Am I getting in the way of your sulking, Keller?

Keller: *middle finger emoji*

Hutch: I'm with Keller here. Out with it already.

Me: Fine...

Me: PARROTS MASTURBATE

Hutch: What in the actual fuck is wrong with you?

Locke: That was not at all what I was expecting.

Fox: Wow. That was...a piece of information I'm not sure I ever needed to hear.

Fox: Say it again.

Me: Parrots masturbate.

Keller: Nope. No. I'm out.

Hayes: Wait. How do you even know this?

Fox: ^ What he said

Fox: Have you, like, SEEN it?

Me: Don't be fucking weird, Foxy.

Me: I'm sitting at a bar, and I overheard this guy telling his buddies about his brother's pet parrot who got attached to him and literally masturbated to death.

Keller: That's not possible.

Me: I thought you left?

Keller: You've reeled me back in. Congrats.

Fox: I need more information on this. For example, HOW? WHY? WHEN? WHERE? And most importantly… WHAT THE FUCK?

Hayes: That pretty much sums up all my questions, too.

Locke: I really feel like this group chat has gotten out of control. Want to rein it back in, Captain?

Hutch: I've got nothing. I'm at a loss for words after that shit.

Hutch: This is all you, Locke. I have a super-hot girlfriend waiting for me. We're baking cookies.

Me: WHILE YOU'RE TEXTING? GROSS!

Hutch: That wasn't a euphemism for sex, you moron. We are literally baking Christmas cookies.

Me: Booooooo!

Me: Boring old Hutchy, all tied down and not even in the sexy way.

Hutch: Fuck off, Lawsy.

Me: Nah.

Me: Also, are you even allowed to be part of the club anymore? You're not single...

Fox: That's an excellent point.

Keller: If we're voting people out, go ahead and write me down for nixing Lawsy.

Me: Dick.

Keller: And proud of it.

Hayes: Wait...if we start dating someone, we can't be in the club anymore?

Fox: Appears so.

Hutch: How about nobody gets kicked out because we're not a fucking club.

Me: Aww, you like us. You wanna stay.

Locke: Just dug your own grave, Hutch.

Fox: You SO like us.

Hayes: He REALLY likes us.

Keller: You can not like me. I'm good with that.

Me: Wow. You're like SO cool, Keller.

Keller: Wow. You're like SO fucking annoying, Lawson.

Me: Admit it, you miss me.

Keller: Not a chance in hell.

Hutch: Would you all just shut up? This conversation has taken a weird turn.

Locke: Parrots masturbating not weird enough for you?

Hutch: Oh, that was incredibly weird, and I'm recommending Lawson for a psych eval when we get back.

Me: GASP! You would never!

Hutch: GASP! I would too!

Hutch: Now, everyone (ESPECIALLY YOU, LAWSON), please shut the fuck up so I can spend time with my girlfriend.

Me: Ooooh. Hutch and Auden sitting in a tree...

Fox: K-I-S-S-I-N-G

Hayes: First comes love...

Keller: Gross.

Me: Then comes marriage...

Keller: Extra gross.

Fox: Then comes a baby in a baby carriage!

Keller: Absolutely vile.

Hutch: I hate you all.

Keller: Ditto.

Me: Can't wait to see you all after Christmas break!

Keller: Delete my number.

Me: Not a chance. *kissy face emoji*

I laugh, shaking my head at my teammates.

It's no secret I wasn't too pleased I was left unprotected in the expansion draft and was picked up by the newest team in the NHL, the Seattle Serpents. I gave St. Louis my all for three years, but it was never good enough. Not good enough for the coach, my fans, or my teammates, and apparently not good enough to keep around either.

The Serpents were my chance to start over, and the very first thing I did was make sure I bonded with my team and let them know I'm not just here for hockey—I'm here for them, too. While I consider all my teammates to be friends, I'm closest with the guys in the group chat. Being the only single dudes on the team, we quickly gravitated toward one another and started a group chat to keep in touch easily. Now, these knuckleheads couldn't get rid of me if they tried.

"Another round, Lawson?"

I glance up at the bartender, Chaz, who has been generously serving me and the rest of the bar all evening by himself. Given that it's Christmas Eve, it's not busy, but I'm sure he's still taking time away from his family to be here with all these other lonely assholes.

I look down at my nearly empty beer. I've already had three, and that's usually my limit in public, but it's a holiday, so why not? Besides, I'm not driving. I'm good.

"Sure, and you can close my tab out too."

"You got it, man."

Chaz pours another lager, then slides my card and

receipt to me, and I'm unsurprised to see he's given me happy hour prices. He usually does, even though he knows I don't need his discounts. He's just that good of a dude.

I continue my eavesdropping as I sip on my last beer. The parrot guys are long gone, having taken their highly informative conversation elsewhere, leaving a few stragglers and me behind. I catch pieces of stories about the Vietnam War and a sad one about a woman planning to divorce her abusive husband. I want to lean over and high-five her for it, but I know I shouldn't intrude.

Instead, I keep my opinions to myself, letting my eyes wander around the sports bar, appreciating all the Serpents memorabilia hanging on the walls, some of which I donated myself. Though I'm sure most people wouldn't believe it thanks to all the rumors surrounding me, I don't spend much time out partying. But this place? This place feels like a little bit of home. I suppose that's not entirely surprising since I practically grew up running around a bar in Colorado while my mother poured drink after drink for the locals.

I'm sure that's why I gravitated here tonight. I was unconsciously nostalgic for home since I'm not returning during the break like I usually do.

I toss cash onto the bar for Chaz, add enough to

cover the tabs of everyone else hunkered down here, and then take my leave. I push open the doors of Top Shelf and step into the cold December air, tugging my jacket closer around me. The air smells faintly of impending snowfall, and I hope we don't get too much of it. Trying to drive in the snow on these hills is a bitch, and I have big plans to take in a movie tomorrow.

Holiday music plays from several shops as I walk along the mostly empty streets, everyone else tucked safe and warm inside with their families. Not me. I was getting antsy at home by myself. I had to get out of my apartment, even if just for a little bit.

Usually, I'd be back home at this point, huddled under piles of blankets while a cheesy movie plays in the background, my mother feeding me too many cookies and hot chocolate while we wait for Christmas morning to come, but she's on a trip with her best friend to the Bahamas. I schemed for months with Lydia to make it happen. I knew full well my mother would never accept a gift like that from me—hell, she turned down a new house—so I knew I had to go through her best friend to make it happen. Even though I'm alone on Christmas, I'm glad I did it. She's already been sending me pictures, looking happier than I've seen her in a long time.

I could call my father and see what he's up to, but

I'm sure he's wrapped up in whatever his newest wife has planned for him. After separating, I thought they would call it quits, but they surprised me by sticking it out. For now, at least.

There's always crashing my half brother's break, but I'm sure he's busy with his girlfriend and her kid in North Carolina.

Of course, I could call up one of the other Serpents Singles and bother them until they agreed to hang with me, but they all seem to be busy with their own stuff. Hutchinson—or Hutch as we all call him—is off with his new billionaire babe somewhere. Locke is out of town spoiling his ten thousand nieces and nephews. Fox is back home with his family like the good son he is, Hayes is doing whatever he does, and Keller, who would have certainly been my last option, has plans, too. It's the only reason I was sitting in the bar feeling like the star of a Celine Dion music video about being alone.

God, I have to get out of this funk.

Nothing a night rolling in the sheets can't fix, I'm sure.

I pull out my phone, scrolling through the list of saved names to find someone, hovering over a few. Niki would let me come over and help keep her bed warm on this cold December night. Ashley wouldn't even let the first ring finish; she would answer immediately and demand I come over ASAP. And I bet even Jo, who I haven't talked to in three months after slipping out of her bed in the wee hours of the morning and have since effectively ignored, would pick up, and *not* just to tell me off.

But none of those options are enticing enough to get me to tap the screen.

I don't know why, either. One-night stands and short flings are my thing, but lately, I'm not as into it as I once was. Maybe it's the time of year, or perhaps it's the pact I made with the guys to focus solely on hockey this year. It's not like Hutch stuck to that deal now that he's gone and fallen in love with Auden, but I'm not a flake like him. I intend to see this vow all the way through. I want that Cup, and nobody is important enough to distract me from achieving my dream.

I slip my phone back into my pocket as I take long strides toward my empty apartment for another night of flipping through Netflix until I finally click on something I've already watched a hundred times. Maybe I'll mix in a glass of good bourbon tonight because why not?

See? Pathetic.

A loud clang echoes off the buildings as I pass a dark alley. I've seen my fair share of horror movies in my twenty-six years, but that doesn't stop me from pausing and straining to hear what's happening.

Another clang. A soft whimper.

I should walk away. I know I should. I should call the authorities and let them handle this.

But…

I move into the alley, taking two tentative steps before stopping again when I hear another distressing whimper. It's a familiar sound, but I can't place what it is.

Another step, another soft whine.

I keep this up, getting closer and closer to where the sound is coming from until I hear something *entirely* different.

A growl.

I stop because it's close—too close.

I turn right. There's a dumpster, a few pieces of cardboard, and some trash scattered about. Another clang, this time coming from right in front of me, and I jump back as fear races through me. I see it as I'm about to turn and run like a big, totally macho man.

A puppy.

It's a tiny, chestnut-brown little thing, and the only reason I can spot it in the shadows is because of the bright blue eyes staring up at me with a mix of trepidation and helplessness.

"Oh. Hi," I say stupidly as if the thing can understand me.

I take a step closer, and the puppy lets out another

soft growl, this time sounding much less menacing and much cuter than before. Crouching down, I reach out for the dog to show it I'm friendly.

"Hey there, buddy," I murmur softly. "I'm here to help you, that's all."

The puppy's eyes flick from my outstretched hand to my face, then back to my hand. It inches closer, its little body shaking and struggling to rise off the ground.

My heart fucking breaks.

I let the puppy take its time coming to me, coaxing it with soft words every step of the way until I'm certain it won't run, then I scoop it into my hand and bring it to my chest, tucking my new friend into my jacket for the warmth I'm sure it so desperately needs.

I run my finger over the pup's nose and up between its ears. It whimpers at my touch, pressing into my hands and seeking the comfort I'm providing. Fuck if it doesn't make me the perfect combination of sad and pissed off. I genuinely hope this is just a case of a dog sneaking out of the house and this sweet baby isn't out here because some asshat dumped it.

I push up to my full height and pull my phone from my pocket, searching for the nearest and best animal clinic to get the puppy somewhere safe and warm. Luckily, one not too far from me is open for a little longer.

I hit the navigate button, then follow the directions it calls out for the next ten minutes, turning this way and that way, hoping like hell they're still open by the time I get there. The snow that was clinging to the air has started falling, and it's coming down fast and thick. There has to be a quarter inch on the ground already. I need shelter, not just for the little thing in my arms, but for me.

The building comes into view as I round yet another corner, and I pick up my pace, breezing by an older man carrying a rust-colored Dachshund. I'm running out of time, and it's getting late, most places having already closed their doors for the night. Even if I took the pup home, I have no supplies and no indication if it's healthy. I'm barely equipped to care for myself, let alone take care of a puppy that's probably on the verge of hypothermia.

A woman in green scrubs is walking up to the door as I approach. Our eyes connect. I dart my gaze down to where the dog is tucked into my jacket, and the woman frowns. She pushes the door open, and the warmth of the veterinary office smacks against my cheeks almost instantly.

"We're closed, but there's an animal hospital a few blocks over," the woman says, pointing in the direction of the other clinic I most certainly am *not* going to.

I gnash my teeth, irritated she would try to turn me away. "I fou—"

"Our office opens back up at six AM on the twenty-sixth."

Is this lady serious? She can't be.

"Please, I—"

She attempts to close the door, but thanks to all my years of playing hockey, I'm much faster than she is. I shove my foot against it, blocking her from closing it farther.

"Sir—"

"You don't understand," I interrupt. "I found a puppy in the alley, and it needs attention. It won't stop shivering. I think the thing has hypothermia, and it's probably thirsty and hungry, and I don't know what else. I need help."

"I understand that, but we're closed."

I groan. "So you've said, but I—"

"Sir, please calm down. You can go up the street to—"

"Let him in."

The eyes of the woman in front of me grow to about twice their size, and her back goes straight. She turns her head to look behind her at the other person who has spoken.

"But—"

"Let. Him. In."

The employee blocking the entrance huffs, then steps aside, letting me into the warm office. I hurry in, wiping my wet feet on the welcome mat.

"Thank you. I'm sorry to come in so late. It's just—"

I lift my head and realize what a big mistake this night has been. This isn't just a random veterinary clinic, and that isn't just a random veterinarian staring at me with sharp, bright green eyes. This place belongs to Rory Sinclair, the twin sister of my teammate's girlfriend.

She's standing right in front of me.

And she hates me.

Chapter 2

My ideal Christmas Eve would be spent sitting in front of a fire, wrapped tightly in my softest blanket with my hands curled around a cup of peppermint tea and my favorite holiday film playing in the background while Hades, my cat, sits at my feet.

It just so happens that tonight is Christmas Eve, and I'm doing none of that. I'm still at the clinic, trying to convince my ever-faithful client, Mr. Duhaime, his dog does *not* need his anal glands expressed simply because Petey licked his butthole.

"I understand Petey was licking himself, but his glands are fine. I checked him at his appointment last month and just looked again. His glands are doing exactly what they need to do. Petey is perfectly healthy."

Mr. Duhaime—who, if I'm being honest, is a bit of

a pain in the ass sometimes—opens his mouth to argue, but I'm guessing my hard stare does its job because he snaps it back shut.

"I promise, Mr. Duhaime, Petey's fine," I say more softly this time. "I would never, ever put my patients at risk. I'd tell you if I were worried or thought you should be worried."

That earns me a smile.

"Thank you, Dr. Sinclair." He gives me a crooked grin, the wrinkles on his cheeks deepening.

"Rory," I remind him, even though I know it's pointless. He's been coming here for years, and no matter how many times I've asked, he refuses to call me by my first name. It's both endearing and annoying.

"I'm just glad Petey's okay. I know I worry, but he's all I have. After my kids moved away and we lost Betty…" He shakes his head solemnly, his gray hair—still full and lush—moving right along with him.

I know all this too. He tells me every time he comes in, which is entirely too often. His children live only an hour away, and though Betty might sound like his wife, she was the calico cat he lost over five years ago. His wife divorced him about fifteen years back because he cheated with his much younger secretary.

"She was feisty, and I'm sure she misses you as much as you miss her."

"Yeah, yeah. I know." He waves me off with a grin. "Are we all good here?"

"Yep. I recommend keeping an eye on Petey."

"I thought you said—"

"He's fine," I assure him. "I only meant giving him extra love for Christmas."

I shoot the older man a wink, and he laughs heartily.

"Always such a flirt, Dr. Sinclair."

As frustrating as he can be sometimes, I like Mr. Duhaime fine, but there is no way in hell I'd ever flirt with him. Not only because he's older than my father, but because I don't flirt. At all. Ever.

Just like I don't do relationships. Neither is my thing. I'm perfectly content being the zany cat lady all my life if it means I get to avoid the same pining and heartbreak I had to watch my father suffer over the years thanks to my mother. Love and relationships lead to nothing but agony, and I'll keep my feelings locked up tight where I can control what happens to my heart, thank you very much.

"You got me," I deadpan, but he doesn't pick up on the sarcasm. He just keeps grinning as I lead him out of the room and back to the front lobby.

I hand Petey's folder to Casey, my tech helping close the clinic tonight, then crouch down.

"You be good, okay, buddy?" I say to Petey,

running my hand over his head and scratching behind his ears like I know he likes.

He drags his tongue over my hand, his way of saying *Thanks for putting up with my dad's shit, Doc.*

"Thanks again for seeing us tonight. I'm sure you have much better things to do on Christmas Eve than entertain an old coot like me."

I chuckle. "It was no problem. That's what I'm here for, and there's no place I'd rather be than here."

I mean those words with my whole chest. This business is my baby, and taking care of it is priority number one because helping animals is my calling. I was meant to do this, and I'd give up all the Christmas Eves in the world to keep doing it. I'm not a people person by any stretch of the imagination, but give me an animal in need any day, and my heart pours open like a fresh cut.

I don't know exactly when my love of animals started. Maybe when I was five? My twin sister, Auden, found a wounded squirrel on the brink of death and immediately ran to my father to "fix" it. His solution and mine didn't exactly line up, and I won when he faced grouchy five-year-old me. He gave me that squirrel, took us both to the vet, and I got to watch as the doctor performed a miracle and brought that little thing back to life.

Right then, I knew what I wanted to do with my

life—I wanted to fix animals *my* way, and that's precisely what I've been doing, building this place day by day, year by year, long night after long night. Now, we're the best clinic in the Seattle area, and my second location on the opposite side of the peninsula is the second best.

These are all things I'm proud of, but it also means I work myself to the bone. Case in point, we're minutes from closing, and I have at least another hour's worth of paperwork to complete before I can call it a night.

"See you later, Doc," Mr. Duhaime calls as he files out the door with Petey in tow.

I send him a wave and a grin, which quickly turns into a frown when I get my first glimpse of the outside world since the sun went down.

"Is it supposed to snow the rest of the night?"

"Yes."

"Crap." I sigh. "All right. Let's get this place locked up, then hit the road."

"On it."

I head for my office as Casey crosses to the front door. I begin mentally going through the paperwork waiting for me. I need to read over some charts and arrange for flowers to be sent to the Johnsons, who recently lost their cat. Then I need to—

Two voices carry through the clinic, and I slow, straining to make out what they're saying.

"*Please*," a deep voice says, the desperation evident even from here.

I make my way out into the hall, inching back to the front lobby, where I can now clearly hear Casey refusing service to the customer, and it has my blood boiling. I made a rule when I decided to buy the clinic, and Christmas Eve or not, I'm sticking to it. We don't turn anyone away. It doesn't matter if the door is locked for the night. If I'm here and someone comes for help, I'm helping them.

"Let him in," I instruct, interrupting her trying to send him up the street to the shitty clinic I can't believe is still running.

"But—"

I grind my teeth. "Let. Him. In."

She lets out a grumble but steps aside. The man walks past her, head down, stomping his snow-covered feet on the rug I've replaced so many times over the years when it gets too stained to keep around.

"Thank you. I'm sorry to come in so late. It's just…"

The words trail off as the stranger lifts his head.

Because this isn't a stranger. Not at all. This is someone I know.

Someone I hate.

Fine, maybe I don't hate *him*, but I certainly hate everything he is—a total playboy who thinks he's God's gift to women. It's obvious in how he carries himself, that swagger that says, *Hey, look at what you're missing out on, ladies.* How he lets his deep brown hair lie all chaotically like he doesn't have a care in the world. And that grin of his that promises he'll do dirty, dirty things to you, but only if he deems you worthy of his attention.

I know guys like him far too well, and I want nothing to do with them. Why he's in my clinic, I don't know. All I know is I want him gone.

I cross my arms over my chest, swallowing back an agitated sigh. "Lawson."

A smile overtakes his face, putting on display bright white, perfectly straight teeth that I am sure are fake. They have to be, right? He's a hockey player. No way he has teeth that good looking playing in the NHL.

"Well, isn't this a nice surprise," he says in that voice of his that's just a little gruff.

"I think our definitions of nice are entirely different."

Somehow, his smile grows. "You sure about that, *Rory?*"

I hate how he says my name like it's familiar to him. Like it's a name he's said a hundred times before, even though I only met him two days ago at a hotel bar when he and his band of hockey bros worked together to get my sister and her boyfriend back together. It was a nice gesture if you're into that sort of thing, but it was also enough for me to know I don't like this guy. At all.

"What do you want, Lawson?"

He reaches into his jacket, and even though I have no idea what I expect him to pull out, it certainly isn't a tiny Labrador puppy. He holds the dog up like this is *The Lion King* and he's showing off his cub, and I swear the pitiful thing frowns at me as it shivers in his grasp.

I cross the room instantly, taking the shuddering pup into my own hands, working overtime to tell my heart to stop doing what it's doing. I will *not* get weepy over this dog, especially not in front of Lucas Lawson. I try not to laugh at his ridiculous name and focus solely on the animal that needs my help.

"Who is this little lady?" I ask, bringing the dog to my chest.

"It's a girl?"

"She sure is. And I'm guessing, based on her weight, she's around six to eight weeks old, right?"

He lifts a shoulder, his eyes not straying from the shivering dog, who has now added soft whimpers to the mix. I need to get her warm and fast.

"Come on." I turn and head for the exam rooms, following behind the now highly motivated Casey, who I'm sure has picked up on my frustration with her.

"I don't know how old she is or anything about her.

I just found her," Lawson tells me as we make our way down the hall and into one of the empty rooms I know Casey cleaned before Mr. Duhaime interrupted our lockup process.

"Found her? Where? When?"

I set the pup on the table, running my hands over her, checking for any signs of broken bones, wounds, or anything that seems out of the ordinary, while Casey runs to grab heated blankets to get her back to a safe temperature.

"Like fifteen minutes ago? I was walking home from Top Shelf off Westlake Ave., heard something in the alley, and went to investigate. She was just…there."

I don't bother scolding him about how foolish it is to creep around dark alleys this time of night. I'm too focused on my job.

"There was no one else around who she could have belonged to?"

"No."

"No other pups?"

"No."

"Her mom wasn't nearby?"

"No."

It's the same calm and collected answer, making me wonder if he's even paying attention to what I'm saying to him. I look up, ready to snap because I truly need all the information I can get, but Lawson's attention is on the dog Casey is now wrapping in a blanket.

He looks…worried. Scared, even, like this puppy's survival is solely on his shoulders. I try my best to ignore how it makes him entirely too human. I'm not sure I'm ready to picture Lawson as anything other than…well, Lawson—a jock with a cocky walk and an even cockier mouth.

"She's been crying," he tells me, gaze still locked on the dog. "The whole time I carried her. Is that normal?"

"For a cold and hungry animal that's been left on the streets? Yes, that's perfectly normal."

He works his jaw back and forth, shoving his hands deep into his pockets like he's trying to convince himself not to reach out for the dog when she gives the softest of cries.

"You don't have to stand over there."

He finally snaps his focus from the silver table to me. He swallows when our eyes connect, then shakes his head. "I'm okay."

I huff. "Just get over here. She clearly wants you to."

A slow grin curls his lips. "Does she now?"

I narrow my eyes, knowing exactly what Lawson is insinuating—that it's *me* who wants him closer.

Not a chance, I tell him with my hard stare.

It doesn't stop his lips from rising higher as he saunters closer to the table, where I ignore how big his shoulders look with his hands still tucked into his pockets. It's not until he's an inch or two away that he removes them, reaching out to the pup. He allows her to sniff him before petting her head, and she pushes into his touch, absorbing every second of it.

She's smitten with him because *of course* she is. I'm sure every woman—other than me, of course—in a hundred-mile radius is obsessed with him. He's just that kind of guy.

"Is she okay?" he asks after a few seconds, concern dripping from every word.

"Nothing seems to be broken. She's not whimpering when I touch her, and there are no knots or swollen spots. There's a good-sized cut on her back right leg, likely from walking around the alleys. I'll give her a shot for it and some antibiotics. What we need to do now is keep her warm, get her fed, and hope no infection spreads."

He works his jaw again, leaning closer to the dog and ruffling her ears with both hands, carefully covering them before saying, "I swear, if I ever find the fuck who dumped her, I'm beating their ass myself."

I fight a smile—but only barely. "She can't understand you, you know."

"I know." He drops his hands and tucks them back

into his pockets, rocking on his heels. If I didn't know any better, I'd say he was embarrassed, but I *do* know better. The guy has far too much confidence to be embarrassed.

I reach for a cotton swab and check her mouth for any signs of injury or disease. Luckily, I don't find anything.

"Considering she's been on the streets, she's in good shape."

"Really?" There's no mistaking the happiness in his voice. "I mean, good." He clears his throat, nodding. "That's good."

"Very good. And lucky. Casey?"

"I'm on it," Casey says, darting from the room, knowing exactly what needs to be done.

Lawson is back at the table now, his hands roaming over the puppy, who is just as eager for his touch as he is to give it. She's pushing into him, trying to climb out of the heated blanket and toward him, but he doesn't let her.

I like that he doesn't let her. That means he knows how important it is for her to get warm.

"It's Christmas Eve," he says after several quiet moments, and my eyes fall to his full lips, watching as the words tumble from them. "What are you doing here so late?"

I don't want to tell him I have no plans tonight

except to work. Auden is off in New York reuniting with her boyfriend, Hutch, and my father is spending the holiday with one of his old hockey buddies. It's just me this year.

"Not sure you have room to talk, Mr. Out Roaming the Streets at ten PM," I counter, dragging my eyes away from his mouth.

"No one to go home to."

He says it so simply, like it's the most logical answer in the world. I guess it is, but it's also sad. So damn sad, especially when I see the pain mixing into his gray eyes.

I'm sure I'm imagining it. There's no way Lawson is lonely. I bet he has a slew of girls ready and willing to warm his bed. Loneliness is not a thing a man like him experiences.

"I have plans for tomorrow, though." He rushes out the declaration like he knows how pitiful he sounds. *There it is.* "I always spend Christmas at the theater. A bit of a tradition."

I would think his Christmas traditions would include baking cookies with Satan or stealing toys from kids with the Grinch and Max, but I guess spending it at the movies works too.

Casey comes back in, saving me from having to say anything. She's carrying a tray of different food types —hard, wet, and a syringe, just in case the dog doesn't want to eat and we have to coax her into taking it like she would from her mother.

I'm not surprised when Casey tries the dry bits and the wet mush and the dog doesn't bite. She's too skittish, inching away from every attempt my vet tech makes.

"Let me try," I say, taking the food and giving it a shot, but I'm just as unsuccessful as she is.

After several more tries, I'm ready to give up. Just as I'm about to toss the syringe to the side and try again later, my hand begins to burn.

A second later, I realize what's happened: Lawson's hand is covering mine. I steal my gaze from where he's touching me—where his hand is burning against mine—and peer into his nearly gray eyes.

"Let me," he says, his words somehow a request and a command all wrapped into one as he stretches his other hand out toward me, palm up.

I want to kick myself for how easily I hand it over, like his words have some sort of effect on me other than grating. And then I want to kick *him* because, like some damn expert, he holds the syringe of food out to the puppy, who takes it eagerly with zero coaxing.

"How did you do that?" The words sound harsh even to my ears, so it makes sense that Lawson gives me a smirk I want to slap away.

"Chicks just dig me."

I groan, unsure if it's because of what I just had to hear or because there is a tiny, minuscule—and I mean so, so small it's practically nonexistent—part of me that wants to laugh at his lame joke.

Not Casey, though. She doesn't groan. She laughs. *Loudly.* And when I look over at her, I am utterly unsurprised to see a flirty smile gracing her lips and stars practically dancing in her eyes.

Oh, man. She might have been against him when he first tried to get into the clinic, but she's now fallen for him hook, line, and sinker. I want to grab her by the shoulders, shake her, and ask, *"How could you possibly fall for this shit? Don't you see what a player he is?"*

I certainly do. I saw it the moment I met him. He had that whole *I'm a pro hockey player, everyone worships the ground I walk on* vibe, and there was no way in hell I was going to fall for it.

The dog continues to eagerly lap at the food Lawson is offering as he slowly brings over the bowl of wet mush, pushing it closer. Eventually, the syringe is long forgotten, and the dog only cares about the bowl. It's just minutes before she finishes off every bit of the horrid-smelling slop, then looks at her new friend, a bit of food stuck beside her mouth.

"Feeling better, girl?" Lawson asks softly, scratching between her ears once more. "Yeah, you are. I can tell."

"She's no longer shivering, which is a good sign. It's clear she has an appetite, another good sign. I'm going to take blood samples, just to be sure she's not carrying any disease or infection I can't see, but aside from the scratch, she looks perfectly healthy."

Lawson beams—but not at me. No, he's too entranced by the puppy, who is now licking at his hands, kissing him like he's the greatest thing she's ever encountered, and to her, he likely is. The needy thing just doesn't know better, I guess.

I give her flea and tick meds, clean up her cut, wrap some gauze around it to keep her out of it, and then get her to take a dose of liquid antibiotic. The whole time, Lawson stands close, so close there's no way I won't still smell his cologne—a mix of leather and cedar—long after he leaves.

"All right." I step back—from him and the dog—then nod toward Casey, signaling I'm ready to wrap up. "She'll need a checkup and her vaccines soon. You'll have to decide if you want to spay her as well, but I've done all I can for now."

"Yeah? She's good?"

"She's good."

Lawson nods a few times before clearing his throat and giving the dog one last heavy pet, then taking two steps back. The dog immediately begins to whimper at the loss of touch, and she's not the only one. Even

Lawson lets out a soft sound, but it doesn't last. He pushes his shoulders back, looking over at me with a slight sniffle. "So, um, see you later?"

My head whips back at his words. "Excuse me?"

"I'll pay for everything, of course, but are we all set here?"

"Um, no. Not even close. Over my dead body are you leaving this dog here." I pick the puppy up from the table, then thrust her into Lawson's hands. "Take her."

He holds her out like he did the first time, like he's showing her off to the rest of the pride, and says, "I can't take her."

"Why not?"

"Because… Because hockey!"

"So?" I challenge.

Lawson sighs, tucking the dog under his arm. "I can't get a puppy. I'm on the road too much."

"What are you going to do, then? *Abandon* her?"

I know what I'm doing in this moment, playing on his emotions, and I try hard to fight my smile when his shoulders deflate, my words working just as I intended. It's mean, I know that, but I also don't want to see this puppy have to go into the system. Sure, she'll get adopted quickly because everyone loves puppies, but I like the idea of Lawson taking responsibility. I have a feeling it's not something he does too often.

"But I… She's not mine. What if she belongs to someone else?"

"Then we put her information out and see if anyone is looking for her, even though I highly doubt that's the case. She's young. There's no way, if she had just slipped out of the house, that people wouldn't be calling and looking for her. I'd put money on her being dumped. Hell, I wouldn't be surprised if the whole litter was dumped somewhere. I've been doing this for many years, Lawson. I know the signs when I see them. If by some miracle someone claims her, we'll deal with it then, but for all intents and purposes, she's yours."

"But…"

My lifted brow halts his refute, and I know I got him. His mouth snaps shut, and he nods.

"Okay. All right. I'll take her."

I grin victoriously. "Good. I'd watch her throughout the night just in case there's a reaction to any of the medication I administered, but other than that, she should be perfectly fine. Casey will get you squared away at the front desk."

I turn my attention to the folder Casey set on the counter, my pen at the ready to start filling in the blanks so we can get this filed in our charts. I hear one set of feet shuffle from the room, but not the second.

It's not like I'd need that to indicate whether or not Lawson's left. I know he hasn't; I can feel his stare on me. When he doesn't say anything or make a move to leave, I peek over my shoulder to find him standing a couple of feet away, his silver eyes boring into me.

"Yes?"

"I…" He clears his throat, giving his head one shake. "Thank you."

And that's all he says before he darts out of the room, leaving behind the scent that's distinctly him and leaving me suddenly wishing I wouldn't be alone this Christmas Eve night.

Chapter 3

LAWSON

"Stop looking at me like that."

Blink.

"Knock it off."

Blink.

"Come on. Quit it."

Blink.

I sigh, shoving off the couch and padding across my apartment that I desperately need to do something with. I still have boxes stacked in the corner despite having lived in Seattle for over a year. It's time I deal with those and accept that Washington is my new home.

I bend at the waist, scooping up the little ball of coffee-colored fluff and bringing her close to my chest. "You're already spoiled, you know that?" I press a kiss to her head. "Merry Christmas, whatever your name is."

Between waking up every few hours to check on the puppy and sleeping on the couch, I got next to no sleep last night. I didn't mean to pass out there, but when I finally got home after a quick stop for her to pee outside, she beelined straight for the couch and curled into herself, falling asleep almost instantly. I wasn't about to disturb her, so I sat on the opposite end. I must have fallen asleep myself at some point.

I look down at my new companion. I've always wanted a dog, but hockey has always been too big a part of my life for a commitment like that. Last night though, when Rory shoved her into my arms and told me I was taking her home, I couldn't say no—to the dog or to Rory.

The creature in my arms makes a noise, like she knows she's the subject of my thoughts, and for the hundredth time since I brought her home, I pray nobody claims her.

"Guess I should probably find some supplies for you today, huh?"

She lets out the softest little grunt, approving of my suggestion.

"You're lucky the pharmacy down the street is open, or else I'm pretty sure you'd be eating bacon for breakfast."

Another grunt.

"You're right—bacon does sound good. Maybe I'll make some when I get back."

She tips her head at me, and then I swear she rolls her eyes. She must have picked that up from Rory last night.

I still can't believe out of all the clinics in the city, I walked into hers. I vaguely recall Hutch mentioning she's a vet, but that was the last thing on my mind after finding my new roommate in the alley. I wanted to get her to safety, and I would have taken her anywhere, even to someone who openly hates me like Rory does.

I only met her a few days ago, but I knew immediately she didn't like me, and not just because she had me tongue-tied, something I *never* get. I saw her across the room before we even approached her twin sister, Auden, and my eyes were instantly drawn to her. It wasn't just because she looked like my teammate's girlfriend either. It was something else I don't quite have the words for. All I knew was I wanted to talk to her. I *needed* to talk to her.

So, I did, and she shot me down faster than lightning strikes. It stung, just like seeing the disdain in her eyes last night stung. But my mom didn't raise a quitter, and I'm determined to make Rory like me, even if she doesn't want to.

After a quick shower where the dog sits beside the

door the entire time, I dress, lock her in the spare bathroom, and truck the short quarter mile to the store. I stock my basket full of everything I can think of that a dog might need—food, toys, training pads, and treats—and toss in a six-pack of beer for myself for good measure, then quickly return to my apartment.

I hear her the second I push my key into my door, and my heart fucking breaks at the sounds coming from inside. Little yelps and whines, like she can't stand to be apart from me either. I didn't want to leave her, but I needed provisions if we're going to make this work.

I shove the door open, not bothering to drop my bags on the counter before I head for the bathroom and let her free. She bounds out of the room and past me to the living room, jumping back onto my gray couch like she's done it a thousand times before.

"You're not claiming that as your spot," I warn. "That's mine. I already called dibs."

She ignores me, sniffing at the bandage on her leg, something she's been doing all morning. I have no clue if it's normal or not, but I *do* know someone who can answer that for me.

I set the bags on the kitchen counter, pluck my phone from my pocket, and shoot off a text.

Me: Merry Christmas, dickwad. Can I
have Rory's number?

Dots dance on the screen almost instantly.

Hutch: Abso-fucking-lutely not.

Me: Why not?

Hutch: Because I've met you. And
because you annoy her. And me. Now
go away.

Me: Be nice. It's Christmas.

Hutch: Exactly. It's Christmas, so why
are you bothering me?

I pad over to the couch, snap a quick picture, then send it to my new captain.

Me: She's why.

Hutch: What the…

Hutch: When the fuck did you get a dog? And HOW?

Me: It's a long story. Now, can I have Rory's number? It's a vet thing, I promise.

Hutch: Hang on.

I unpack my bags, checking my phone every couple of seconds as I wait for a response from my teammate. Several minutes go by, and I'm sure he's discussing this with his new girlfriend, Auden, Rory's twin. I'm sure she's telling him not to do it, especially since her sister has made it abundantly clear she's not my biggest fan, but I hope she'll give me the benefit of the doubt because of the dog.

Five minutes later, I get a Christmas miracle.

Hutch: 206-555-1989

Me: I knew you loved me.

Hutch: Not in this lifetime or the next.

Me: But definitely the one after that, right?

Hutch: Go. Away.

Me: Kisses!

Hutch: *middle finger emoji*

I laugh, then click on the number he sent and bring the phone to my ear. It rings three times before she picks up.

"Hell…o?" Her greeting is apprehensive…and maybe a little sleepy. Did I wake her? It's almost nine on Christmas morning. I figured she'd be up by now, but I guess not.

"Rory?"

"Who is this?"

I clear my throat. "It's Lucas."

"Lucas who?"

I can't tell if she's screwing with me. The sleepiness in her tone is keeping me from detecting her usual sarcasm.

"Um… It's, uh, Lawson." *Fuck, I sound like a bumbling fool.* "Lucas Lawson."

She groans, and there's a shuffle on her end of the line. I let my mind wander for just a moment, imagining what she looks like when she first gets up.

Do her pajamas match? Better yet, is she even wearing any? Are her eyes puffy, or does she wake up like women in the movies, already sporting perfect hair and makeup and wearing the sexiest set of silk pajamas money can buy?

"What do you want."

Just like that, the vision shatters. Her question isn't even a question. It's a demand and everything I could have expected from her.

"Good morning, Rory."

She grunts. "Lawson."

I can't help but smile at how she says my name, like she's completely annoyed by me. It's not the first time I've had it happen, and I'm almost sure it won't be the last time. I'm a bit of a handful for just about everyone.

"Why are you calling me."

Again, not a question.

I grin. "This is your Christmas present."

"I wasn't aware I was on Santa's naughty list this year."

"This year? You say that as if you've been on the naughty list in previous years. Tell me, what'd you do to earn that?"

"Wouldn't you like to know."

"Yes."

A pause. An audible gulp.

Have I stumped her? The few times I've met her,

she's been mouthy. Now, though, she's quiet. Is it wrong that I prefer the mouthy version of her?

"Can you just tell me what you want, Lawson? Because so far, this is the worst Christmas present I could imagine."

"Even worse than getting a stocking full of coal? Or dog turds?"

"Did you forget I'm a veterinarian? I'm surrounded by dog turds constantly."

"That's kind of why I called."

"For dog turds?"

"No. Because you're a vet."

More shuffling in the background. "Is everything okay with the puppy?" Rory asks, her voice full of much more emotion than she's ever shown me. "Did something happen?"

"No. No—"

"No, nothing happened, or no, everything isn't okay?"

I laugh at her impatience. "No, nothing happened. Everything is okay. I think."

She blows out a relieved breath. "You think?"

"Well, yeah. Dog has been—"

"Dog? You named her Dog?"

"No. I haven't named her anything yet. And could you please stop interrupting me?"

"Could you please just get to the point?"

I'd ask her if she's always this grumpy, but I know she is.

"Anyway, as I was saying, Dog has been sniffing at her bandage. And if she's not sniffing it, she's nipping it. She doesn't want to leave it alone except when sleeping."

"Well, that's not surprising. She's not used to having something wrapped around her leg. I'm sure she also smells that she has a cut and wants to investigate it, especially with her young age. But she's fine. It's perfectly normal."

"Are you sure?"

"Which of us is the veterinarian with years of experience under her belt who runs not one but *two* highly rated clinics here in Seattle?"

She has two clinics? How does she even have the time to run two?

"I'm going to go out on a limb here and say you want me to answer with *you*."

"Unless you somehow went to school for eight years while playing professional hockey, then yes, I mean *me*."

I had no idea how long it takes to become a veterinarian. They're doctors, so I figured it would require a good amount of school, but *eight years*? That's almost a decade, and she's under thirty. How is she running two clinics successfully after spending so much time in school? That's…impressive.

"You're doing the math, aren't you?"

"Maybe."

"I graduated high school early," she explains like I'm sure she's done so many times before. "I immediately started on courses for my bachelor's, then went on to graduate school. I was twenty-five when I became a vet, and I bought my clinic from a retiring doctor with whom I did my clinicals when I was twenty-seven. I opened my second office earlier this year."

It's the most she's said to me at once outside of being in the exam room last night. I wonder if her willingness to talk to me is because it's early and she hasn't had a chance to wake up and adequately tell me off, or if maybe—just maybe—she's starting to come around to me.

"Go on, call me a nerd. You know you want to."

"Nah. Never." Okay, maybe. If I were back in high school, yeah, I probably would have called her a nerd for liking school enough to graduate early, but that's because I was young and dumb and embarrassed by the fact that I was struggling to barely trudge through my own classes. Hell, I *still* think the only reason I graduated was because of my hockey skills. "I'm actually impressed by it."

She makes a noncommittal noise like she's calling bullshit on my words. "Why did you call me, Lawson?"

"Pardon?"

"Why did you call me? You could have just as easily hopped on Google."

"I'm sorry, but are you, a doctor, encouraging the use of the internet to diagnose something?"

"You're right. You'd probably put in the wrong thing, assume she's dying of gangrene, then take her into an emergency clinic and get charged out the ass for something as simple as her being curious about her bandage. Actually, on second thought, take her in. I'd love to see the bill on that one."

"Anything to see me suffer, huh?"

"Don't feel too flattered. That's not exclusive to you. I love watching the world burn."

I laugh, mostly because I know she's being honest. From what I've gathered from Hutch, it's not just me Rory Sinclair hates—it's everyone. She's like a little dark cloud, ready and willing to rain down on anyone's happy day. I want nothing more than to see her cloud burst.

"I wanted the opinion of someone I trust to take care of…Dog. Besides, we're kind of like co-parents."

She sighs. "First of all, no. Absolutely not. We are not even kind of co-parents. She's my patient, and you're…well, you. Secondly, you really must come up with a better name than that. Literally anything is better than Dog."

"I'll work on it."

"Before the next visit, preferably. I am *not* writing down *Dog* in my patient files."

"You keep files on the animals that come through?"

"Well, duh."

"And their owners?"

"Nope. I don't care about them. I'm there for the animals and animals only."

Another chuckle escapes. "Duly noted."

The line goes quiet. It stays that way for several moments. I'm not entirely sure why, either. I don't have anything else to say, and she doesn't either, but I still can't bring myself to hang up. Maybe because it's Christmas Day—a day usually filled with joyful music and laughter and presents—and I'm sitting alone in my apartment. I'll take this company over no company at all, even if Rory does hate me.

"Is that all you need?" she finally asks.

"I…just…"

"Yes?"

I have nothing else to say, not really. I just don't want to get off the phone, and I *hate* talking on the phone. Am I that desperate for companionship?

Yes.

"I…"

She sighs. "Out with it already, hockey boy."

I smile. Only she could be this grumpy on the most joyful holiday there is. "Merry Christmas, Rory."

"Oh." A pause. "Um…merry Christmas, Lawson?"

It comes out a question this time, and it makes me laugh.

She groans. "Shut up."

The line goes dead, and even though I was hung up on, I'm still grinning. Maybe today won't be so bad after all.

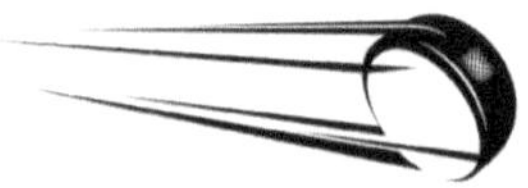

"One for *A Christmas Story*, please."

"Sure thing."

The person behind the counter mashes buttons and then gives me the total. I hand over my card with a smile. They hand it back seconds later with a frown.

Why is everyone so testy today? It's Christmas, for crying out loud!

"Thanks," I tell them, and all they give me is a grunt.

I take my ticket inside, arm myself with a large bucket of popcorn and a massive Coke, and then find a spot tucked away in the back of the theater. Only then do I pull open my coat, looking down with a grin.

While I knew I'd be spending my afternoon at the theater today no matter what, I never anticipated I'd be sneaking a dog in right along with me. I couldn't help myself, not with the look she gave me when I tried to leave her behind, locked in the bathroom again. There was no way I could leave her there and still enjoy the movies. Besides, it's a holiday. Most people will be home with their families and not at the theater. As long as she stays quiet, I'll be fine.

"You good?" I ask, running a single finger over the tip of her nose.

She lets out a soft grunt but doesn't budge otherwise. She's been sleeping so much since I brought her home, but I'm not surprised. I think she's worn out from having to survive on the streets.

I leave her be, tossing a bit of popcorn in my mouth while I wait for the movie to begin and try hard not to think about the one person I'm missing the most —my mom.

I'm not scared to admit I'm a total momma's boy. Is it really such a surprise I would be? My mother raised me on her own since I was one, working as a bartender into the wee hours of the morning to provide for us. My father and her never married, and when I was a lot older, I learned that was his thing. He was the *love 'em and leave 'em* type, an approach I also tend to use, only unlike me, he always left behind a kid, which is why I have five half-siblings scattered across North America.

Even though my dad wasn't always present, he was still a good father. He called weekly, sent birthday cards and gifts, provided school clothes, and paid for my hockey training. Hell, he even stopped by a few times a year, even if it was only for a day or two.

He loves me, and I love him, but our relationship is vastly different from my one with my mother. Outside of hockey, she's been the only constant in my life for as long as I can remember, and doing a Christmas without her feels a lot like what I imagine it feels like to lose a limb.

I shove away those thoughts before I do something irrational, like get emotional while sitting alone in a theater with a bucket of popcorn in one hand and a sleeping dog in the other. The same five commercials play across the screen as I plow my way through my snack before the previews even start, and a few stragglers make their way into the auditorium.

I'm mouthing along with the same lawyer commercial I'm now on my sixth watch of when someone shuffles into my row. I try not to be annoyed on the happiest day of the year, but there's a whole theater open, and they pick this section?

"You have got to be kidding me."

I *know* that voice. Hell, I just heard that voice a few hours ago.

I whip my head up, taking her in. Her dark hair that's usually slung back in a low bun is hanging loose around her shoulders, she's wearing a pair of lounge pants that look about two sizes too big with an equally oversized shirt that reads *Cats Over People*, and a bulbous jacket is draped over her arm as she glares down at me.

She looks ridiculous, yet I can't seem to take my eyes off her, which isn't all that surprising. When Hutch first brought Auden around, I thought she was gorgeous. Then I met Rory and realized, as pretty as Auden is, Rory is even more beautiful. They may be twins and look alike, but they couldn't be more different in the way they carry themselves.

This is a prime example of that. The other Sinclair scoffs, then plops into the seat four chairs away from me. She sits, staring at the screen, refusing to look at me and acknowledge me further. Naturally, this makes me want to *make* her notice me.

"Miss me that much, Rory?"

"In your dreams, hockey boy."

I grin. "What are you doing here?"

Another huff, but she finally glances my way, gracing me with the greenest eyes I've ever seen.

"Watching a movie."

My lips twitch. "No shit?"

"No shit." She rolls her head back toward the screen where the car dealership commercial is now playing.

"I didn't take you as a Christmas-movie kind of person."

"Why? Was my cheerful disposition not a dead giveaway?"

"You know, now that I think of it, you're right. You're definitely a cheerful person. There is no reason you wouldn't love Christmas movies. What's your favorite?"

"*Black Christmas.*" Her answer is automatic, leading me to believe it truly is her favorite. *Of course* her favorite holiday film would be about people getting slaughtered.

"Which one?"

"The original, obviously."

"Right. *Obviously.*"

"And yours?"

"My favorite version of *Black Christmas*?"

"No. What's your favorite Christmas movie?"

I try to hide my surprise that she's actively engaging in conversation and asking me about myself instead of completely ignoring me.

"*The Spirit of Christmas*," I tell her.

"Is that the one where the heroine falls in love with a ghost?"

"Sure is."

The way her brows rise tells me she wasn't expecting me to admit that. What I'm not telling her is that it's my favorite because it's my *mother's* favorite. She's a sucker for any Hallmark-style movies, and I've seen far too many of them to count over the years. At first, I moaned and groaned and, at one point, actually started to loathe Christmastime because I knew I'd have to suffer through at least twenty films where the plots were all incredibly similar. Then, when I stopped complaining and started paying attention, it all made sense—my mother didn't love the movies because they were masterpieces. She loved them for exactly what they offered: a happily ever after, something she'd been yearning for since my father dipped out of the picture.

As much as I love my mother, I don't want to be her, still sitting around years after I've gotten my heart broken and wishing someone would come along and fix me. I just want to have a good time and play good hockey. Is that too much to ask for?

"I...was not expecting that."

"Why? Guys can't like movies like that?"

"Of course they can. I just don't exactly consider you a guy."

I choke out a laugh. "What am I, then?"

"I'm not sure you want me to answer that."

"Oh, but I do."

"Fine." She sucks in a deep breath, then turns fully toward me, pointing a finger my way. "You, Lucas Lawson, are a player. And I don't mean a hockey player. You use. You take, take, and discard like it's nothing. You think you're a godsend to everyone and walk around with a smug, obnoxious grin. You're the exact kind of guy I want nothing to do with, and your whole schtick of playing cute and innocent with rescuing the dog last night isn't going to work on me. I see through you, and I don't like what I see."

Whatever I expected Rory to say, it certainly wasn't that. I knew she didn't like me, but I assumed it was because I tried flirting with her the first time we met.

But this? I wasn't expecting this at all.

The worst part is…she's not exactly wrong. It's no secret I don't do commitments of any sort outside of my hockey contracts. But am I truly that bad, or does it just *sound* bad when she says it? I feel the answer to that question isn't what I want it to be.

She arches a single brow, challenging me to refute her words, and when I don't, she lifts a shoulder, settling back into her seat. I sit there dumbfounded, staring as she watches the screen, those damn commercials still rolling.

We're just minutes away from the movie starting when a big family of about ten steps into the theater… and heads directly to our row.

"Um, hi," a woman says to Rory.

"Hi…" Rory says tentatively, her brows crushed together.

"I was wondering, since it's Christmas and all, could you possibly move down a few seats?" She gestures behind her. "My family would love to sit together, and this is the only row that will allow us to. If you move down, that is."

"I…"

Rory leans forward, taking in the group of people eagerly waiting for her to say yes, then turns toward me, looking as confused as I am. Are these people serious? If they wanted to sit together, they should've gotten to the theater early, not minutes before the show starts.

But…the not-so-Grinchy part of me mouths to Rory, *It's Christmas.* She rolls her eyes, and I know she's about to tell the people to go away. When I raise my brows, she groans, and I can tell I've won.

She smashes her lips together, then looks at the woman with a tight smile. "Sure. I'll move."

"Oh, really? Thank you *so* much. You're too kind."

"Mmm." It's the only response Rory gives before she shoves to her feet and heads my way.

The scent of pears and something flowery hits my senses as she settles next to me. I'm stunned by this development and rendered more speechless than I have been in a long time. She realizes she's sitting next to me, right?

"Can you believe these assholes?" She thrusts her thumb toward the group. "Get here early if you want to sit together. Dicks."

I'm still sitting with my jaw dropped, unable to reconcile the fact that she's not only sitting next to me but engaging in conversation…again. This really *is* a Christmas miracle.

"You know, I—" Her words die on her lips, eyes shifting down, down, down. "Um, Lawson?"

"Yes?"

"Is your jacket moving?"

I follow to where her stare is trained, and yep—my jacket *is* moving.

"Is that…" She looks around before leaning in just an inch closer. "Is that the *dog*? Did you bring a *dog* into the movie theater?"

I can't help the grin that stretches across my lips. "Maybe."

"Lawson!"

The reprimand is loud and piercing and certainly

draws the attention of several people in the theater, the couple sitting two rows in front of us turning around to cast glares our way. I smile, sending them a wave before wrapping my arm around Rory's shoulder and dragging her to me.

"Stop it. You're causing a scene," I say out of the corner of my mouth.

"And you're"—she shakes off my arm, adding an extra jab of her elbow that doesn't hurt nearly as much as I'm sure she hopes—"an idiot. Why would you bring her here?"

"Because I couldn't get a sitter?"

"She's a *dog*, Lawson. She'd have been fine for a few hours at home."

"Maybe, but she gave me *the look* when I tried to leave, and well, call me a sucker because there was no way I was going to leave her home alone after that."

"Sucker." She says it so matter-of-factly. So…Rory-like.

I like that about her, that she's so unapologetically her. Most women in my presence would be tucking their hair behind their ears or fluttering their lashes to get my attention.

Not Rory. Never Rory.

I like that. She's wholly her. A little grumpy and gruff, but her.

"What are you going to do if she needs to go potty? Or she's hungry? Or starts to bark?"

"First, she won't bark. She doesn't do that—she whines, and she won't do that unless I'm away from her. Second…" I reach into my jacket, plucking free the bag of snacks I have tucked in my pocket. "I brought her some turkey bacon since I read that was a better alternative than regular bacon."

"You… I…" She shakes her head. "I'm sorry, you brought *home-cooked* bacon for the dog?"

"Uh, yeah? Everyone likes bacon."

She wrinkles her nose. "I don't."

"Oh, fuck off."

The words slip out of my mouth before I can stop them, and I sit in absolute horror as the realization of what I said settles over Rory.

One.

Two.

Three.

That's how many seconds it takes her to let out the loudest, most obnoxious laugh I've ever heard.

For the second time, we've drawn the attention of the theater, only this time, I don't care. I'm too enraptured by Rory tossing her head back, her body shaking as she makes the most awful noise. It's terrible. Truly so loud and embarrassing.

Yet, somehow, I can't seem to look away…or hate

it. I should really, really hate it, and I should really, really not want to hear it again. But I do.

"Oh, wow. Sorry." She swipes at her eyes, wiping away the tears that have welled. "Sorry. I just was not at all expecting you to tell me to fuck off."

I wasn't expecting to say it. It just rolled out, and I instantly wanted to take it back. But I'm not telling her that, not if it's going to make her laugh that hard.

"I didn't expect you to say something so psychotic like you don't like bacon."

"Of course I like bacon, Lawson. I'm not a savage. Anyway…" Another swipe at her eyes. "You were telling me how bringing the dog along to the movies wasn't the worst idea you've ever had. Please continue because I'm curious."

"I feel like I've addressed all your concerns."

"Potty issues?"

"Oh. That." I pat my jacket where the pup is curled up. "She's wearing a diaper."

A weary sigh. "You got her doggie diapers, didn't you?"

My cheeks heat. "There's such a thing as doggie diapers?"

"Oh, no. No, no, no. She's wearing a people diaper, isn't she?"

I nod, my ears now heating up too.

"Did you at least cut a hole for her tail?"

I grin, feeling pretty damn proud of myself for remembering. "Yep."

Rory shakes her head. "You are… You're…"

"What?"

She studies me with her emerald eyes, her lips parting far too many times until she finally says, "Something. You're something, Lawson."

I grin because I *know* that something is a good kind of something. "I know."

That earns me yet another huff and eye roll. I should really start counting them.

"What if she gets loose?"

I point down to the dog. "Does it look like she's going anywhere? I'm telling you, this thing is lazy."

"That *thing* still doesn't have a name, does she?"

"She does."

Rory lifts a brow. "And that would be?"

"It's…" I glance down at the dog, who hasn't bothered to move an inch since we sat down. She's completely dead to the world, and completely adorable. "Daisy."

"You totally pulled that out of your ass, didn't you?"

"Of course not." I grin, but it's a lie, and we both know it.

Somehow, the name fits her perfectly, and I couldn't imagine it being anything else.

"Daisy," I whisper, testing it out. I run my finger over her nose, and she stirs for the first time since I settled into my seat.

"She likes it," Rory says just as quietly, watching the pup blow out a breath, then let out a soft grunt before falling back into a peaceful slumber. "How's it really going with her? Did she do okay last night? Some dogs have reactions, but it's rare."

"She was good. No issues at all."

And I would know since I had my alarm set to go off every two hours to ensure she was okay. Every time I got up, she was in the same position as before, sleeping probably more soundly than ever. It was certainly more soundly than I did.

"Good. That's good. Just make sure you bring her back in for more shots. I'll have Casey send you a reminder."

"Aye, aye, Wednesday."

She pauses. "Wednesday?"

"Yeah, Wednesday Addams." Her brows shift inward. "From *The Addams Family*. Black hair, black dress, black outlook on life. She's pale and—"

"I know who Wednesday is, Lawson. I'm asking why *I'm* Wednesday."

"Why, your sunny disposition, clearly."

"Clearly," she says dryly.

I try not to comment on the irony of that.

"You're unemotional and matter-of-fact like she is," I tell her. "You remind me of her, Ms. My Favorite Movie is *Black Christmas*."

She shrugs. "Moving on, then…"

"How Wednesday of you."

"What are you going to do with her?" she continues. "When hockey starts back up, I mean?"

That's the million-dollar question, one I don't currently have any kind of answer for. That's the biggest reason I never got a dog. The guys on the team with one have partners at home to take care of them while we're on the road. While I might be able to sneak Daisy into the theaters, I can't sneak her onto the plane or into the rink to keep tabs on her. I have no clue what I'm going to do, and it's something I need to figure out sooner rather than later.

The lights dim, signaling the movie's start and saving me from having to answer—another Christmas miracle.

"Shh. The movie's on."

I nod toward the screen, and Rory narrows her eyes at me but gives me this win, settling back in her new seat. The previews begin to roll, and I sneak my hand back into my popcorn, holding it out to my seatmate because I'm not a total monster.

To my surprise, she takes it.

And then goes back for more. And more. We're

sharing popcorn, our hands brushing repeatedly, but Rory doesn't move to take her hand away, and neither do I.

This is not at all how I expected this day to go, but I can't remember the last time I was so content.

Chapter 4

RORY

"How was your Christmas?" my twin asks. From the sound of it, she's in the airport waiting on her flight back from New York to Seattle.

"It was good," I tell her.

"What'd you end up doing?"

I hesitate. I could tell her I spent yesterday with Lawson, but I know her well enough to know she'd have about a million questions, and at least ninety-nine percent of those would be questions I'm not ready to answer.

So instead of bringing down the inquisition, I simply tell her, "I went to the movies."

"What? Why?"

It's a fair question, especially since I can't recall the last time I went to the theater. Thanks to Lawson awkwardly telling me he was spending the holiday at the movies, I knew he'd be going somewhere in the city. I just never in a million years thought out of all the places he could go, he'd wind up at the same theater as me.

The strangest part is I didn't even intend to go to the movies. I was sitting at home alone, bored out of my mind and not enjoying anything on TV, so I slid on my shoes to go for a walk. The next thing I knew, I was walking up to the theater off Queen Anne Ave and asking for a ticket to *A Christmas Story*, a movie I don't even like. That's how I ended up spending a holiday with the guy I can't stand, the same guy who snuck in a damn puppy to the movie theater. Who even does that? And why…why do I find it so adorable?

Lawson and adorable aren't words that go together. Lawson and hot? Yes. I have eyes; it's very clear he's attractive. Lawson and annoying? An even better combo. But Lawson and adorable? No. They don't work together, ever…except for when they do, I guess.

I should tell my sister the truth. So we spent an afternoon together, sharing a bucket of popcorn, letting our hands brush? Big deal. I still don't like the guy and never will.

But if it's not a big deal, why am I so hesitant to talk about it?

"I don't know. Just something to do since everyone else ditched me."

That's right, Rory. Deflect. That's what you're good at.

"I'm sorry," my sister says, and there's no mistaking the remorse in her voice, remorse that shouldn't be there. It was her first Christmas with her boyfriend; she was right where she was supposed to be. "I hope you at least had a good time."

"I did."

And truthfully, I did. Sure, Lawson talked way too much, analyzing each second of the movie and leaning over to inform me of his every thought throughout it. He ate far too much popcorn, and more than once I caught him licking his fingers and sticking them back in the bucket. He hogged the armrest, got popcorn all over the floor, *and* clapped at the ending. It was annoying, but I still had a good time, probably a better time than I've had in years.

That's not to say I haven't loved spending my Christmases with my father and sister, but in years past, Auden always snuck off to work and my dad always fell asleep on the couch before dinner was even served. It always felt so…boring, so bland.

Yesterday didn't feel like that at all, and I'm sure that was because it was something outside the norm. It had absolutely nothing to do with Lawson.

"Oh! Did I tell you the latest gossip? Hutch told me Lawson got a dog. Lawson! A dog! Can you believe it?"

"I can't imagine he's capable of taking care of a dog, let alone himself, so no, I can't believe it."

"Right?" Auden laughs. "I swear I didn't know, or I would have sent him to your clinic."

She means it, too. She's been incredible about sending people my way. I think she brags about me being a veterinarian as much as I brag about her building a hotel empire and becoming a billionaire before thirty.

If Lawson was impressed by my work ethic to graduate high school early and become a veterinarian by twenty-five, I'm certain my sister's accomplishments blow his mind. They blow *my* mind, and I watched it all happen. She gave up so much to make her dreams of establishing a successful upscale hotel chain happen, and I was worried for a long time she was running herself into the ground, never taking a day off, let alone a vacation. She worked and worked and worked, never being satisfied when she laid her head down at night, and I could tell it was wearing on her.

When she started seeing her boyfriend, Hutch, I didn't believe it at first. She *never* did anything for herself, and she really never put it all on the line for a guy, but that's exactly what happened. I was surprised when she told me she was selling her company to focus on other things that made her happy. I was even more surprised when that "thing" was a guy, especially since she's as bad as I am with relationships and swore them off like I did long ago.

"I know," I say to Auden, "and while I love the support, I would have cursed you for sending Lawson my way. He's…something."

"Exhausting. So exhausting. Did you know he once tried to scale The Great Wheel? Hutch said he had to physically restrain him. And he was completely sober."

I wish I could say she's full of shit, but I have no doubt Hutch isn't lying. Lawson seems like the type to do anything for attention.

"Of course, it was a dare from Keller, so maybe that's why he did it, but still." I can picture her rolling her eyes. "Enough about Lawson. What movie did you see? Ugh, I still feel terrible I bailed on you."

"No, you don't, and I'm glad for it. You had better things to do."

She giggles, and I love the sound of it because I love hearing how happy she is. "Fine. But I do feel a little bad."

Now *that* I believe.

"Well, don't. It was fine. After the movie, I went home and ate about two dozen cookies while I watched my favorite Christmas movie, *B*—"

"*Black Christmas*, the original. I know, I know. Did you at least open your gift from Mom?"

"Oh, you mean the *Halloween* card she sent me? Yes, I loved it. It's hanging on my fridge right this very moment."

Auden laughs. "Of course that's what she sent. Can't wait to open mine when I get back."

"You'll have to tell me which holiday you got this year. I'll shit a gold brick if it's Christmas."

"That'll just mean I'm the favorite."

"Please, the only favorites that woman has are her favorite bottle of wine and her favorite crystal."

We laugh, both of us having come to terms with the fact that our mother just is who she is. She and our father, a retired NHL player, got together after his career in hockey, and their marriage was tumultuous at best. They spent a good portion of it traveling the country in an RV before Auden and I came along, then we settled in Washington, flitting from place to place within the state. That didn't last long for my mom, and it was just six months before she packed her bags and left my father for another man who promised her adventure.

She came back, of course. Then she left again. Back, gone, back, gone. They did this song and dance until I was sixteen, when my father finally said no more. My mother was more than happy to hand over custody, and it's just been me, Auden, and Dad since then. Mom will occasionally call or text, but she knows very little about our lives and, apparently, even less about what time of year it is.

It is what it is.

"I—oh, shoot. Hang on."

There's some shuffling, then a tinny voice in the background before Auden returns.

"Sorry. That was them announcing our flight is delayed by twenty minutes. What? No! That is *not* plenty of time for bathroom sex, Reed."

Hutch laughs in the background, which makes my sister giggle even more, which makes *me* smile. I might not be interested in love, but man am I happy that my sister is happy.

"Sorry," Auden says again, coming back to the phone. "Ignore him. He's a rake."

"A rake?" I laugh. "What is this, Regency London?"

"He wishes. He's clearly into the whole forbidden thing most of those books are about."

I swear I hear Hutch growl at that, which is my cue to get off the phone.

"Hey, I just had a patient come in," I fib, reaching for a pen and spinning it through my fingers.

"What? You're at the office again? Do you ever take a break?"

"We were closed yesterday. That was a break."

"Sure, but I'd bet big money that after the movie, you went back into the clinic and stayed until the wee hours of the morning."

I don't answer, which is answer enough for Auden.

She gasps. "You did, didn't you? Ugh, Rory. Come on. You need a break. You work too much."

I try to ignore the irony in her words since until a few months ago, I was telling her the same thing.

"I take breaks," I argue, though we both know it's a lie.

"As your older sister, I demand you take *more*."

I roll my eyes because she *loves* throwing in my face that she was born first. "Three minutes, Auden. Three whole minutes."

"Those are three very important minutes, thank you very much."

"Are you going to ask her about the thing?" Hutch says.

Ask *me*? "What thing?" I ask.

"It's nothing. I can tell you when I get home if you're too busy."

"It's okay. Casey is still checking the patient in."

I am such a liar. I have no clue if someone is in the lobby. We don't even open for another half hour. Either Auden doesn't realize this, or she knows me too well and is letting the lie slide.

"All right, so, Hutch had a fun idea to do a team calendar featuring the Serpents with animals to help get dogs and cats adopted from local shelters. The guys could even use their own animals too, do a mix or something, to bring awareness to a real issue and to showcase the players off the ice. He still needs to run it by management, but could you get us in touch with a shelter who would be willing to help on such short notice? We already have a photographer in mind. Do you think people would be interested in that though?"

Do I think people would buy a calendar that not only supports a local animal shelter but also showcases the eye candy the Serpents have on their team? Uh, hell yes. I'd probably even buy one. I'd rip Lawson's page right out, but I'd buy one.

"It's a great idea. There are far too many pets out there in need of good homes."

"And then, because you're so amazing, they could funnel work your way. That way everyone is getting something out of it."

I'm already running the numbers in my head for what it would cost to offer first visits free. It would be expensive and have to come out of my own pocket and mean extra hours on my end, but I'd gladly give my time and expertise to get those animals into loving homes.

"I—oh, hang on," Auden says as another voice comes over the intercom. "Crap. That's our flight. I guess we're good to go now, so we'd better get going."

"Ah, yes. Let's rush to the gate even though we're first class and can board whenever."

"Don't smart back, Mr. Grumbles," Auden tells Hutch in a sharp tone, and I have no doubt she's sending him a glare that's just as piercing.

"Or what?"

"Or I won't do that thing you like. You know, when I use my tongue on your—"

"Auden!" I cut her off. "I'm still here."

"Oh. Right." Another giggle. "I'd better let you go."

"I'd love that very much. Have a safe flight. I know it's not your favorite."

"It's not so bad now that I have Hutch. Oh my gosh, stop it!" She groans, but I can still hear a smile in her voice. "Love you, little sis."

"Love you too," I grumble.

Hutch says something I can't make out, and my sister giggles for the fourth time in this short conversation. For the first time ever, I'm a little jealous of what she has, and I'm not sure how to reconcile that fact.

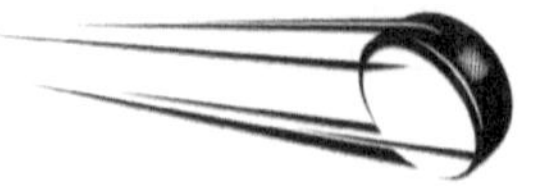

Hutch pitched his calendar idea the day after he and Auden got back into town, and the team ate it up. Between helping Auden coordinate things with a local shelter and keeping up with patients, I've been running around like a madwoman for a week straight. We've been up to our elbows in appointments and walk-ins all day. It's been nonstop since before we even open to close. I should have never lied to Auden about clients coming in early because I think it triggered something. I even had to come in on Sunday to tackle some things on my to-do list because there haven't been enough hours in the day.

I'm exhausted. If I can just get through today and tomorrow, I can sleep in on Sunday before the shoot.

"Knock, knock."

I look up from my mountain of paperwork to find Casey standing in my doorway. "How's it looking out there?"

My tech's eyes widen, but to her credit, it only lasts a second before she collects herself and sends me a reassuring smile. "Great. Things are great. Hillary just got back from break and Tyson started on the Murphys. It's a little full out there, but we got this."

Despite how she handled Lawson's late arrival on

Christmas Eve, I believe her. I wouldn't have hired her if I didn't think she could manage busy days like this.

"Good. Anything else?"

"Actually, yes."

I lift a brow, urging her to go on when she pauses. "That is?"

"Um, Lucas Lawson called for you."

"He did?" *Why the hell does my voice sound so high?* I clear my throat. "What did he want?"

I haven't talked to Lawson since Christmas.

"He didn't say, but I told him you'd call him back."

I wonder for a moment why he didn't call me on my cell, but I don't voice that thought out loud. The last thing I need is for Casey to start asking questions about why I'd have a client calling my personal phone instead of the office, and I really don't need her wondering if something is going on with me and Lawson. Not that there's anything to tell, but still.

I nod. "Is that all?"

"Yes, except that Mr. Duhaime is in room four with Petey."

I groan. "What is it this time?"

"He thinks Petey might have fleas."

My jaw slackens. "He doesn't. He's on the best preventative out there."

"I think we *all* know that, but..." Casey shrugs, knowing as well as I do that no matter what we tell Mr.

Duhaime, it's not going to stop him from coming into the office at least once a week. At this point, I think he's just lonely.

I guess it's a good thing I stopped charging him for unnecessary visits like these long ago. He'd be broke by this point if I hadn't.

"All right." I sigh. "Tell Mr. Duhaime I'll be with him and Petey in a moment. I need to check on room three first."

"I'll go let him know. Room six is ready too."

"On it."

Casey rushes from the room and I push away from my desk, rising to my feet with a tired sigh. It's always wild around here after Christmas thanks to the number of people who get new pets as gifts. I've given the speech that a new critter is a serious responsibility for life and not just for fun over and over and have probably administered no less than a hundred vaccines over the last week. And yet, I still have five hours of work ahead of me.

I stop off in room four, and after looking Petey over, I tell Mr. Duhaime exactly what I knew I'd be telling him—there are no fleas. Petey is perfectly healthy, and as I walk his owner to the front office, I swear the dog gives me a look that says, *"He's back on his bullshit, Doc. See you next week."* And I truly have no doubt that I will.

After finally getting Mr. Duhaime out the door, I stop by rooms three and six, where, thankfully, the visits are quick and easy, one needing vaccines and the other a prescription for allergy meds. After that, it's not so simple between a few dogs who got into leftover Christmas candy, one who ate a sock, and a cat that took a tumble from the top of the tree and now has a broken leg. It's a long, exhausting day, and by the time I'm able to finally sit down, it's nearing eight o'clock and I still have phone calls to make.

I place an order for some Chinese to be delivered, then begin tackling the calls. After my fourth one, my food arrives, and I take a break for the first time. Only it's not really a break when one name keeps jumping out at me from my list, and I stare at it as I eat my fried rice and spicy chicken.

Lucas Lawson.

Lucas Lawson.

Lucas Lawson.

I set down the box of takeout, trading it for my cell. I don't usually make business calls from my phone as I tend to have a strict *when it's my personal time, it's my personal time* kind of policy, but I pull up Lawson's name anyway.

He answers on the first ring. "Wednesday!"

I can *hear* the smile in his voice, and I'm not sure if it's because I've been working my ass to the bone for the last week-plus and I'm utterly exhausted or what, but I find myself smiling too.

I remedy this almost as quickly as it happens.

"Lawson," I return, far less chipper than he is.

"Aw, come on. Don't pretend you don't miss me already."

"I miss a full night of sleep, not waking up with my back aching, and Tamagotchis. You, however, are not on the list of things I even kind of miss."

"Lies."

"Truth. I know it hurts sometimes, but if you're going to cry, do it when we get off the phone, please."

"You know, you should be much nicer to me. I just lost a hockey game. I need support, not sass."

"I'd say sorry, but sass is just who I am." I glance at the clock: it's now twenty after eight. "Where are you?"

"Why? You miss me?"

"Only in your dreams, Lawson."

He laughs. "Philly," he finally answers. "We sucked, they didn't. We'll be in D.C. tomorrow if you want to tune in."

"You know, I just might. I'm sure D.C. would *love* more fans out this way."

"So mean."

"Your point?"

Another deep laugh. "No point. Just an observation."

"I think you like my meanness."

"Maybe," he hedges, and his tone indicates I might just be right.

I don't know how I feel about being right.

"Why'd you call, Lawson?"

"Ah, right. I have a neighbor kid watching Daisy while they're on winter break. He said Daisy tore off half her bandage. I wasn't exactly sure what the protocol with that would be."

"Is she acting like she's in pain?"

"No? I mean, I had the kid video-chat me and she seemed fine, but he's twelve, so I'm not entirely sure what all he actually knows about taking care of a dog."

"Says the new dog dad."

"Hey! I'm a great dog dad. I feed her turkey bacon."

"And take her to the movies. Can't forget that."

"She's loved."

"She's *spoiled*, and you're a sucker."

"You say sucker, I say good dog dad."

"Hmm." He chuckles at my noncommittal answer. "Is it red or warm to the touch?"

"Is… Wait, what?"

"Focus, Lawson. I'm talking about Daisy."

"Ah, right." He laughs awkwardly. "I didn't realize we'd circled back to that. Uh, um, no. Not red and not warm."

"Are you sure? Because you don't sound sure, and I need you to be sure."

"I'm sure, Wednesday."

I roll my eyes at the nickname even though he can't see me. "If she's not in pain and there's no redness and it's not warm, it'll be fine without the bandage. I gave her antibiotics, and it's been wrapped for over a week. If something were going to go wrong with it, it would have by now."

"So she's good?"

"She's good."

He breathes a sigh of relief. "Good. Because I'd hate to have to miss hockey because I had to fly back home to take care of her."

"You'd do that?"

"Since I want to win Best *and* Hottest Dog Dad of the Year, then yes. I'm expecting big trophies, too."

"I'm not giving you a trophy for doing the bare minimum, Lawson."

"But what you're saying is if there were a trophy to win, I'd win it for being Hottest Dog Dad?"

A laugh bubbles out of me before I can contain it, and I regret it instantly, especially when Lawson gasps loudly.

"Did you… Did I… Did I make you *laugh*? Again?"

The pride in his voice is evident, and I can imagine him puffing his chest out proudly. He's that obnoxious.

I sober myself. "No. I was clearing my throat."

"Uh-huh. Sure. That sounded an awful lot like a laugh to me."

"Well, then you're hearing things."

"Are we sure about that?"

"Positive. Anyway, you know you still need to bring Daisy in for a more comprehensive checkup, right?"

"You kidding me? Trophy-winning dog dad here. Of course I know this." A pause. "Can you remind me of the time again?"

"You're not even on the schedule."

"Sure I am. For whenever you schedule me."

This time, I don't laugh, but I also don't miss the twitch of my lips. I force them to still, annoyed I'm finding him amusing. It must be the lack of sleep. "I'll make sure Casey gets you on the schedule. She'll send you the info."

"Excellent. Daisy and I both thank you."

The line goes quiet, neither of us knowing what to say next. I should hang up. I have a pile of work left, and I'm sure he's beat having just played a game.

"What time is it there?" I find myself asking anyway.

"After eleven."

"What are you doing?"

"Currently on the bus to the airport. We're traveling to D.C. tonight, so we can rest in the morning. Are you going to ask me what I'm wearing next?"

"N—"

"Because it's a suit, in case you were wondering. We have the option to wear whatever, but I like how I look in a suit, so I figure why not?"

Of course that would be his reason.

"I wasn't going to ask."

"Sure you weren't." His laugh rumbles through the phone.

"You're on the other side of the country, yet you're still so damn annoying."

"It's a gift."

"More like a curse if you ask me."

"Yet, I didn't."

"Oooh, sleepy Lawson is sassy Lawson."

"What? You can dish it but can't take it?"

"Oh, I can take it." The second the words are spoken, I regret them. "I—"

"I have no doubt that you can, Rory." His voice is gravelly and low and so...*hot*. How did I never notice how hot Lawson's voice is?

No. Not hot. Annoying. Lawson is annoying. Everything about him is annoying, especially his voice.

I sit forward in my chair, ignoring the sudden throb between my legs. "Is that all you need?"

He laughs darkly, like he knows exactly what his words did to me. "Yes, that's all."

"Good."

"Yeah, good." But I can still hear the humor in his voice. I hate it. "I'll see you Sunday," he tells me.

"Wait…what? Why Sunday?"

"The photoshoot, remember? I'm bringing Daisy."

Oh god.

Why did I assume I wouldn't have to see Lawson again until his appointment? Why didn't I think about him being at the photoshoot? Ugh. I'm regretting this more and more by the second.

"Oh."

"Don't sound so excited, Rory."

"I'm not."

"Are too."

"Am not," I argue, though it feels childish and pointless because I know whatever I say, he's going to take issue with it.

"Whatever you need to tell yourself."

"You're impossible."

"Impossibly good looking maybe."

I sigh, shaking my head. "Goodbye, *Lawson*."

"Good night, *Rory*."

I groan, and he laughs. I can still hear it as I pull the phone away, hitting the red button on the screen. He's the most exasperating person I've ever met, and no matter what he says, I am *not* excited about seeing him on Sunday.

Which is why I choose to completely ignore the spark that flits through me at the thought and bury myself in Lawson-free work.

Chapter 5

"Left, left!" Locke hollers across the ice, and because we've been playing together for a while now, I know he's talking to me.

I do a spin-o-rama to avoid the incoming hit, laughing when the Washington player slams hard into the glass, missing me completely. He doesn't find it as funny as I do, charging down the ice after me, the puck now on my stick as I push my legs as hard as I can to outskate him.

He's fast, I'll give him that, but I'm faster, dangling the puck between two defensemen and charging into the offensive zone. I flick the puck toward the net, not really aiming for the goal but hoping the goalie flips his pad out and saves it, creating a scoring chance on the other side where Hayes is stationed, ready to fire it in.

We couldn't have set it up better—Hayes giving it

his all, the puck soaring past Washington's goalie, the lamp lighting up behind him. Hayes lifts his stick in the air, and we swarm him.

"Fuck yes." Keller bumps his helmet against the young forward's. "That's my boy!"

"Let's keep it rolling, boys," Dulak, one of our defensemen, encourages.

"Now that's what I like to see!" Hutch grabs Hayes by the shoulders, giving him a shake before letting me in the circle, and I fist-bump the kid.

"Nice play," Hayes tells me.

I shrug, pointing at him as I skate backward. "All you, man. All you."

We bump fists with the bench, then get back to work. By the end of the first period, we're up 1 to 0 and feeling damn good, but all that changes when we hit the ice for the second period. Washington scores twice in the first five minutes, then gets a power play on a shitty call and scores again, and we're officially in an uphill battle.

"Fuck!" I scream, banging my stick against the boards until it snaps in half.

I'm sure the TV cameras are trained on me and my outburst, but I don't even care. I'm fucking pissed. We're playing like absolute ass, and I swear I catch Coach checking his watch instead of trying to get us in a good headspace and back in the game.

"This is rough, man," Keller says to me as I settle back on the bench. "Playing like shit."

"We can do this," I promise, but it's a useless sentiment.

Washington doesn't score again in the second, but they do in the third, picking up not one, not two, but *three* more goals, and we skate off the ice with our heads hanging low. It's a brutal loss after such a beauty of a goal in the first, and sadly, it's not our only game like it this season. We've been up and down the ranks all year long, and I'm tired of it. I want consistency. I want to win. I want to be good and prove to everyone I'm not the castaway St. Louis treated me like.

We file into the dressing room, not even one of us saying a word as we start stripping off our gear. Coach strolls in after a few quiet minutes, and we all pause what we're doing, giving him our full attention.

"Need to be stronger on the puck. Check harder. Move faster. Better luck next game."

And that's all he says before heading back out of the room.

The team sits dumbfounded. We're all exchanging looks, disturbed by the lack of leadership we just witnessed.

My eyes find Hutch. "Is that really all he has to say after that?"

Hutch shakes his head. "I guess so."

I'm not saying our coach is a bad coach—he definitely knows how to win and get things done—but whatever he's been bringing to the table here in Seattle…it's not good. Not at all. We got our asses handed to us 6–1, and that was his response? Sure, he's not the one out there on the ice making the mistakes, but he should sure as hell be the one here in the locker room helping us get back in the game. He didn't even come in during the second intermission after we gave up three of those six goals. He left it to Hutch to get us motivated, and he hasn't even officially been named captain yet. Makes it damn hard to root for yourself when your coach doesn't seem to believe in you.

We shower and dress, then head for the bus. I can't remember the last time I was so excited to get home. I just want this road trip to be over with. I want them to announce Hutch as captain and get this team fired up again. I want to snuggle my dog.

"You ready for tomorrow?" Hayes asks, settling into the seat next to me on the bus.

I quirk a brow. "Tomorrow?"

"The shoot with Auden's sister."

Ah, right. I guess with getting decimated tonight, I momentarily forgot about tomorrow.

Tomorrow, when I get to stand in front of a camera for far too long.

Tomorrow, when there's no doubt in my mind my face is going to hurt from smiling too much.

Tomorrow, when I get to see Rory again.

"Damn, man. Didn't realize you were into her."

"Huh?" I look over at Hayes.

He dips his head toward me. "That smile when I mentioned Auden's sister. You're into her, aren't you?"

"Who, Rory?"

"*Who, Rory?*" he mocks with a laugh. "Yeah, *Rory*. You got a thing for her."

"I do—"

"Don't. Don't try to bullshit me. I watched several idiots on the Carolina Comets fall in love. I know that look when I see it. You like her."

"I don't even know her." It's not a denial, but it is the truth. I *don't* know Rory, so I really can't say if I like her or not.

"Maybe not, but you *want* to know her."

"I…" I start, but I swallow the words because truthfully, I can't refute his accusations.

I *do* want to get to know Rory. I don't know why, but she intrigues me. It could be the mean words she slings my way like she's completely unimpressed by my *pro hockey player* status or the fact that she's so uninterested in me it makes me interested in her. Whatever it is, it has me looking forward to seeing her.

"Yeah, that's what I thought." Hayes smiles arrogantly.

I look past him to find Hutch staring at me, brows furrowed, lips tugged down into a frown. I can't decide if he heard our conversation just now and doesn't approve or if that's just the way his face looks since he appears angry about ninety-five percent of the time.

His hard stare sharpens momentarily before he flicks his chin my way and turns to scowl out the window. Only then do I release the breath I wasn't aware I was holding.

Hayes laughs, drawing my attention back to him.

"Don't worry," he says quietly. "Your secret is safe with me."

I want to tell him there is no secret and it's all in his head, but for some reason, I can't find the words. Which leads me to believe that maybe he's not wrong to think there's something between me and Rory after all.

Guess I'll see tomorrow.

I couldn't stop thinking about what Hayes said the entire flight home.

Was it obvious I'm eager to see Rory again? Do I

actually like her, or do I just like riling her up? Did Hutch hear our conversation? When he murders me for being into his future sister-in-law, will he stuff my body in a dumpster or feed it to pigs? The questions kept repeating in my mind all night and I couldn't decide which, if any, I could answer with yes.

So, this morning when my alarm went off, I popped out of bed faster than I have in a long time and raced around my apartment like a fool to get ready for the photoshoot.

Not because of Rory. Nope. Not at all. Had absolutely nothing to do with her. I was just eager to get to Daisy and get today over with. That's the absolute *only* reason I'm annoyed by the sight in front of me.

"Tell me again what happened," I say to Jaden, the twelve-year-old neighbor kid I've recruited to watch Daisy for me.

"Well, Daisy had to pee, so I took her outside. There was a cat, and Daisy saw it. She was trying to say hi—*just* hi—but the cat got scared and swatted. So Daisy barked, and the cat freaked, then tried to run and well… Daisy chased it. She didn't go far, I swear, but there was a puddle and…" He gestures toward where my dog is sitting with her tail wagging and her tongue hanging out. She's completely covered in mud, and we have to be at the photoshoot in half an hour, and it's a ways away. "She's a little messy."

"A little?" I rub the now-throbbing spot between my eyes. He's a good kid and I know it's not on him, but damn. I am so going to be late for the shoot now.

He hooks his thumbs into his belt loops, kicking at something invisible on the ground. "I'm really sorry, Mr. Lawson."

I cringe at the name, not because it reminds me of my dad or anything, especially since I have my mother's last name. No, it's the *mister* part. I'm under thirty; I'm not a mister.

"It's okay, Jaden. It's not your fault." I reach into my back pocket and pluck my wallet free, grabbing a hundred bucks and shoving it his way. "Here you go."

His eyes widen as he takes the bills, fanning them out with a megawatt grin. "Thanks so much, Mr. Lawson. I swear I'll put it in my piggy bank and won't touch it unless I really, really need to. I won't even go buy the new *Zombie Wars: The Dead Awaken...Again (This Time They're Really Dead Deluxe Edition)*, I promise."

I laugh, ruffling his dirty-blond hair. "It's your money, kid. Do what you want with it. And please, just call me Lawson."

I scoop Daisy up, trying to hold her far enough away to not get me messy, but it's pointless. She's dripping wet, and there's no way I'm going to make it back without getting dirty.

"Thanks again for watching her."

"No problem. I've always wanted a dog, and Mom said this was good practice, so maybe…" He rocks back on his heels, and I know what he's asking without him saying it.

"I promise to give her a glowing review." I wink at him, yanking open the front door. "Oh, and don't forget to ask her about that game. I meant it when I said I'd get you and your friends some tickets. Just tell me the date and I'll make it happen."

Unlike most of the guys on the team, I chose to live in a more modestly priced apartment. My ample salary means I could afford somewhere much nicer and more secluded, but I know hockey isn't going to last forever. I want to squirrel away all the money I can while I'm still making it. The longer I live here, the more I think I made the right choice. I don't know what I'd do if I didn't have Jaden and his mom around to help pick up my slack when I'm not here. Paige has been such a help when it comes to getting my mail and packages. In exchange, I take Jaden out whenever I get the chance and spend some one-on-one time with him. His dad walked out of the picture a long time ago, and I guess I can relate to him, being raised by a single mom and all.

The kid's grin grows, and he shoots me a thumbs-up. "Will do, Mr. Lawson."

"Later, Jaden." I don't bother correcting him this time, pulling the door shut behind me.

I trudge back down the hall to my apartment and make my way straight to the bathroom. Luckily, Daisy doesn't fight me through the bath. In fact, she loves it, splashing in the water like a little kid. I get her cleaned up, dried, and in the carrier I had delivered to Paige's place while I was gone, then I change my clothes before heading out the door.

By some miracle, there's little traffic on the way there, and I'm only ten minutes late when I pull into the lot.

"I'm here! I'm here!" I say, rushing into the building where the shoot is happening.

"Ah! Finally!" Auden claps excitedly, rushing over to grab my bag of supplies for Daisy and taking it from me. "We're all running a bit behind, so we haven't started yet. Drinks and snacks are over there, and you can either hold on to this little angel"—she sticks her fingers into the crate, wagging them at Daisy—"or set her over with the others."

She points to a spot where several carriers are lined up, some housing dogs and some cats. A few crates are empty, some of the other guys on the team already bonding with the animals. I wonder briefly if we'll even get a chance to advertise them to the public or if the players will adopt them all after today.

"Thanks," I tell her. "Is Rory here?"

Auden's brows pull together, probably wondering why I'm asking after her sister. Hell, *I* don't even know why I'm asking about her, but I can't take it back now.

"Uh, yeah," my teammate's girlfriend tells me. "She's over there."

I follow where she points, finding Rory standing on the other side of the table. Her dark hair hangs loosely around her shoulders, and the dark jeans she's wearing cling to every curve. She's wearing a simple navy top that must be low-cut. I know this because Gregor, the slimiest guy on the team, is staring right down her shirt, never mind his wife and three kids at home.

I march right on over to the table, stopping opposite them.

"Rory."

She startles, peering at me with those damn green eyes I swear are the clearest I've ever seen. They narrow when she realizes it's me.

"Yes?"

"I'm here," I announce.

I don't know *why* I announce it. Maybe because I hate how close she's standing to Gregor. Maybe because I want it to be *me* standing so close to her. Or maybe I've finally lost my mind. Who knows?

She lifts a single brow. "Would you like a cookie?"

"Yes."

She smirks, then reaches down and grabs one off the table, holding it out to me. "Here you go."

I grab it, shoving it in my mouth and eating it like a man gone mad, not caring about the crumbs falling out all over my shirt. The corners of her lips tip up, and now I *really* don't care how ridiculous I look because *I* made her smile. Not stupid Gregor. *Me.*

"Wow. Look at you."

"Yep. Look at me." I look over at my teammate. "Gregor, how's your wife doing?"

He visibly stiffens, a hand coming up to squeeze the back of his neck. "Uh, she's g-good." He takes a sip of his drink. "I'm, uh, going to go get my costume on for the shoot."

"Yeah, you do that, man." There is absolutely no mistaking the venom in my words, the growl to my tone.

"Excuse me," he mutters, rushing off without another glance in Rory's direction.

When I look back at her, she rolls her lips together, fighting a laugh.

"You happy?"

"Yep."

She shakes her head, walking away with a hint of a smile on her face, and I'm...relieved. I don't have the right to feel that way, but I do. I've been his teammate for over a year now. I know exactly what Gregor was up to, and I wasn't about to let Rory fall for his shit.

Hell, I don't want her to fall for *my* shit either, but I'd rather it be mine than his. I shake that thought away, grabbing another cookie. I'm going to need the sugar to get me through these next few hours.

We have a quick meeting, going over the process, pose ideas, and other details. Six of the guys brought their own pets to showcase, and we're filling the other months with dogs and cats from a local shelter with the goal of getting them adopted within thirty days of the calendar's release, which is just next week. It's a short window to get the project into production, but we're all up for the challenge, especially if it means getting these little guys a home.

Up first are Keller and Cheddar, an older orange tabby whose owner passed away six months ago. She's been with the shelter since and is looking for a new family to take her in.

"Smile!" Rory instructs after two shots where he's sitting there with a dead face.

"I am smiling."

"You're frowning."

"No, this is a smile," the surly centerman argues.

Rory huffs, clenching her fists. I try my best not to laugh at how ridiculous my teammate looks, at how irritated Rory is. She doesn't know that this truly *is* him smiling. I know she wants a traditional, teeth-baring grin, but Keller's face doesn't move that way.

The cat in Keller's arms tries to wiggle free for the third time in as many minutes.

"She can feel that you're uncomfortable," Rory tells him.

"Well, that's because I *am* uncomfortable. Do I really have to wear a turtleneck?"

"Yes. It makes you look distinguished."

"I look like a fucking nerd," he growls, rearranging the cat.

"We're only on January and this is easily my favorite project I've ever done," Ryan Bell, the photographer, says from behind the camera, watching the scene unfold with a smirk. "Please nobody tell Adrian I said that."

Her eyes flit to the side of the set, where her husband, Adrian Rhodes, a defenseman for the Carolina Comets, who we're playing on Tuesday, stands talking with Hutch. Ryan is not only a mega YouTube star known for her makeup videos, but also an accomplished photographer, and you'd have to be living under a rock to not have seen her stuff all over the internet, especially her piece on flaws where she got the big, grumpy hockey player she married to cry on camera.

"I heard that," Rhodes yells, not once taking his eyes off the Serpents' captain, nodding along with whatever he's saying.

Ryan flicks her gaze skyward, a smile on her lips. "All right. Now, let's try to smile *with teeth*," she instructs Keller before tossing Rory a wink as she makes her way over to my side to watch the shitshow in front of us.

Keller pulls his lips wider, flashing his teeth at the camera, and it's utterly terrifying. Maybe this is the reason he never smiles.

"Why is that the scariest thing I've ever seen?" Rory remarks, her eyes trained on the shoot as Keller tries to keep the cat calm.

"Downright creepy," I agree.

"Okay, yeah, don't do that." Ryan shoots him what I believe is supposed to be a reassuring smile, but it's wobbly at best. She's as creeped out as we are.

A few guys on the team laugh, and Keller flips them off.

"Can't believe I'm giving up my Sunday for this," Rory says, covering her mouth, trying to hide a yawn.

Not that I'd say it out loud to her, but she looks tired. I bet if there were a bed here somewhere, she'd be the first one to faceplant on it.

"I know why we're here, but what about you?"

She lifts a shoulder. "I guess they figured having a

vet on set would be beneficial in case something happened. Auden asked me, so here I am."

"So you're here to supervise the children?"

"Well, you're here, aren't you?" she counters, a dark brow lifted my way.

I grin. "Fair enough." I lift Daisy, who has been calmly chilling in my arms since I brought her out of her crate. "Did you say hi to our daughter?"

Rory sighs heavily. "Once again, we're not co-parents, Lawson."

"Sure we're not." I grab Daisy's paw, making her wave. "Hi, Mommy. Did you miss me?"

"I swear…" She pinches her nose. I'm not sure if she's more annoyed by the silly baby voice I'm using or because I keep calling her my co-parent. Either way, I don't stop.

"I was such a good girl while Daddy was away. I only had two accidents and got lots of belly rubs. But I missed my daddy so, so much."

Finally, she looks over. "Your dad is an idiot, Daisy, and every day, I regret just a little more making him take you home."

"Hey!" I tuck the dog back into my arms, covering her ears. "She doesn't need to be poisoned by your ill feelings toward me."

"I'm not poisoning her. I'm merely educating her."

"Mean."

Her shrug says indifference, but the twitch to her lips says otherwise.

"Next!" Ryan shouts, fiddling with her camera as several people come in to change up the background.

The team's rented out a massive studio, and there are distinctive scenes set up around the room to represent the different months. Some can be adjusted by quickly switching out a few props, but each has its own flair to it. Right now, we're shifting over to February, which means a little less snow and more pinks and reds. The mountain background is swapped for a bright white, and heart balloons replace the snow-people family that was off to the side. It's nothing too elaborate, but it's enough to create something fun for a good cause.

"Who's February?"

"That's me!" Hayes says, setting his plate of snacks down and moseying toward the set.

"Give me five minutes, then I'll be ready," Ryan tells him. "And don't forget your heart-shaped glasses."

He winces, but it only lasts a moment because Rhodes is giving him a death glare that says, *Listen to my wife or I'll make you listen.*

"Uh, yes, ma'am." Hayes tucks his chin to his chest, then shuffles over to wardrobe to retrieve his accessories.

I'd laugh at the whole exchange if Rhodes' glower

didn't frighten me so much. I've only met Rhodes on the ice and he seems like a nice enough guy, but that nasty scar that drags down the side of his face makes him appear menacing no matter what's coming out of his mouth.

"What month are you and Daisy?" Rory asks.

"March."

"Mmm." It's all she says, cool and indifferent as always. It makes me want to see what it would take to get her to drop the act.

I take a step closer. She doesn't move, but she does suck in a breath.

"Why? Were you hoping I was June or July? Eager to see me in swim shorts?"

"No." But the word is missing her usual bite.

I lean closer. "I'd have to take my shirt off. To match the summer theme, of course."

She swallows. "Ew."

Again, no bite.

Another step, my lips only inches from her ear. "I bet you'd be the first to volunteer to rub the oil all over my abs, wouldn't you, Rory?"

I say it to see her squirm, to see if my words affect her, and they do. Her breaths come in sharper, chest rising and falling rapidly. When her eyes slide my way, there's something churning in them I haven't seen before: *lust*.

"No, thanks. I'd prefer to keep my breakfast down today."

Her words are cold, unemotional. But her eyes…

They tell a whole different story.

"Hmm. Whatever you say, Rory. Whatever you say."

She narrows her eyes before huffing, storming away. I laugh, watching her leave, but I know it as well as she does—walking away isn't at all what she wanted to do. It's what she *needed* to do, because if Rory had stayed, she just may have had to admit she likes me.

And I like the idea of that entirely too much.

Chapter 6

RORY

For the first time in a long time, I show up to work late the day following the photoshoot.

I tossed and turned all night, and when my alarm went off at five, I didn't hesitate to hit snooze—*twice*. Even Hades let me sleep. He didn't wake me up at his usual crack of dawn by prancing across my stomach. It wasn't until Casey called my cell and asked if I was coming in that I finally dragged myself out of bed and raced to the clinic.

I couldn't fall asleep no matter what I tried. Finally, after three hours of trying and two meditation sessions, I was able to drift off only to awaken in the middle of the night in a sweaty mess after the most awful of dreams.

The most frustrating part of all is that it's not my fault. It's Lawson's.

It was the way he acted with his teammate. All we were doing was talking. I mean, okay, so Gregor was flirting a little, but it's nothing I haven't been through before. I was fighting off his advances without Lawson's help. He didn't need to step in and get all growly. Was he jealous? Or was he just being protective because he knows Gregor is married? I don't know, but I had to walk away after that. Not because I was mad at him for stepping in, but because, if I'm being honest, I liked that side of him entirely too much. I can't remember the last time someone showed such… *possessiveness* when it came to me, if ever. I needed a moment alone to gather my thoughts and talk down my racing heart.

When I finally got my shit under control, he just *had* to tease me about wanting to see him shirtless and rub oil all over him, which started a whole new kind of marching in my heart. I didn't want to then and I still don't want to now, but my brain can't seem to work that out. My vagina can't either considering I woke up in a heat, my nether regions throbbing after a dream where I was not only rubbing oil on his abs but also whipped cream.

It was a weird, strange nightmare, and I hated every second of it, which is why it was so annoying that it kept repeating. Over and over, it was just me and Lawson. It would start innocently, then he'd say something stupid and I'd rip his shirt off, running my hands that were miraculously oiled all over him.

It was completely illogical, yet I couldn't stop my body from responding to it. It makes me hate Lawson even more, the way he got into my head, and now, thanks to him, I'm behind on work. Again.

"Hey, boss, I'm going to run and grab lunch. You need anything?"

Ugh, lunch. I didn't even think about that as I was racing from my apartment.

"A large coffee from The Coffee Spot?" I ask Casey.

She laughs. "Late night, huh?"

Oh, if she only knew. "Something like that," I mutter. "And can you get me the schedule when you get back? I want to go over it and make sure everything is good."

"Will do."

She taps the doorframe twice before bouncing off, leaving me to my pile of work.

I manage to get through three patients before she comes back with the coffee, also dropping off a sandwich because she knows me well enough to know I likely didn't pack a lunch. I'm in the middle of scarfing it down when my phone rings.

I smile when I see the name on the screen.

"Sister," I answer.

"Rory! I was hoping I'd catch you during a down moment."

"You just saw me yesterday. What could you possibly want?"

"Gosh, your love for me never, ever ceases to amaze me."

I laugh. "It's not just you."

"Yes, yes, I know—people are the worst. Blah, blah, blah."

"They really are. Especially when they bother me in the middle of a workday. Why are you calling, Auden?"

"I just…" She trails off, then sighs heavily.

I set my lunch down. This feels like it's going to be a lengthy conversation. "You're bored, aren't you?"

"No. I just don't know what to do with my hands." She laughs a little. "I mean…a month ago I was running a billion-dollar empire. Now I'm… here."

"You're supposed to be relaxing."

"I am relaxing!"

"Really? Is that why you spearheaded an impromptu calendar photoshoot? Because you're *relaxing*?"

"Shut up," she grumbles because she knows I'm right.

I can't really blame her. I'm sure it's hard for her to

turn it off after working nonstop for so many years. I have the same problem turning it off too.

"Do you think you made a mistake selling your company?"

"No." Her answer is instant, which is how I know it's true. "Not in the least. I'm glad I sold it. Hell, I wish I would have sold it sooner. I know people are talking and ragging on me because I apparently sold my company for a guy—don't even get me started on that crock of shit—but I don't care. It wasn't for Hutch. It was for *me*. I was unhappy. I was tired of being *on* all the time and constantly go, go, go. Don't get me wrong, I love what I built, but I gave up so much for it. We're not supposed to spend our twenties working our asses to the bone. We're supposed to have fun and make mistakes and maybe even find love, not be killing ourselves. You don't even know the amount of stress that was on my shoulders that's now gone. It's truly a relief. I'm just…"

"Yes?"

"I don't know. I'm so used to running myself ragged and now I'm supposed to…what? *Relax?* What do people even do to relax?"

I can't answer her because I don't know. I never relax. Even on my "off" days, I'm still likely to be found here at the clinic, and if I'm at home, I'm probably reading up on the latest treatments and medical news. I don't know how to relax either, but I sure would like to figure it out.

"You are asking the wrong person. I think Dad would be better suited to giving advice. He's a pro at being retired."

Auden laughs. "He really took to it, didn't he?"

If my father isn't on the golf course, he's doing something hockey-related, a fundraiser or visiting the rink. He hasn't played in a long time, but he couldn't stay away from the game if he tried.

"Well, raising two kids practically on your own will do that. Speaking of our parents…what holiday did you get?"

"Easter." I'd laugh if it wasn't so sad. "Hutch wants to give her a piece of his mind. I keep having to convince him it's fine and I'm used to it."

"He's a good one."

She lets out a dreamy sigh. "He's the best."

I fake a heave. "Gross."

"Shut up. I used to be like you, you know, swearing off love and feelings and stuff. Now look at me—head over heels in love with a hockey player. It'll happen to you too."

"Not in this lifetime."

"Don't be so sure," she singsongs. "It's going to sneak up when you least expect it. Just watch."

"I'll pass, thanks."

I'm almost certain I hear her eyes roll. "Whatever. Just wait."

"Oh, I am—with bated breath and all."

"You're so cynical."

"It's my most flattering trait."

"That's one way to put it. I saw a couple of the guys looking longingly at you yesterday, you know."

"You did not," I counter.

"Did too. Hayes was one of them."

"What? The new guy?"

"You sound like Hutch, calling him that."

"Well, he *is* the new guy." Hayes was traded to the Serpents before the start of the season. It was a major move by the team, and nobody saw it coming, least of all Hayes. He's been a bit of a problem child in the NHL so far, so I'm surprised the team would want to take that on. "And he wasn't looking at me. He was probably just checking out the snack table. I did stand by it an awful lot."

"You're impossible, you know that?"

"And yet, you love me."

Casey stops in front of my office, a piece of paper in her hands: the schedule I requested. I wave her in.

"Look, Auden, I know you're like super retired now and all, but some of us *do* still have to work."

"Shut. Up," she says for the third time during this conversation.

"So original."

"Hate you."

"Lies," I tell her, grabbing the paper from Casey and mouthing a *thank you* before she takes her leave.

"Fine. I love you, Aurora Rose Sinclair."

I want to gag at my full name. I hate it. Why would they name me after a Disney princess? Lawson was right—I'm much more like Wednesday Addams than a princess any day of the week.

I hate that Lawson was right.

"Stop it," I demand.

"I loooooove you," she sings, dragging out the word *love* obnoxiously. "Favorite little sister of mine. I love you forever and ever and ever."

"I swear I'll hang up."

"And ever and ever."

I hit the red button, tossing my phone onto the desk.

Less than thirty seconds later, I get a text with about a hundred hearts. I reply with a middle finger, and she sends back a bunch of laughing emojis, knowing me far too well. I'm never going to be one to send "I love you" texts or regale her with my feelings. My sister knows I love her, and that's all that matters.

I take a sip of my piping-hot coffee as I start going over the schedule. I like to be prepared for what patients are coming in so I can know if it's going to be a difficult day or a good one.

Tomorrow looks like a good one so far. The Hallsteads and their Boxer Kenneth. Mr. Oliver and his cat Legolas. Ms. Winters is bringing in her spoiled yet sweet Chihuahuas. Then there's Lucas Lawson and—

Hold up.

I read over it again. *Lucas Lawson with Daisy. 1 PM. Dr. Sinclair.*

Tomorrow.

Lawson's coming into the clinic *tomorrow.*

How did I not know this? Why wasn't I warned? Why did he not say something yesterday? Sure, it could have been because I spent much of the day ignoring him and left without saying goodbye, but still. He could have said *something.*

My mind drifts to what Auden said during our call, and I wonder who she was referring to when she mentioned the guys looking at me. I know she said Hayes, but she used plural words, which means it was more than one guy.

Does she mean Lawson? My heart resumes that same hurried beat it had every time I woke up last night in a haze. *Thump-thump, thump-thump.*

Do I...do I *want* her to mean Lawson? No. *No.*

That's absurd. I don't want her to mean him. I *can't* want her to mean him. It's Lawson. I don't like him. I'm sure all this heart pounding is because of yesterday and my lack of having sex for over a year. That's all it is.

I look at his name on my schedule again.

Thump-thump, thump-thump, thump-thump.

I push to my feet in a hurry, grabbing my white coat and slinging it over my shoulders, forcing myself away from the stupid schedule. I'm not excited about seeing Lawson tomorrow. Not at all.

I don't care what my damn heart says.

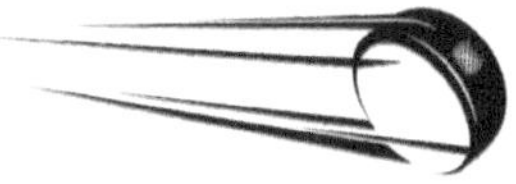

I check the clock for what feels like the hundredth time today. Thirty minutes to go.

I don't know how, but I managed to sleep through the night. It doesn't matter, though; I've been on edge all day, and I know exactly who to blame for it.

Casey. Why couldn't she have given Lawson's file to Dr. Helms? She's an incredible veterinarian. I'm sure she'd love having him as a patient far more than I would, but alas, it's me she decided to torture. Is it because I was here that night he first came in? Either way, I'm screwed. Sure, I could have refused it, could have passed it on, but that would have created even more questions that require answers I don't have.

I check the clock again: twenty-five minutes to go.

I do everything I can to distract myself, even going so far as to begin organizing the supply closet that's already organized. The techs and receptionists are looking at me like I'm bananas, but I can't stop. I have to keep myself busy. If I don't, I might stop and think about *why* I'm all amped up, and I *really* don't want to do that.

When I check the clock again, it's one, which is when Lawson should be here, but he's not. I keep one eye on the door, my heart leaping into my throat every time the bell goes off, but it's pointless because he doesn't show.

Not at five after, not at ten after, and not even at thirty after.

He's late—like *really* late—and now I'm just annoyed. How can he be so irresponsible? He's supposed to be taking care of Daisy; how can he miss such an important appointment? She needs a checkup after being on the streets like she's been.

When the clock strikes three, I'm officially pissed. There's been no communication at all from him. Not even a *Fuck you, I'm not coming in* message. It's been nothing at all.

I don't bother trying to call him. Instead, I march

to my office, find his address, then shuck off my white coat, trading it for a different one before grabbing my bag and storming to the front of the clinic on a mission.

"Dr. Sinclair?" Casey questions, brows cinched together.

"I had a house call come up. If my next patient comes in early, send them to Dr. Helms."

Thankfully she doesn't have anything to say to that. She simply nods, then agrees to do what I asked, and I push out the building.

It's only then do I take a deep breath.

I'm being reckless. I know that. But I can't seem to stop myself. I'm too damn frustrated.

I push forward, pulling out my phone to navigate to Lawson's apartment. It's not far from here. And who knows? Maybe I'll have cooled off by the time I get there, and I don't mean literally.

I pull my wool jacket closer around me, turning right, left, right, then right again. I'm nearly to his place, and I still haven't calmed down. Who does Lawson think he is? Wasting not only my time but others' too? We work hard to keep that clinic a well-oiled machine. One client missing their appointment is time taken away from someone else, from someone who actually cares about their pets.

Sure, I'm probably being a little dramatic, but it's

Lawson. I knew he was irresponsible, but I didn't realize he'd bail on me altogether.

My footsteps slow when I come up on his building. It's far from what I expected from him. I figured he'd be at one of the massive high-rises, living in utter luxury, but that's not the case at all. The building in front of me is sleek but modest. It's clearly a newer build, but it's not lavish.

It's not at all what I was anticipating, but still, I pull the door open and step into the lobby. I'm greeted by a gentleman in a pressed navy uniform who tips his hat to me as I push my shoulders back and make my way to the elevator.

My dad taught me something long ago—if you go somewhere you're not supposed to, pretend you belong there anyway, and that's just what I do in this moment. Nobody stops me on my way to the elevator, and I push the button for the twelfth floor. I count the floors as they pass by, taking another steadying breath when the lift stops at my destination. I poise my hand to knock, then stop.

What am I doing? This is insane. *I'm* insane. I'm—

A bark sounds on the other side of the white door, and it's all the go-ahead I need. I pound my fist against the wood.

Nothing.

I knock again. Still nothing. I lift my hand to knock

a third time, but it's pointless because the door isn't there anymore. It's been wrenched open, and standing in front of me is Lawson…and he's shirtless.

No. Not just shirtless.

He's wearing nothing but a pair of low-slung gray sweatpants that leave little to the imagination, and *holy hell* is my mind running wild. I know logically it's because of what he said at the photoshoot on Sunday to get me all riled up, but that doesn't stop my body from responding to the sight before me.

There's a smattering of hair across his chest and his abs. I didn't know it was possible to have that many or for them to look that sharp. I figured with hockey, Lawson wouldn't look bad shirtless. I guess I just never expected he'd look this good either.

"Rory?" he says, his voice scratchy and low.

It's only then that I drag my eyes from his semi-dressed form and to his face. The first thing I notice is that he needs a shave. The second is that he looks good *un*shaven. The third is that he's wearing a pair of black-rimmed glasses that have no business looking so good. And the fourth is that it is very, very clear I woke him up.

He reaches up and scratches at his chest. "What are you doing here, Rory?"

I swallow thickly, crossing my arms over my chest,

hoping to hide the way my nipples are straining against my thin shirt. "You're late."

His thick brows hitch up. "Excuse me?"

"Your appointment. You're late."

He tips his head to the side, clearly not understanding what I'm getting at. His sweet little Labrador pads across the apartment, her footsteps *clunk, clunk, clunking* over the hardwood floors. She forces her head between Lawson's legs, making her presence known.

That's when I see it—realization.

"Oh fuck." Lawson drops his head backward on a sigh. "Shit."

He bends to scoop Daisy into his arm, his bicep popping as he snuggles her close.

I will not be jealous of a dog.

I will not be jealous of a dog.

I will not be fucking jealous of a dog.

"We're sorry," he says, waving Daisy's paw my way. "We were taking a nap."

A nap? That's his big excuse?

I don't budge. In fact, I don't even *think* about budging. I continue to stare him down, waiting for a better explanation.

He lifts his arm, raking his hand through his hair. Why is it suddenly so hot in his building? They must really be cranking the heat. I get that it's January, but damn.

"Do you want to come in?" he asks, moving to the side.

I don't know why I do it, call it curiosity or whatever, but I walk right past him and into his apartment. I stop short when I notice the boxes stacked in the corner.

"Do you live here or are you squatting?"

He laughs, closing the door behind me. "I know it doesn't look like it, but yes, I do live here. I haven't gotten the chance to unpack yet."

"You've been here over a year, though."

He lifts a brow my way. "Been keeping tabs on me, Rory?"

"You wish. I've heard Auden talk about the Serpents. She's super into hockey now, I guess."

"Comes with the territory of dating a hockey player." He sets Daisy down; she doesn't move from beside his feet. He points behind him. "I'm going to go put a shirt on."

"That would be preferable."

The grin he gives me tells me he doesn't believe me, but thankfully, he says nothing, shuffling off into his bedroom, Daisy right at his heels.

I take the chance to look around his apartment. It's

clean, I'll give him that, but it's empty. The walls are an off-white with nothing on them. Aside from the couch, the coffee table, a bookshelf, and the TV setup, there's not much else going on either. It really looks like he hardly lives here at all. I'm not sure exactly what I was expecting his house to look like. Maybe more hard lines, furniture that looks uncomfortable to sit on, fancy gadgets, and perhaps a bikini-clad woman sitting by his too-big outdoor pool. Something that screams rich playboy hockey player.

This is a far cry from that.

I'm perusing his collection of books—mostly biographies and crime novels—when he comes back out of his room and heads for the kitchen. Much to my chagrin, he's wearing a shirt and he's swapped his glasses for contacts.

He opens the fridge, then peeks over his shoulder at me. "Drink?"

"No, thanks."

He shrugs but pulls out a pitcher of water anyway. He reaches into the cabinet next to the fridge and grabs two cups, pouring water in each before stepping over to two bowls he has set up on the opposite side of the kitchen and pouring water into one of them.

He's giving Daisy filtered water. I *love* that he's giving Daisy filtered water.

He slides the pitcher back into the fridge, then pushes one of the full glasses of water across the counter and toward me. Only then do I move forward, farther into the apartment. I sidle up to the counter and accept the drink, suddenly feeling thirsty. I down half of it in one go.

Lawson arches his brow at me when I'm finished, then crosses his arms over his chest as he leans back against the counter behind him. "So, Rory, what brings you by?"

"I told you, you're late. You—"

"I know that. I guess I'm just confused. Do you make house calls to all your patients?"

"Yes."

It's a lie, and we both know it. But somehow Lawson doesn't call me on it.

"I was worried for Daisy," I tell him, pushing my shoulders back and lifting my chin higher.

"That so?" He smirks. "Well, there's nothing to be worried about. As you can see, she's fine." He nods to where the pup sits, right beside his feet again, her tongue lolling out as she looks up at her dad.

Yeah, me too, Daisy. Me too.

I shove that thought away, looking back at the cocky hockey player standing across from me. "What are you doing sleeping in the middle of the day?"

"*Game* day," he corrects, and a heavy feeling sinks into my gut. I didn't realize today is a game day for him. If I had known, I probably would have thought a little harder about marching over here and confronting him. "I always take a pre-game nap. I was wiped out after morning skate and just passed out. I didn't even think about my appointment. I'm sorry."

Standing across from him now, I see he *does* look tired. I'm sure it's from all the travel, playing games, and adding in press, the photoshoot, and everything else that comes with being a pro athlete. Not to mention he has a brand-new puppy at home. It'd be a lot for anyone.

I lower my defenses, letting my shoulders relax. "Well, I'm here now, so I may as well give Daisy her shots."

"What? Here?"

I nod, setting my bag on the chair next to me. After taking off my wool jacket and slinging it over the back of the stool, I dig around for the medicines I tucked in there before I left, then set the case they're in on the counter.

"I didn't realize veterinarians did house calls."

"We have patients who don't travel well and older owners who don't get around the best either, so we offer home visits for special cases."

"And I'm a special case?"

"No, Lawson. You're not. You're just an idiot who missed his appointment."

He mashes his lips together, nodding. "I deserved

that." He scoops Daisy up again. "Where do you want us?"

"Wherever she's most comfortable."

He nods his head toward the couch. "There is fine."

I let him lead the way, then settle down on the couch, leaving a cushion open between us. He sets the dog down and she looks between us like she's confused by what's happening.

Don't worry, Daisy, so am I.

"Think you can hold her?" I ask him, plucking free the first vaccine.

"Are you kidding? All I do is hold her. She's obsessed with me, aren't you, baby girl?"

Baby girl. I don't know why, but Lawson has never struck me as a pet name sort of guy. Hearing the word fall from his lips just now though… Well, I don't hate it.

I will not be jealous of a dog.

"Bring her closer," I instruct, and he draws nearer, the mixed scents of leather and cedar hitting me all at once. My head goes a little fuzzy and I swear it's getting hotter in here.

Seriously, what kind of heating system does this building have?

"How should I hold her?" he asks, running his hand over top her head to soothe her.

"Like this."

I show him the best way to get her to hold still and keep her calm just in case she jumps at the needle poking her. Once we're settled, I ready the needle.

"You ready?" I ask.

He takes a deep breath. He's more nervous than Daisy is, and it's…cute.

Ugh. What is wrong with me? This is Lawson for crying out loud. He's not cute. Not at all.

I give myself a mental shake, then administer the vaccine with a steady hand. Daisy doesn't flinch, taking the shot like a pro. Could be because she's too busy licking a huge wet spot onto Lawson's navy t-shirt, or it could be all the words he's whispering to her to keep her relaxed.

"You're doing so good."

Then…

"I'm going to give you so many pieces of bacon after this. The homemade turkey kind, just like you like."

And…

"That's it. Just keep staying still. Yeah, like that. Good girl."

Good girl.

Fuck me if those two words don't zing right between my legs. I ignore it, especially since I know it has absolutely *nothing* to do with the man saying them, then pull free the second shot. Again, Daisy does well with it, and Lawson keeps holding her while I check out the cut that was on her leg.

"How is she, Doc?"

Doc.

I've been called it so many times before, daily even. But when Lawson says it…I don't know. I like it, perhaps a little too much. I can't help but wonder if I've slipped off into another dimension where I'm suddenly into Lawson or something. Because if so, I'd like to return to reality now.

I clear my throat. "Really good, actually. She's put on some weight, which is good because she needed it. Her leg is healing nicely, and considering she's been on the streets, her temperament is surprisingly docile. I like that. She's a little warrior, that's for sure."

I boop her nose, and she presses into my touch, seeking more. I offer it, running my hand over her head.

"She likes you," Lawson tells me softly.

"She likes everyone," I say, running my fingers through the dog's soft fur. "So that's not really the compliment you think it is."

"Mmm. I think you're wrong, but I'll let you keep believing that."

I peek up and find him staring down at me with a look in his smoky eyes I haven't seen before. It's a mix of sincerity and something else I can't quite name. Whatever it is, it makes me shift in my seat. Not because it bothers me, but because it's just the opposite —I like it.

I hate that I like it.

"Oh fuck!" Lawson propels off the couch, his hands going to his hair, then to Daisy when he realizes he's scared her. He scared me too.

"What? What is it?" I ask, panicked. He's looking at the space just over my shoulder, right into the kitchen. I glance behind me, trying to see what he does, but there's nothing in my line of sight except for the oven.

"I'm late. I have to be at the rink in less than an hour and it's Seattle and I haven't showered or dressed and I don't have…" He trails off, raking his hand through his hair once more. His teeth sink into his lower, full lip, and I've never seen him this stressed out before. "I… *Shit!*"

Daisy begins to whimper, sensing his anxiety.

"No, no. Shh. It's okay. I'm okay," he tells her, pulling her into his arms and snuggling her close. He looks at me finally. "I have to get to the arena."

"Oh." I rise to my feet. "Okay. I'll just…go." I head for the kitchen to gather my things so I can get out of his way. "I'll—"

"No, Rory, I have to get to the arena."

I pull my eyebrows together. "You said that."

"I…" He gives Daisy a shake. "I don't have anyone to watch her."

"Oh. Well, she should be fine on her own for now, no?"

He grimaces. "I, uh, kind of haven't told the building super about her yet."

He's had her for nearly two weeks; why would he not say anything? "Why not?"

Another cringe, and I just know I'm not going to like his answer. "Because I wasn't sure I was going to keep her?"

"Lawson!" I hiss, stomping my foot because he just brings out that side of me. This is unbelievable! How could he abandon her like that?

"Hey, I said I *wasn't* sure. Now I *am* sure. Like *sure*, sure. She's mine."

I huff. He did say that, didn't he? "Fine. But you need to let them know."

"I know, I know, and I will. But until then, I can't leave her here by herself. You know, just in case she makes a ruckus."

"A ruckus?" I don't know why, but I didn't expect him to use that word. I shake my head. "What about that neighbor kid who was watching her?"

"He has band practice after school on Tuesdays."

I want to ask him how he knows the kid's schedule,

but now doesn't seem like the time when he's standing in front of me with panic in his eyes, looking at me like he wants *me* to fix this.

I cross my arms over my chest. "Out with it."

He blows out a long breath. "Can you watch her? Please? *Pretty please?*" He juts his bottom lip out.

He looks so ridiculous standing there, hair messy from running his hands through it and bottom lip sticking out like he's some little kid who dropped his ice cream cone.

He's not winning this. Not a chance. Not even kind of. Not even—

Daisy whimpers, and I fold.

"Fine."

"Really?" Lawson looks like he's a dog I just gave a treat to.

I nod. Even though it's going to be incredibly inconvenient and I'll need to call the clinic and let them know I'll be out the rest of the day, I'm going to do it. Not for Lawson, but for Daisy.

This is *just* for Daisy.

"Yes, really. Give her over."

I hold my hands out and he crosses the space, forgoing placing Daisy into my outstretched hands and instead doing the absolute last thing I ever expected.

He hugs me. Wraps his dog-filled arms around me and squeezes.

Leather and cedar and warmth blanket me as I stand there stunned, completely unable to move. I want to move. I want to move so damn badly I'm tingling. That has to be the reason I'm tingling. *Has to.* It definitely has nothing at all to do with how good his hard body feels pressed against mine, or how perfectly I seem to fit against him.

Nope. That's not it.

"Uh, Lawson?" I ask, and he tenses.

"Yes?"

"Are you going to hug me forever?"

"Oh." He peels himself off me and—I swear to never, ever admit this out loud—I miss him almost instantly. He takes a step back, then another, clearing his throat. "Sorry," he murmurs, darting his eyes anywhere but at me. "I, uh… Here."

He steps forward long enough to shove Daisy into my hands, then he's back to putting distance between us. Then more. And more. He backpedals toward the hall, hitching his thumb over his shoulder.

"I'm, uh, going to…uh…" he starts, and only then do I realize his cheeks, which are usually pale, are stained red.

He's embarrassed. It reminds me of the night he came into the clinic.

Have I been wrong about Lawson all along? Is he

really the stereotypical manwhore jock I made him out to be? Or is he…nice?

"Change," he blurts out. "I'm going to go change."

Images of Lawson like the ones from the other night flood into my head again, only this time, he's not just shirtless—he's taking everything off. He's pulling his shirt over his head, dropping his hands to his sweats, sliding them down over his a—

Nope! No. No. I am not *going there.*

I shake away the thought, inhaling, then exhaling just as slowly. I swallow. "Okay."

"Right. Okay." Another step. "Going."

He turns, darting down the hall. Daisy squirms in my hands, whining the second he's out of sight, so I set her down, watching as she chases after him.

I will not be jealous of a dog.

I will not be jealous of a dog.

I will not be fucking jealous of a dog.

Chapter 7

LAWSON

My stomach churns like an ocean during a storm, enormous wave after enormous wave hammering against me, unease curling through every inch of me.

I am such a moron.

"Come on, Lawson. It's not that bad." Hutch pats my shoulder in the most awkward of ways.

I'd never admit this to him, but I don't want a *shoulder pat* at this moment. I want a hug. I want a good, old-fashioned hug, maybe even one from my mom.

Oh god. I want a damn *mommy hug*. That's how shitty I feel.

"So you scored on our net. It's fine. It happens," Fox, our goalie, adds, but his signature *It'll all be okay* grin is missing. He thinks I'm a dumbass too.

"Even I've done it before," Thomas, another teammate, chips in from across the locker room before pulling his wedding ring from his necklace and slipping it back on his finger. It's the first thing he does after every game. All the married guys do it. I'd probably find it funny and make a snide comment if I wasn't feeling like absolute dogshit.

"I've never done it."

All eyes in the room snap to Hayes, my new number one enemy.

"Dude," Fox hisses. "Come on."

"What? I haven't. It's a dumb move." Hayes shrugs, then begins unlacing his skates.

The urge to use *him* as a test dummy to see just how sharp his skates are surges through me. That may be a little dramatic, but it's one hundred percent justified. I already feel like shit. I don't need him piling it on.

"We won," Hutch says. "That's all that matters."

"How very captain-like of you." I flick my eyes down to the C adorning his jersey.

Hutch was officially named captain before the game today. We all knew it was coming. He's certainly the most deserving of it. I just wish I hadn't tainted his first game as captain by scoring on our own net, and I don't mean the puck bounced off my leg or off my skate or something like that.

No. I literally used *my stick* and scored.

I was driving toward the net, trying to get to the puck before the other team could, and that's when it happened—the puck landed on my stick, and the next thing I know, the buzzer was going off and the Carolina Comets "scored."

In my rush to get it away from their top scorer, Grady Miller, I flipped it right behind Fox and that was it. It felt horrible doing it in front of a sold-out crowd, and it feels just as bad now recalling the incident with all my teammates gathered around.

A hush falls over us as Coach walks in.

"Good effort. Let's keep it up." And then he's gone again.

Another lackluster speech. Another minimal response. It's so…odd.

Next up is Coach Steen. "Great game out there, boys. Let's keep that going into our next one. For media, we have—"

I hold my breath. *Please don't be me. Please don't be me. Don't. Fucking. Be. Me.*

"—Hutch, Thommer, Kells. You're up," our assistant coach concludes, and I release my breath.

Thank fuck. The last thing I want to do is go on camera and be asked the same question five different ways and try to explain what happened tonight five different ways.

The coaching staff clear the room, and we all look to the captain.

Hutch shoves off the bench. With his hands resting

on his hips, he addresses the team. "We played hard out there, and I'm proud of us. It's been a rough season, up and down and up again. We know how to win. We just have to find the right drive to keep winning. Let's use tonight as an example that we can overcome adversity and do whatever it takes to win. I believe in this team. If you carry nothing else forward, carry that."

He sits back down, the room quiet. We'd normally be celebrating a win, but it was so hard fought, especially after my mistake, and nobody in this room feels like cheering for that when we know we didn't deserve it. We weren't the better team out there by a long shot. The hockey gods must have felt bad for me after I fucked up and gave Carolina that goal to tie it, because we were blessed with a puck that took a weird bounce and barely snuck into their net with only thirty seconds to go.

I just hope we can somehow take this win and finally pull our heads out of our asses and *keep* winning. It's been our struggle all season so far. We'll win two games, then lose three. Back and forth. It's hard to keep your spirits up when you're always waiting for that other shoe to drop.

I try to shake off that feeling as I remove my gear, then hit the showers. I rinse off quickly, eager to get out of here and get home so I can put this night behind me. As I'm tugging on my clothes, my phone buzzes, and I snatch it up.

Greer: You hiding?

I grin.

Me: From you? Yes.

Greer: Get your ass out here, little bro. Bus is leaving soon, and I want to roast you to your face.

Me: Give me five.

With my half brother being in the league too, I hardly ever get to see him. We didn't grow up together, only seeing each other when we both happened to be at our dad's place during summers, but we've maintained a good relationship throughout the years, especially since we both love hockey so much.

A few minutes later, I find Greer standing out in the hallway, ready to head to the bus. The Comets are playing in Vancouver tomorrow, so they're flying out tonight so they aren't traveling on game day.

"Ah, there he is, my favorite Comets player." He pushes off the wall, snapping his finger, then pointing at me. "Wait—you're not a Comet. You're a Serpent. Huh…weird, because earlier, I could have sworn you scored on Fox. You—"

I punch at his stomach, but Greer, being the two-time Stanley Cup–winning goalie he is, stops me before I can make contact.

"Ah, ah, ah. Nice try, little brother. I'm too fast for you."

"Really? You didn't seem that fast when we scored those two goals in the third and won the game."

His eyes narrow, then he yanks on my fist, hauling me to him and wrapping his arms around me. "Shithead," he says, hugging me tightly.

"Learned it from my brother," I respond, patting his back twice.

We pull apart, and he grins at me.

"Good to see you. Sorry I couldn't get together for dinner last night. Had a thing with the Comets."

"Don't sweat it. If anyone knows how grueling this hockey life can be, it's me."

He nods. "It's exhausting. You should have come to North Carolina for Christmas. We could have caught up then. My mom told me Cassidy actually took some time away from the bar and went on some trip, so I know you didn't go home."

Not only have Greer and I stayed in touch over the years, but our moms are friends too, both having been burned by our father. I always appreciated that no matter what crap he pulled, our mothers kept us out of it and made sure we had a good relationship not just with our father, but with each other too.

I shrug. "Was busy here."

"Bullshit."

I laugh at his crassness. "Fine. Just didn't feel like flying out and flying back, ya know? Besides, it turned out good for me. I got a puppy."

"For real? Show me."

I'm already pulling out my phone and firing up photos.

"Her name's Daisy," I tell him proudly.

"She's cute as hell. Don't let Macie get wind of her. She'll be begging me to come out here so she can play with her. Stevie too."

He rolls his eyes, but there's no malice behind the gesture at all. In fact, it's the opposite, and it makes me want to laugh. If someone had told me *the* Jacob Greer would settle down with a single mom, I'd have laughed in their face. Not only has he always hated kids, until his girlfriend, Stevie, he was even more opposed to relationships than the entire Serpents Singles club put together. Seeing him settled down and completely in love now is comical, but I'm happy for him. He deserves some happy, just like Hutch deserves happy with Auden.

I deserve happy too, but I'll get it once I win my Cup.

"Yo, Greer, are you coming or what?"

We turn to find Cameron Lowell, captain of the Carolina Comets, standing up the hall, ready to hit the road.

"Be right there," my brother tells him.

Lowell lifts his chin my way. "Good game, Lawsy."

"Thanks, man."

"No, no. Thank *you* for the goal. Boosts my stats."

I flip him off, and he laughs, shaking his head as he heads off to the bus.

"Can you believe that asshole?"

Greer laughs, but it lasts only a second before he sobers, his face going flat and his eyes hardening, narrowing to slits. "That asshole is my captain. Watch it."

He's kidding. I think.

It still has me pointing in the direction of their bus. "You'd better get going before they leave you here. Nobody wants that, least of all me."

What I really mean: *I'll miss you, big bro.*

He sniffs, shoving his hands in his pockets and

looking anywhere but at me as he says, "Right? Wouldn't want that."

What he really means: *I'll miss you too, little bro.*

We're quite the duo. Guess we got our lack of sharing feelings from our father.

"You have any plans for the All-Star break?" Greer asks.

"Probably hang around here with the puppy."

My brother nods. "Well, if you change your mind, we're taking Macie to Disney. She gives zero shits about the princesses, but she's stoked for the *Star Wars* land." From his tone, I'd say *he's* excited for it too. "Anyway," he says, checking behind him, "I'd better get going before they send Miller in to look for me. We lost tonight, and I'd rather not be annoyed for a second time."

"That kid is something else."

"Dude...you don't even know." He drops his head back on a heavy sigh. "He's dying to propose to Stevie's sister. I already see far too much of him, and him marrying Scout would be too much Miller in a world where I already have too much Miller."

"Aww, you don't mean that." The man in question saunters down the hall with a grin. He grabs Greer by the shoulders, giving him a hard shake. "You love me. You want *all* the Miller time you can get, buddy."

My brother shakes him off, giving him a glare that has *me* shaking.

Miller is completely unbothered by it, laughing and jabbing his elbow into Greer's ribs. "Come on. They're doing headcounts. You can tell your brother you love me more later." He looks over at me. "'Sup, Lawsy? Thanks for the goal."

"Shut up, Miller," I tell him, shooting daggers.

Miller laughs, pointing between me and Greer. "Yep, you're definitely brothers. Same glare and all." He pats his teammate's shoulder again, and once again, Greer shakes him off. "Makes me wish I had time to see my sister while we're here in Seattle, but I'll have to hit her up over summer break. Now, let's get to the bus so we can go kick Vancouver's ass."

"Please do," I tell him. "Don't need them getting any more points. We're close to catching up."

"Oooh. Maybe we can get them to score goals for us too." He flexes his hands in the air. "These silky mitts could use the break."

"Miller, I swear…" I take a step toward him.

He backs away laughing. "And that's my cue." He flicks his head toward the exit. "Let's move it, FBIL. We have karaoke to sing."

"FBIL?" I question. "Karaoke?"

Greer sighs, shaking his head at Miller's antics.

"Future brother-in-law, and I plead the Fifth on the other thing."

I laugh. "Anyone ever tell him he's exhausting?"

"Only every day." Another headshake. "Anyway"—he holds his fist out—"see you later, little brother."

"Yeah, man, later." I tap my fist against his.

He smiles.

I smile.

Suddenly he's wrapping me in a quick hug and ruffling my hair before shoving me against the wall and stalking off as he mutters, "Dork."

I laugh in return. We might not have grown up together, but he's *such* a big brother.

I head the opposite direction, waving to our security guard Andrew and hopping into my black BMW X5 M, a splurge I allowed myself after moving to Seattle. I check my phone before heading out and am surprised to find a text from Rory waiting for me. I click on it and my screen fills with a photo of Daisy curled up on the couch fast asleep with a text that reads, *And that's how it's done, folks.* In my misery from scoring on my own net, I forgot that while tonight was embarrassing, I still have something to look forward to.

Rory.

It took every ounce of strength I had earlier to let her go. I don't know why I hugged her to begin with—

it was a natural reflex—but once I put my arms around her, all I could think was, *Why haven't I done this before?*

She was warm and soft and felt *so* fucking good pressed against me. The whole drive to the rink I tried to convince myself that the only reason I liked having her body against mine was because I haven't been laid in over three months and maybe that's why I was so into it, craving human touch and all that. But the farther away from Rory I went and the closer I got to the rink, I realized I didn't hug her just because I was missing touch. I hugged her because I wanted to touch her.

No—because I *needed* to touch her.

It wasn't because she was saving me either. It was more than that. It was me giving in to something I'd been wanting to do for far too long. Something I want to do again.

I race home faster than I have in a long while, and before I know it, I'm jamming my finger against the button for the elevator. It feels like it takes forever for it to arrive and even longer for it to take me to the twelfth floor. When I finally step off, I'm practically shaking with excitement. It's so fucking stupid, especially because I don't have a reason to be excited other than seeing Rory, but I can't help it. I unlock my apartment and push open the door.

"Honey, I'm ho—"

"Shh! I just got her to sleep!" Rory chides, but that's not what has me stopping in my tracks. It's not seeing Daisy swaddled in a blanket. It's not her little puppy snores and twitches as she snoozes away on the couch.

It's something else.

"Is that my jersey?"

Rory glances down at the dark green sweater that has the face of a furious snake with a hockey puck coming from its mouth right in the center.

"Oh. This." She peers back up at me, worrying her bottom lip through her teeth. "So, I know this probably looks weird," she says, rising to her feet, holding her hands out like she's trying to calm a rabid animal. "But it's not. Daisy began whining the second you left, and she wouldn't stop no matter what I did to try to calm her. So, I sort of went into your bedroom—which, by the way, looks like the room of a serial killer with your bed still on the floor and those boxes in there—and found this in your closet. It smells like you, so I put it on and held her, and well..." She gestures to where Daisy is still snoozing away. "It clearly worked. She's been out ever since. I, uh, hope you don't mind."

Hope I don't mind? Is she serious?

"I didn't think you'd care, to be fair," she tacks on.

I care that she's wearing my jersey. I care entirely too fucking much. I'm standing here trying my damnedest not to cross this room and rip it off her, and not for the reasons she thinks.

"Here, I can take it off." She reaches for the hem.

"Stop!" I yell, my voice echoing off the empty walls.

She pauses, tipping her head to the side as she stares at me with surprised eyes.

"Stop," I repeat quietly this time, taking two tentative steps toward her.

Another.

Another.

Another.

I keep going until I'm only a foot away from her. One more step and we'll be touching. *One. More. Step.*

She swallows hard, tipping her head back and training her bottle-green gaze on me.

"Lucas…"

She never calls me Lucas. It's always Lawson.

But not tonight. Not now, not when we both know what is about to happen.

I take that last step, my body sliding against her so easily, just as it did earlier. I slip one hand around her waist, tugging her that last bit closer, then cup her face, tipping it back just a little more.

Her lips part, eyes darting to my mouth, then back to my eyes again.

"Don't take it off," I instruct. "Turn around."

Another swallow, but she heeds my instructions, turning slowly.

Her dark hair that was pulled back when she first arrived is now hanging loosely around her shoulders. I reach out, gathering the silky strands and brushing them aside. I see it then: my name and my number stitched across her back.

Lawson.

25.

A hunger I've never experienced builds inside of me as I stare at it. A desire I didn't know lay so deep rises to the surface, and before I can fully comprehend what I'm doing, I spin her back around and I kiss her.

No—I *claim* her.

Because kissing Rory isn't just a kiss. It's more than that. I know it, and she does too.

She pauses under me for only a moment, then all at once she's kissing me back, winding her arms around me, pulling me closer as she moans against me.

It's everything I thought it would be. She's soft where I'm hard. She's cautious yet needy, pliable but dominant in a way only she can be as our tongues tangle together, dancing to music only we can hear. Her nails dig into my back, and I haul her even tighter against me, my grip tightening on her waist. There's no way she doesn't feel what this kiss is doing to me, no way she doesn't feel my hard cock aching for her, feel how badly I want her.

I'm uncertain how long we stand there, exploring one another, but all I know is I don't want it to end. Hell, I want *this* to be the beginning, but that's not up to me. That's up to her.

As if she can read my thoughts, Rory pulls away, and there's no mistaking the panic in her eyes. I release her and she immediately takes several steps back, putting distance between us, even though it's the last thing I want in this moment.

"Lawson..."

And just like that, I'm back to being just Lawson.

"I..." She shakes her head, taking another step away. "We can't do that."

"Why not?" I sound fucking pathetic, but I don't give a shit. I want this. *She* wants this. I know she does.

"Because I..." She trails off.

Then I see it: the minute she makes up her mind that this isn't happening. Rory shoves her shoulders back, lifting her chin up high.

"Because this can't happen, Lawson."

I want to argue with her, want to tell her she's wrong, but I have a feeling she already knows she is.

"I should go," she murmurs, shoving past me toward the counter and snatching her bag, then a pizza box I'm sure contains what's left of her dinner before making her way to the front door. She pulls it open and pauses, looking over at me. "If you need help with Daisy…"

I nod. "I'll call."

"Okay."

She hesitates only a moment before shaking her head and walking out the door. It shuts softly behind her, yet somehow, the sound is deafening.

I look over to the chocolate Lab. She's awake now, and she's staring longingly at the door, like she misses Rory already. I sigh, plopping down onto the couch next to her. She curls into my lap, letting out a soft whine. I drop my hand to her head, running my fingers through her soft fur.

"Me too, Daisy. Me too."

Chapter 8

RORY

I kept his jersey.

I don't know when exactly I realized I was still wearing it, but I'll admit I was fully aware it was still on when I crawled into bed as the clock struck midnight. I couldn't bring myself to take it off. I was tired. That was the only reason why. I'm sure of it.

I woke up this morning to the scent of leather and cedar engulfing me, and it took entirely too much convincing for me to crawl out of bed and into the shower because of it. It felt like it would be washing away the memory of last night, and despite how quickly I ran out of there, I'm not sure I *wanted* to wash it away.

Lawson kissed me.

Not only did he kiss me, I kissed him back.

Hard.

It was reckless and I had no business doing it, yet I couldn't seem to stop my lips from working against his. I'm certain it was because I can't remember the last time I was kissed and had nothing at all to do with Lawson himself. At least that's what I keep telling myself over and over.

"Then Hutch asked if we could do that thing I haven't done with anyone else and I said yes, so we went to the store and bought a butt plug and—"

I snap my head up. "A butt plug? What the fuck, Auden?" I glance toward my open office door, thankful nobody is nearby to hear this.

She laughs. "I was testing to see if you're paying attention. I guess you are."

"Sort of." I sit back in my chair, looking down at my nearly untouched lunch. "Sorry. I'm a bit distracted this morning."

"I can tell. What's going on?"

"It's…" *Tell her. Tell her.* "It was just a late night, that's all" is what I settle on.

"Hmm." My twin's hazel eyes bore into me, and I wish like hell I could hide from her curious stare. She knows me too well, and the last thing I want is for her to discover what happened last night.

Besides, there's no reason for her to know. It was a one-time thing that will never, ever happen again. It's fine if she doesn't know about it.

"You work too much," she tells me for the millionth time, then takes a bite of her sandwich. She chews, swallows. "You should come on vacation with us for the All-Star break that's in two weeks. The Serpents are sending Locke, so Hutch and I are going to Banff."

A vacation with my sister and her boyfriend? Yeah, no, thanks. I'd rather not be the third wheel the whole week, not to mention that I truly do have a lot of work to do around here. It's not easy running one clinic, let alone two. I've been meaning to hire another doctor, and maybe it's finally time to admit it needs to happen. We're so busy it's getting hard to keep up with, even for me.

"I appreciate the offer, but I've got an assload of work to catch up on."

"And while I don't doubt that, it's precisely why you need a vacation. You wor—"

"Work too much. I know, Auden. I heard you the first eight million times."

"That sounds like an awfully high number." I narrow my eyes, and she laughs. "I wouldn't say it if it weren't true, though. You kept trying to convince me for years to take a break, and now look at me." She stretches her arms out.

"Oh, I'm looking at you—invading my office and barging in on my lunch, the one break I get throughout the day."

She shrugs. "I missed my sister."

"You *just* saw me over the weekend."

"At the photoshoot? That hardly counts. We were both busy the whole time."

"It counts. You're only here because you're horrible at relaxing and don't know what to do with all this time on your hands."

"That's not true. I have a packed schedule, thank you very much."

"Oh yeah? Lunch with me, drinks with Lilah, and dinner with Dad?"

"No," she argues, but her cheeks pinken. "Fine. Yes." She sits forward, resting her elbow on my sprawling white desk and pointing a finger at me. "But I *get* to do all that stuff because I'm not working my ass to the bone anymore like *someone* I know."

I sigh. "Taking time off isn't that easy, Auden. You should know that better than anyone."

"I do. I *do* know, and that's why I'm telling you to take a break before you get to the point I was at. I was hardly sleeping, I was traveling all the time, and I lost all passion for what I was doing. Sure, I still *loved* it, but it drained me more than excited me. I don't want the same thing to happen to you."

"It won't," I promise. "Besides, I have plenty going on in my life to keep me busy."

She perks up, and I know immediately it was the wrong word choice.

"Ha! I knew it! You might have had a *late night*, but that's because you weren't alone, isn't it? That's why you didn't seem interested when I told you Hayes was checking you out. You're seeing someone."

"I didn't seem interested in Hayes because it's Hayes. I don't even follow hockey and *I've* seen the shitstorms he's caused. I already have enough chaos in my life. I don't need to add more."

"That's not a denial of you seeing someone though."

I should tell her I'm not, should shut this down right now, but for some reason, I find myself saying nothing, which to her is like saying everything.

"Oh my gosh, you are! Who? What's his name? Do I know him?" She leans even closer. "Is it someone from the photoshoot?" she whispers conspiratorially.

I scoff. "Ew, no. It's..." I shake my head. "It's nobody you know, and it was one date. No big deal."

It's a lie. All of it is a lie, and I hate the feeling that settles into my gut. But telling Auden I kissed Lawson? That sounds a hell of a lot worse. Maybe because it's Lawson, or maybe because I liked the kiss way more than I'm willing to admit and can still feel his lips on mine. Or maybe it's just because sharing my feelings is the most dreadful thing I can think of.

Either way, I let the lie permeate the room and let Auden get excited about it. I'm an awful sister, but I'm a cautious one too. The last thing I need is for her to find out about Lawson, then tell Hutch, who will tell his whole team and suddenly everyone is going to know and I'd rather them not for too many reasons to list.

"Was it at least a good date?" my sister asks, knowing all too well I'm not about to gush about it—and not just because it's not real.

I think back to last night when Lawson was pressed against me. His hands on my waist, holding me close. The feel of his perfectly sculpted body on mine. The way he kissed me with authority and determination. No, not just kissed. He *possessed* me, and I was more than willing to let him.

The one thing I don't let myself think about is how hard he was, how wet I was. It's pointless. Utterly futile.

"He was a perfect gentleman," I tell her, and it's true. He *was* a perfect gentleman, letting me walk away without an ounce of protest despite clearly wanting to push back.

And I meant what I told him. I'll still help with Daisy if he needs it. She's young and clearly has some abandonment issues. It would go against everything I swore to when I became a veterinarian to flake out on her. I'm not going to leave Daisy hanging just because Lawson and I kissed, especially when there's no way in hell it's happening again.

Never. Ever.

I wonder how many times I'll have to repeat it for me to believe it.

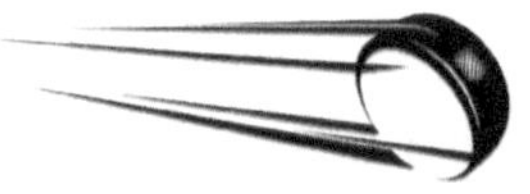

My cell phone rings at three o'clock three days later, and I only hesitate for a few seconds before answering it.

"Hello?"

"Wednesday! You answered!"

I ignore his new nickname for me, even though it *is* starting to grow on me a bit, not that I'm telling him that. "Why wouldn't I answer?"

He pauses. Clears his throat. "Well, because you're madly in love with me, of course."

I laugh. Maybe a little loudly and a little too hard and a little too forced. "Keep dreaming, Lawson."

He chuckles, but I hear the discomfort in it. "Anyway, I was wondering if you were serious about helping with Daisy."

"Are you asking a veterinarian if they're serious about helping an animal?"

"Uh, yes?"

I don't even dignify that with a response.

"Right," he continues. "Any chance you're available tonight? I'm sure you're busy or have a date or whatever, so no worries if you say no. Daisy is going to be upset, but she'll get over it. It's just that Jaden, the neighbor kid, has debate tonight, and…"

"You still haven't told your super?"

"Uh, no. We had practice yesterday, then we did a trip to the children's hospital, and I spent most of the day there with the kids, helping them make early Valentine's Day cards. Then practice again this morning, pre-game presser, lunch, then—"

"Lawson?" I cut him off, mostly because I do not at all want to think about him at the children's hospital. Sure, it was probably a required activity, but after what happened earlier this week, I cannot think about Lawson doing something sweet like making Valentine's Day cards with sick kids. It's too much. It makes him too real, which makes what happened too real.

"Yes?"

"I'll help."

"Oh, thank god." He sighs. "That would be amazing. I owe you big-time."

"It's fine. I don't mind helping. Daisy really did seem stressed as soon as you left."

"I know. I should probably do something about that, huh?"

"You should. There are some techniques you can use to help desensitize her to your departure. I'll print a list of things you can try."

"Really? Fuck, that'd be amazing. The last thing I want to do is be worrying about her during the game. We're already sucking. I don't need to pile on the stress."

"Why are you sucking?"

He laughs derisively. "Your guess is as good as mine. We just are. Can't pull out a win streak to save our asses."

I remember Auden talking before the short Christmas break about how the Serpents would go from playing well to playing poorly and it was weighing on Hutch. I guess it's still going that way from the sound of it.

"Anyway, you're a lifesaver, you know that?"

My face heats at his praise, and I don't even kind of know why. People have said as much to me before, said similar things. This isn't new, but coming from Lawson? I don't know. It just hits me differently.

I wiggle around in my chair, telling myself I'm just getting more comfortable though I know it's more than that, and clear my throat. "It's no problem."

"Could, uh, could you be here by five?"

Crap. I have a client coming in at four thirty. It *should* be a quick appointment, but it could run long. Maybe I can check with Dr. Helms and see if she'd be willing to take it instead.

"I'll try," I tell him, not wanting to promise when I can't.

"Thank you. I appreciate it so much."

"It's no problem," I repeat.

This is the part where we both say goodbye and hang up, but neither of us is making a move to do so. I can hear him breathing on the other end of the line, can hear the *clack clack clack* of Daisy's paws against his hardwood floor.

"So, uh, see you at five?" I finally ask.

There's shuffling on the other end. "Yeah, definitely. Definitely. See you at five."

"Okay."

I pull the phone away, ready to hang up, when I hear him call my name.

"And, Rory?"

"Yes?" I ask, bringing it back to my ear.

"Maybe try not to kiss me this time." And the line goes dead.

I sit in stunned silence, trying to figure out just how badly I messed up kissing Lawson and why, even despite that, I want to do it again.

Chapter 9

LAWSON

"Fuck, come on. Come on, come on, come on," I chant under my breath as Hayes glides down the ice, the puck on his stick as he approaches the Calgary goalie.

Because we can't seem to stay ahead to save our lives no matter how hard we try, we're in a shootout after leading for the first two periods. The Calgary netminder inches back into his crease as Hayes gets closer, his glove up and ready to catch whatever the forward sends his way. Hayes slows, moving the puck quickly back and forth on his stick. Slower, slower. Then he flicks it up on his backhand, and it soars past the goalie's shoulder and into the net.

We cheer, but it's not over yet. Now it's Fox's turn. We need him to stop this for us. This shootout has already gone far too many scoreless rounds for our liking.

"What a beaut," I tell Hayes as he settles back onto the bench next to me. "Perfect execution. Got him to bite."

He spits onto the ice, then sniffles. "I thought for sure he was going to catch it."

"Nah, man. Your speed messed him up. He wasn't expecting that."

"Let's just hope Fox can stop this."

The Calgary player goes wide and skates into the puck, pushing it forward. He tries a move similar to what Hayes just did, slowing down and trying to get Fox to bite, but what he doesn't know is Hayes practices that move all the time. Fox faces it on the regular, and there's no way he's going to give in like this guy wants him to.

And he doesn't. Fox catches it in his glove with ease, and the bench explodes. We're over the boards in an instant, meeting our goalie halfway and taking turns bumping our helmets against his.

"Oooh, Foxy. What an incredible save. My man!" I wrap him in a hug and, unlike some of the other assholes on this team, he hugs me back with just as much fervor.

We hit the locker room, strip out of our gear, grab showers, and we're out for the night. Even after pulling a win out of our asses, Coach never once steps foot in the room. I don't know what his deal is, but he's not performing like he should be. We aren't either, but that doesn't mean he's supposed to lose all faith in us.

I climb into my SUV and race home, eager to see if Rory's wearing my number again. If she thinks I didn't notice she went home wearing it, she's wrong. I noticed. Oh fuck did I notice.

I noticed so damn much that when I climbed into bed, it was all I thought about until my cock was aching again and I had no choice but to fist it. I should have felt ashamed jerking off to images of her in nothing but my jersey, but I couldn't be bothered. Not after that kiss.

God, that kiss. She bolted right afterward and I let her, but only because I knew without a doubt that wouldn't be the last time it happened.

I get lucky with traffic again and soon I'm pulling into the parking garage, then making my way into my building in record time. I'm hardly ever home this early, and I want to take advantage of it.

Rory wasn't too far off the mark when she called me a playboy before. I'm not exactly known for settling down. It's not who I am, and because I'm a very no-strings-attached kind of guy, it means I don't bring my dates back to my apartment. *Ever.* The last thing I need is for one of them to get clingy and for me to wind up having to move or get a restraining order. I already made that mistake once, and I'd like to not make it again.

The elevator drops me on the twelfth floor, and I waste no time pushing my key into the door and swinging it open.

"Honey, I'm home," I whisper, but it's pointless.

Daisy bounds across the hardwood floor, her paws —which seem like they're growing an inch a day— clapping loudly against the floor. I close the door behind me, then lift the spoiled princess up, hugging her close.

"How was your night? Were you good for Momma?"

Rory sighs, rising off the couch and making her way over to me. "How many times do I have to tell you we are *not* co-parents?"

"I guess until I believe it."

I have the oddest urge to bend and press a kiss to her cheek, like two spouses after a long day apart, but since I'm rather fond of my balls, I suppress the desire. She walks past me and into the kitchen, where her coat is once again draped over the chair and her bag is up on the counter. Tonight, though, instead of pizza, there's a half-eaten sub sandwich from my favorite deli down the street.

"You go to Bernie's?"

"Only about four days a week," she says, wrapping up what's left of her dinner and shoving it into her bag. "I'm obsessed with their buffalo chicken and blue cheese sandwich."

"And those potato chips? To die for."

"The sweet-and-spicy barbecue ones? Ugh. They've been out of them for months, and it makes me so mad." She shakes her head. "Okay, we have to stop. You're making my mouth water and I still have my drive ahead of me before I can finish my dinner."

"Wait—did you just order it?"

She bites the inside of her cheek, then nods. "Yeah. It got here about ten minutes ago."

"Rory, it's nearly eleven. Why didn't you eat earlier?"

She narrows her eyes. "Wasn't aware you were in charge of my eating schedule."

I'm not, but I also know it's way past dinnertime and I hate the thought of her sitting here hungry in my house. This is the second time she's been here and the second time I didn't even bother to offer her anything besides water. She's doing me a huge favor here, and I'm a fucking moron.

"You're welcome to use the kitchen, you know."

She wrinkles her nose. "No, thanks."

"You don't cook?"

"Not really. I can if I really need to, but I don't

enjoy it at all. The smells and the touching of raw things and the time it takes…" She shrugs. "Not my thing."

"Raw things gross you out, yet you're a vet?"

"Fine, I'm lazy. Sue me."

I laugh. Lazy is not a word I'd use to describe Rory. I'd go more for words like strong, determined, smart, hardworking, beautiful, gorgeous, probably looks incredibly sexy in nothing but my jersey…

And there goes my mind, slipping right back into the fantasy I can't seem to shake. I tuck away the thought, then nod toward her bag. "Stay. You need to eat."

"Lawson, I—"

"Please." I'm not afraid to beg. I'm also not afraid to use the word against her. I noticed before that even when she's being exceptionally stubborn, simply uttering that word will have her folding. I might be a bit manipulative, but it's for a good cause. She needs to eat and take care of herself. That's priority number one right now.

She sighs, then drops the bag that was halfway to her shoulder back onto the counter. "Fine, but only because it's a really, really good sandwich and I'm starving."

I toe off my shoes at the door, letting Daisy down, then cross to the kitchen. Unsurprisingly, she follows behind me like my little shadow. I don't think I paid much attention to it before, but her attachment really is serious. That's going to be an issue if I don't take care of it right away.

"Is this little one the reason you didn't eat earlier?" I ask, pulling open the fridge and grabbing a beer. I seldom drink during the season, but tonight it feels right. "She didn't cause too much trouble, did she?"

Rory shakes her head, chewing a bite of sandwich. Once she swallows, she says, "She wasn't too bad. A little fussy when you first left, but I grabbed a pillow off your bed and gave her that."

I try not to think about Rory being in my bedroom too much, nor do I think about the fact that she didn't grab a jersey this time. *Nor* do I think about her having one of my jerseys at home and neither one of us making an effort to mention it.

Instead, I grab a second beer and hold it up. "Beer?"

"I shouldn't, I—"

She stops mid-protest when I lift my brows her way, silently saying, *Come on. Stay for one beer.*

She concedes. "Okay. Just one."

I twist off the top, then slide the bottle over to her. She doesn't take a drink right away, setting it beside her and picking up her sandwich again.

I close the fridge, pop the top off my drink, and

take a big swig. I move to the small pantry, and it illuminates when I open the door, making what I'm looking for easy to find. I grab the bag, then slide those across the counter next.

"Shut up! No way! You have them here?"

I shrug, settling against the counter with my own beer. "I might be the reason you can't find them."

"You're joking."

I grin.

Her jaw slackens. "You're *not* joking. What the… How? And why?"

Another shrug. "I told you I love them. They're my favorite, so I always make sure I'm never without them. I even take them on the road with me."

"You do not."

"I do too. What do you think my plane snack is?"

She shakes her head with a grin, her expression something between disgust and pride. "I hate you."

"Nah, you're just mad you didn't think of it first."

I take a swig of my beer as she pops open the chips, shoving two in her mouth right away. She moans, and I hate it. I hate it so, so much because I know exactly what that moan tastes like. I take another drink…then another for good measure.

"So," I say, swallowing down the lump lodged in my throat, "if it wasn't Daisy keeping you busy, then why didn't you eat?"

"I, uh, got distracted." She doesn't look at me when she says it. Her eyes are focused elsewhere.

I should be absolutely ashamed of the thoughts that run through my mind. Her writhing on my bed, my jersey riding up as she plunges her fingers into her pussy. Her in my shower, using the detachable head as a toy. Her bent over the couch, her ass in the air as she—

"I watched the game."

Her four words interrupt all my naughty thoughts, and it's hard work to get them to go away. "Oh."

I sound like a dumbass, but I don't exactly trust myself to say much else, not when those images are still so fresh.

"You know they show you on TV a lot?"

Another drink. "I couldn't tell you. I've never watched myself play on TV."

"Well, they do. Like *a lot* a lot."

"Sounds like someone was bothered by it."

She snorts haughtily. "It was hardly me. More like that one." She points to Daisy, who is lying at my feet, nipping at one of the twenty toys scattered around my apartment. "She'd perk up every time they panned to you. It was kind of cute." She pins me with those damn green eyes, and I just know by the sparkle in them that the next words out of her mouth are going to be something I won't like. "And, hey, good news—looks like you have one fan outside of your mom."

I narrow my eyes at her. *Two can play that game…*

"You would know since you have my jersey at home, right, Rory?"

I take a casual sip of my beer as she stops chewing, that spark giving way to panic. But she keeps her cool, swallowing down her bite, then taking her first sip of beer.

Except it's not a sip. It's a chug, and fuck me if I don't nearly lose my shit when I see her pink tongue dart out and chase the rim of the bottle before she sets it back down.

Well played, Rory. Well fucking played.

My whole body heats as I push off the counter and march over to the balcony door. I slide it open, then step outside into the cold January night. I can't tell if the instant relief is the wintry air or the fact that I'm no longer sharing the room with Rory.

She lets out a soft laugh, and I hear her rise from her chair, the legs scraping against the floor as she pushes it in. She moves around the kitchen, and I listen as her footfalls grow closer. She's not the only one either.

"No, no, no, little princess. Stay."

It's only one set of footsteps hitting the balcony, and suddenly she's right next to me. Rory leans against the railing, her beer in her hands as the city moves below us. Even though it's late, people still mill about in the streets. They're having loud conversations that carry up the floors and playing music that reverberates off the buildings. There are horns honking and tires squealing. It's loud and noisy and kind of annoying, but it's home.

"You know, I never thought I'd settle in the city," Rory says contemplatively.

"No? Why not?"

"I don't know. Never really occurred to me until college, and then after school, I found the place I own now and kind of never looked back."

"So, you're not a big-city kid for life?"

She chuckles lightly. "Hardly. I guess you could say I grew up in a small town."

"How small? We talking one stoplight or two?"

She makes a face. "No, nothing like that. I guess it was an average-sized town? I don't know. It wasn't anything like this, that's for sure."

"Where are you from?"

"All over."

I tip my head. From what I've gleaned, her father played in the NHL way back when, but only before she was born, so I know she wasn't moving around because of his playing career.

"We moved around often," she explains. "My

family traveled in an RV for the first ten years of my life, then eventually settled here after my father put his foot down and decided carting his kids around the country with no real roots wasn't how he wanted them to live. My mother didn't care too much for stable, so she took off. My dad took her back, but it didn't last long. She left again. Round and round they went until he'd finally had enough. It's really just been me, Auden, and him since I was sixteen. I even stayed for college. This was the only true home I ever knew, and I couldn't bear leaving it behind, not after everything my dad went through. So, I stayed. Auden too. Dad moved a couple years ago, and I'm happy for him. He deserves that. Auden does too with Hutch."

It's the most sentimental I've heard her be. It's like I'm getting a look at the real Rory Sinclair for the very first time. I like this Rory.

To be fair, I like the other Rory too, but this version of her...it's different. *She's* different, and I'm realizing I like her kind of different a whole hell of a lot more than I thought I could.

"What a very *un*-Wednesday-like thing to say about your sister."

"Nah. She loves Pugsley, just in her own way, that's all." She takes a drink. "So, now that you've heard my story, what's yours?"

"Like where I grew up and stuff?"

"Yeah. What made Lucas Lawson into *the* Lucas Lawson, pro hockey player?"

"My mother."

"Your mom?" Her brows come together. "How?"

"She gave up everything for me." I lift a shoulder. "She worked her ass to the bone at a bar in our small town—and it was an *actual* small town, by the way. We had two whole stoplights." She looks momentarily horrified by the idea, and I don't blame her. Small towns are a lot more tiring than the Hallmark movies let on. "Anyway, she drove me to and from lessons and practices and games in the big city. She gave up her nights and her weekends and she kept me going when I didn't think I wanted to anymore. She's supported me harder and louder than anyone else ever has. *She* made me into *the* Lucas Lawson, pro hockey player, name and all."

Rory pulls a face. "And what a name it is."

I laugh. "That's fair. It is kind of silly, huh? I'm Lucas after my grandfather though."

"She had to know what a mouthful that name would be…"

"Well, at the time, I think she was planning for her last name to be Greer and not Lawson anymore."

"Greer?" She tries the name out a few more times, and I see the wheels spinning. "I've heard that name. Why have I heard that before?"

"Because he's a goalie in North Carolina. He went viral last year when he was giving lessons to his girlfriend's kid and he pranked her with the water bottle. Pretty sure Macie punched him afterward, which he truly deserves."

"You sound like you admire him."

"Well, yeah. I guess I do. He's my brother."

"I'm sorry. He's your… You have a *brother*? There's another one of you?"

"Careful, Rory, I might start thinking you like me. What's that saying? She doth protest too much?"

She rolls her eyes. "Hardly. I just can't believe there's another you running around out there."

"Jacob and I are nothing alike. We're half brothers. Same dad, different moms. He grew up in Canada and I grew up in Colorado. Where I'm handsome, he's ugly. Where I'm funny, he's not. Where I'm oh so charming, he's the biggest grump I've ever met, and that includes Hutchy."

"I highly doubt your brother is ugly if you share the same father. Your—" She clamps her mouth shut as realization of what she's implied settles between us.

"You telling me I'm hot, Wednesday? You're not going to kiss me again, are you?"

"Shut up," she mutters, taking a long pull from her beer.

I laugh but let it go. We lean against the railing,

watching the bumper-to-bumper traffic below us, a comfortable silence lingering. Daisy grabs one of her toys, the softest little *squeak* occasionally breaking through the bubble we've put ourselves in. It's late and Rory should probably go, but she's not making a move to, and I'm not about to mention it. Sure, I have an early day tomorrow, but I'd rather sacrifice a few hours of sleep if it means extra time with Rory.

"I think I'd like living in a town with two stoplights."

I peer down at her, but she doesn't look my way. Her head is tilted back as she looks up at the stars.

"Really? Because you just looked like you were disgusted by the idea."

"Yeah, maybe. But also, can you imagine the stars? I bet they're gorgeous. No bright lights to wash out the sky. Just stars. Just like—oh my gosh, look! Look!"

She grabs my arm, shaking it hard and fast, pointing up at the sky with her now-empty beer bottle. She looks up at me, and her smile is wide and bright and so easily the most beautiful thing I've ever seen.

"It was a shooting star!" she declares, her eyes ablaze with wonder.

Her lips move, and I just know she's making a wish because those are the rules when you see a shooting star, and as big of a hard-ass as Rory pretends to be, something tells me that's a rule she never breaks.

I want to ask her what it was, but I don't dare. It wouldn't come true, then, and I want nothing more than for all her wishes to come true. It's the happiest I've seen her, and it's the most gorgeous she's ever looked. I couldn't look away right now if I tried.

"What?" she asks after several moments of me staring like a total creep.

My gaze drifts to her lips, her full and soft lips…the ones I want to kiss again so fucking badly I physically have to grip the railing to keep myself from doing it.

"Lucas?" she whispers my name, her tongue darting out to roll over her bottom lip. "What is it?"

"It's…nothing." I give my head a small shake, forcing myself to pull my eyes from her mouth and back up. "Nothing."

"Did you see the shooting star?"

"I didn't."

"Oh." Her excitement wanes. "It was gorgeous."

"It was. It *is*," I murmur, not taking my eyes off her even though she's back to looking at the sky.

"I wish I could see this every night. If I had a balcony, I'd be out here every night looking up."

"Use mine."

Her gaze snaps back to me. "What?"

"Use mine."

"What are you…"

"I'll make you a key. You can use mine."

"Lucas…" She shakes her head. "That's insane. You're…"

I shift closer to her, leaning down until I'm only inches away and that familiar scent of pears and flowers hits me. Her lips part. Her pupils grow to twice their size. Her breaths are coming in sharp and fast.

"For you, Rory, I'd gather every star in this sky and string them high somewhere only for you, just to see you smile like that again." Her breath stutters. "Making you a key is the best I can do until then."

I tear my gaze away, looking anywhere but at her and trying to push down the fact that I mean those words more than I've ever meant anything in my entire life.

And that scares the hell out of me.

Chapter 10

SERPENTS SINGLES GROUP CHAT

Lawson: Not to brag or anything, but I'm pretty sure this chick is in love with me.

Keller: Are you seriously talking about your dog again?

Lawson: No.

Lawson: Yes.

Lawson: But to be fair, she's perfect.

Keller: tO bE fAiR

Lawson: Shut up.

Lawson: Where's everyone else? You're annoying.

Keller: Probably avoiding you.

Fox: I'm here. I was just waiting to see how long you two could go back and forth.

Lawson: Far too long. Keller's mean.

Keller: Are you pouting? Because if you're pouting, I swear to god, I'll run you over in practice for the fun of it.

Lawson: No need to swear. I believe you. You get off on violence, don't ya?

Fox: Boys...

Locke: I'm with Fox. Let's settle down, eh?

Lawson: Eh? Want some maple syrup to go with that eh? Or some sweet, sweet O Canada?

Locke: Hey now...

Hutch: Shut up, Lawsy.

Lawson: Hutchy! I was wondering when you'd chime in.

Hayes: Too soon, if you ask me. This was getting good. He's being a loudmouth today. Ups his chances of getting rocked in praccy tomorrow.

Lawson: Hey!

Lawson: What'd I do? I'm innocent!

Keller: Your nickname says otherwise.

Lawson: Um, my nickname says COOL GUY.

Locke: You just called yourself "COOL GUY" and I'm pretty sure that is NOT cool guy energy.

Lawson: Okay, Gramps.

Lawson: But you guys have to admit Lawless Lawson is a pretty sick nickname.

Hutch: …

Fox: …

Hayes: …

Locke: …

Keller: It's fucking stupid.

Lawson: Aw, come on. It's not that bad.

Keller: Oh, it truly is, and unlike these other fucks, I'm not afraid to say it.

Lawson: Again, mean.

Keller: Honest.

Keller: You're welcome.

Lawson: I hope you adopted that cat from the shoot, Kells. Seems like you could use the cuddles.

Locke: He didn't. That thing hated him.

Lawson: Can you blame it?

Fox: That cat was cute as hell though. Probably should have taken it home, Keller.

Keller: Nah. Not a pet guy.

Lawson: Not a pet guy? NOT A PET GUY? What the fuck is wrong with you?

Lawson: Never mind. You don't have to answer. Pretty sure you don't know that many words.

Keller: Maybe, but I do know two pretty important words.

Lawson: Shut up?

Lawson: Go away?

Lawson: Eat me?

Keller: Fuck and you.

Lawson: Tsk, tsk. Your momma ought to wash your mouth out with soap, using bad language like that.

Locke: I've heard you say way, way,
WAY worse, Lawsy.

Hutch: Wasn't it you just yesterday
yelling at San Jose to fuck off before
you fucked all their moms?

Lawson: GASP! I would NEVER.

Fox: No, pretty sure you did. Heard
you down in the net.

Hayes: Actually, he said, "Fuck you,
you fucking fuck. I'll fuck your mom
next time you come for me. Heard she
knows how to handle a stick, unlike
you."

Lawson: Oh shit. Yeah, I did say that.

Lawson: But they deserved that chirp!
Swear they were out for my blood,
and I did nothing wrong.

Locke: I don't know…that check in the
first was ROUGH, even from the
bench.

Hayes: You tried to send that guy
straight to Jesus.

Keller: Even I was impressed by it.

Lawson: I'm screenshotting this and
framing it.

Keller: Of course you are.

Keller: Your mother really should have hugged you more.

Lawson: Leave my mother out of your mouth.

Lawson: WAIT WAIT WAIT WAIT WAIT

Hutch: Nah, man. You dug that hole.

Fox: Uh-oh…

Locke: Annnd that's my cue.

Hayes: I'm staying. NO ONE START UNTIL I HAVE MY POPCORN.

Lawson: Kells?

Keller: Yes, Lawsy?

Lawson: Please be gentle with me.

Keller: Oh. I'll be gentle with you. But your mother? Not a chance.

Lawson: YOU MOTHERFLUFFER

Lawson: MOTHERFLUFFER

Lawson: MOTHERFUCKER

Keller: Not yet, but I will be.

Lawson: I hate it here.

Keller: Not as much as we hate having you here.

Keller: What's that stupid thing you always send?

Keller: Oh, right.

Keller: *kissy face emoji*

Chapter 11

RORY

I'm not one to avoid people when situations become uncomfortable. I'm that person who sticks it through, who pushes their shoulders back and approaches whatever awkward that's happened head-on and gets it sorted out so nothing else hinders the relationship.

But when it comes to Lawson…well, with him, I'm not so sure I know who I am at all anymore.

I've been over to help with Daisy twice more, once to watch her during a home game, then another time to pick her up before Lawson left for his big road trip before the All-Star break. Both times I was there, I hardly looked him in the eyes, and I bolted as soon as I had Daisy in my arms.

Can I truly be blamed though? It's twice now he's broken through all my defenses and left me wanting more from him. First with the kiss, then with The Balcony Thing.

Yeah, that's exactly what I'm calling it because I *refuse* to think about it. I can't or else I'm going to turn into a puddle of mush again. *"For you, Rory, I'd gather every star in this sky and string them high somewhere only for you, just to see you smile like that again."*

Fuck! I thought about it.

It was cheesy. Beyond so. Something straight out of one of those Hallmark movies. And yet…I felt my knees buckle under me. If not for the railing, I would have gone down hard and fast, and I'm not so certain I'd have been embarrassed by it.

He was right. I *was* smiling. I was smiling, and I didn't even hate it.

As promised, he made me a key. It was delivered to my office the next day before lunch with a note attached to it.

Wednesday,

Maybe don't use this key to poison my coffee or anything else nefarious like putting piranhas in my bathtub. We don't want to leave Daisy without a dad, right?

See you soon.

Lucas

Not Lawson.

Lucas.

I don't know why, but that tripped me up the most. It made it seem so…real. Sure, I was holding an actual key in my hand, but signing Lucas instead of Lawson? It made my knees quake in a way only he seems to be able to cause.

I pull the key out of my desk where it's been tucked safely since he left for his road trip. I know he gave me permission, but it still feels weird to go to his apartment when he's not there. Even so, after these last few days I've had, a night looking at the stars sounds perfect.

As I'm running my fingers over the cold metal and debating a trip to his place, my phone begins to rattle against my desk. I peek over at it, and the name flashing across the screen has me pausing. *Does he know when I'm thinking about him?*

It's happened more than once on this trip of his. He's called every day to check in with Daisy, and while I find it cute, it also makes me wonder if it's actually for Daisy or if he's doing it to torture me further.

I take a deep breath, then swipe up to answer. His face fills the screen, his usual grin in place.

"Wednesday!"

"Lawson." Even I hear that the bitterness I usually put into his name is missing.

It makes his smile grow wider. "How's my girl doing?"

"I'm good."

He tucks his lips together, his already vivid gray gaze burning brighter. "I was talking about Daisy."

My face burns hot. No, not just hot. It's *scorching*. There's no way I don't look like a tomato right now. What the fuck is wrong with me? Why would I say that? Why would I even *think* he meant me? I mean, I didn't *really* think that was what he meant. It was a reflex. That's all.

That. Is. All.

"It was a reflex."

He laughs. "Right. Sure."

He winks at me, and I have the urge to hang up on him, but I don't. Instead, I shift the phone down, showing him how *his girl* is doing. Daisy is currently sound asleep on her bed that's been tucked under my desk since he left. I left her at my apartment a few times and for the most part she did well, but there's still a major attachment issue going on with her, not to mention Hades kind of hates her. I've been bringing her into the clinic to work on it, rotating her between her bed under my desk and letting her roam around the office to get to know other people and not just rely on me and Lawson.

"She's under your desk?"

"Yep," I say, training the phone back on me. "She's been there pretty much all day. I had to bring her in because my cat doesn't like her."

"You have a cat? Why didn't you tell me?"

I shrug. "You didn't ask. His name is Hades."

"How fitting for you, Wednesday." He laughs lightly. "Thank you for taking her while I'm gone. I'd have asked Jaden, but he's going on some trip for band."

"How do you know so much about your neighbor again?"

"I don't know." He shrugs. "I… I guess I kind of relate to him, you know? His mom, Paige, is raising him alone like my mom did. It's rough on a kid to go through that. Your parent is always working and the other one isn't around. It can get lonely. When I realized that was the case for them, I started talking to the kid whenever I'd see him around the building. Now, Paige picks up my mail while I'm gone, and I take Jaden out whenever I can, get him out of the apartment and take him to do stuff he normally can't." Another lift of shoulders. "It's not really a big deal."

Except it *is* a big deal. Not just to Jaden, but for Paige too. Sure, my parents didn't officially split until I was sixteen, but I remember what it's like only having one parent around. It's draining for everyone. What Lawson's doing might not seem like something big to him, but it's huge for Jaden, and that's not even factoring Lawson's superstar status into the mix. It's just another notch for him in the human column, one I can't ignore this time no matter how badly I want to.

"Anyway," he says. "Did you know birds masturbate?"

I bark out a laugh so loud even Daisy stirs.

"What?"

"I said, did you know birds—"

"I heard you the first time. I was just not at all expecting you to say that. Why do you know that?"

"So it's true?"

I nod. "Yeah, it's true. I actually had a client once whose bird got attached to him and—"

"It masturbated itself to death, didn't it?"

I'm stunned. "Yes. How did you…"

"Christmas Eve. Right before I found Daisy, I was at a bar, and I overheard some guys talking about it. That's how I found out. I obviously didn't Google it to make sure it was true because I don't want *that* popping up on my feeds, but holy shit. I can't believe it's real."

"It's totally real."

"Is that what's happening with Daisy? Is she getting attached to me? Or does she just have a foot fetish and that's why she follows me around everywhere?"

I laugh. "She does *not* have a foot fetish. She's scared she's going to be abandoned again. It's common for adopted animals. She's looking to you for support now."

As if she knows we're talking about her, Daisy nudges my legs, wanting attention. I pull her up into my lap, making sure she's in the frame.

"Well, good morning, sleepyhead."

Daisy whines her response.

"Are you being good for your mother?"

"Lawson, for the last time, I'm not—"

"You are, aren't you?" He barrels on, ignoring me. "You're such a good girl."

Good girl. There are those words again. I try my best to ignore them and the way they make me feel—all tingly and balmy—and how they make me wish Lawson wasn't so far away.

Daisy licks at the screen, and I laugh. She's about as eager to see him as I am.

"I think she's excited to see you."

"Well, I'll be home soon. Just one more game and this shitshow is over."

The irritation in his voice is clear, and I don't blame him. I've been following along with the road trip, and to say the Serpents are struggling would be a massive understatement. They've not won a single game since they've been on the road and not by a small margin. Not every game has been a total blowout—though two of them have—but they've allowed at least four goals in each one. That coupled with their back-and-forth playing the rest of the season, and things are officially not looking good for them. They're in a big hole, and if they keep this up, they're going to be too far out of the window to get into the Playoffs.

Auden even told me there are whisperings of a staffing change. Nothing has been made official yet, but it's looking like there's a good chance their head coach isn't going to be around for much longer. A five-game losing skid isn't something to sneeze at, especially not this late in the season where they should be playing much, much better than earlier.

"Who are you playing tonight?" I ask, even though I know the answer.

"Buffalo. Hutch's mom, stepdad, and stepsister are going to be there, so he'd really like a win for them."

I've heard about Hutch's stepsister from Auden. She got married last summer and had filed for divorce by the time Christmas rolled around. Auden isn't exactly the biggest fan of her, but it also sounds like the stepsister isn't the biggest fan of anyone either.

"I want a win, too," he says, voice quieter than before. "I'm tired of losing."

He looks so dejected sitting in what I assume is his hotel room. His shoulders are slumped forward, and it's obvious with the dark circles under his eyes that this losing streak is wearing on him.

"Well, just know all of Seattle is cheering for you."

"Even you?" he asks, a smile teasing at his lips.

Yes. "Not a chance," I tell him, hoping the sarcasm I've laced in my words sounds genuine and not as fake as it does to me.

"Hmm. I doubt that."

And he's right. He's so, so right.

"Tell me something happy, Wednesday." He falls back on his bed, raising his arm up and tucking it under his head.

I don't look at his muscles straining against his simple gray t-shirt. Or at his dark hair that looks so damn silky even on video. Or the rough-looking five o'clock shadow that needs a shave.

Nope. I don't look at any of it.

"It snowed here."

"That's not happy. That sounds awful."

"Nah. I love the snow."

"Really?"

"Oh yeah. The smell of it, the way it blankets a city and quiets everything down, the way it can make even the ugliest of places look beautiful. Besides, have you seen the Space Needle all lit up at night with snow on the ground? It's heavenly."

A soft laugh rumbles from his chest.

"What?" I ask.

"Nothing." He shakes his head, smiling at me. "It's nothing. So stars and snow, huh? That's your thing?"

"And horror movies on Christmas."

"Of course. How could I forget that?"

"Hmm…what else, what else?" I tap my chin, trying to think of good news. "Oh! I got Daisy to give me a high five."

"You did not." He sits up. "Show me."

"All right. Hang on."

I get onto the floor, maneuvering my phone until it's leaning against a stack of patient files and my stapler so that Lawson can see both me and Daisy. I set her down next to me and she looks up at me patiently, her tail wagging.

"Up," I instruct, and she pushes herself to a standing position. "Very good. Now sit."

She complies, tail whipping back and forth, and I look over at Lawson, who is watching with his mouth ajar. I waggle my brows at him, silently saying, *See?*

We run through it a few more times, and each time Daisy listens. Up and down and up again. Each time, I give her encouragement, petting her head and making sure she knows she's doing the right thing. Then it's time for the big test.

"Okay, now we're going to show your daddy the trick I taught you. You ready?"

Another tail wag.

"Gimme five," I tell her, holding my hand up.

It takes her a second…then another…and finally, she lifts her paw, resting it on my palm.

"Shut up!" Lawson shouts, just as excited about this as I am. "She did it!"

As soon as Daisy registers his voice, she abandons me, crossing over to the phone and licking it like mad.

"See? I told you so." I grab her, pulling her back into my lap. "She's been working on that for a few days. Figured we'd surprise you when you got home, but you seem like you could use the cheering up now."

"I could. I really, really could."

He's beaming at me, and it's the most I've seen him smile since…well, The Balcony Thing.

"For you, Rory, I'd gather every star in this sky and string them high somewhere only for you, just to see you smile like that again."

His words slam into me. They're as loud as they were the first time as they rattle around in my head and, even worse, in my heart. I try to shake them away and block them out, but it's pointless with Lawson staring at me the way he is, with pride and happiness and genuine joy.

"I—" A knock on his hotel door interrupts whatever he's going to say next. "What?" he growls at whoever is on the other side. He shoves off the bed, trudges toward the door, and yanks it open, causing it to bang against the wall. "What do you want, Hayes?"

"We were about to grab some grub. You in?"

Lawson's eyes dart to the phone, then back at Hayes, I assume. I can't see him, so I can't be certain. "Uh, yeah. Gimme a minute."

"Who are you talking to? Is that your mom? Don't let Keller know. He'll be in here trying to get her number like that." Hayes snaps his fingers.

Lawson groans. "I fucking swear..." He shakes his head. "It's not my mom."

"Then who is—oh. *Oh.* It's a sexy phone call, huh? Is that why you're in your panties?"

"I'm not in my *panties*, you dick. I'm just..."

But he doesn't continue, which tells me he *is* in his underwear. Why did Lawson call me in his underwear? And a better question is: What kind of underwear is he wearing? Are they goofy with different characters on them? Are they plain? Is he a boxer guy or is he wearing boxer-briefs? Are they—

No! No. Stop thinking about Lawson's underwear!

"Wait. Is it Rory? Is that Rory on the phone? The girl you like? Are you having *phone sex with Rory?*"

Did Hayes just say...

"No! I'm not having *phone sex with Rory.* And keep your voice down, dammit," Lawson hisses at his teammate. "Get in here."

There's a commotion, then the screen goes black, but I can still hear voices.

"You fucking idiot. I'm not having phone sex with her. I'm just checking in."

"Yeah, but you *wish* it was phone sex."

"I… That…" Lawson stumbles over his words. "That's beside the point. The point is, it's not happening, and you need to keep quiet. Hutch doesn't exactly know I've been hanging out with Rory."

"And by *hanging out* you mean having phone sex with her? Ow! Stop throwing shit at me," Hayes yells. "I get it—no phone sex. But why not tell Hutch?"

"Because I…"

He doesn't have a reason, just like I don't have a reason for not telling Auden. It's stupid. It's not like there's anything going on between us, right? I should tell my sister. I *will* tell my sister.

"Because it's none of his damn business, that's why," he finally says.

"Pfft. Sounds to me like you're into her and don't want Hutch to know because he knows you're a total moron and playboy and he wouldn't want you to defile his future sister-in-law."

"Can you shut up for five seconds?"

I laugh, mostly because Lawson telling someone else to shut up is hilarious.

The call goes quiet.

One.

Two.

Three.

Then suddenly his face is filling the screen again. He's smiling. It's big and wide and oh so fake that it's comical.

"Uh, hey," he says, narrowing his eyes at something off screen.

What he doesn't realize is that behind him is a mirror, and I can see Hayes clearly. He's thrusting his hips and pretending to make out with someone. Honestly, he's doing a good job at both.

"You do know holding the phone against your chest doesn't mean I can't hear you, right?"

He winces. "So you heard all that?"

I chuckle. "Yeah, I heard all that."

"And that…is the first draft of my upcoming play!" He forces out a laugh, scrubbing a hand through his hair nervously. "How's it sound?"

"Like two morons wrote it."

"Hey!" Hayes protests.

Lawson throws the hotel phone at him.

"Oh, real mature, Lawson. Injure me before the game tonight—great idea."

"What do you care? You're riding the pine anyway."

Hayes tries to tackle him, but he moves too quickly,

and the kid ends up falling face-first on the bed.

"I should, uh, probably let you deal with him."

Lawson sighs. "Yeah, probably a good idea. I'll see you tomorrow?"

"Tomorrow."

"Hey! Watch it! We're trying to win tonight, and these hands need to be sharp," he shouts at Hayes before disconnecting.

It's ridiculous. He's ridiculous. But that doesn't stop me from sitting there with a smile on my face. It's probably the most fun I've been involved in in a long, long time, which is really sad because it's happening thousands of miles away.

I look over at Daisy, who is now tucked safely under my desk again.

"Your dad is strange, you know that?"

She lets out a long, tired sigh, like she's fully aware of this.

"But he's fun. He's fun and I…"

I swallow down the rest of the words, locking them up and throwing away the key before I admit to something I know is just in the heat of the moment. I don't know how long I sit there on the floor of my office hiding away from my responsibilities while I try to sort out the millions of thoughts running through my mind, but it's far too long.

And it's all because of Lawson.

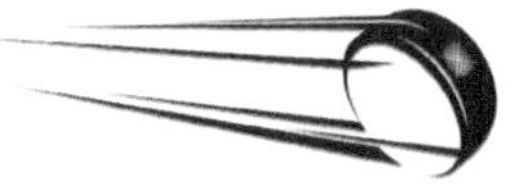

I'm not sure what possesses me to do it, but I leave work early for the first time in who knows how long, walk into my bedroom, tug open my drawer, and pull out the item I stole from Lawson a few weeks ago. I slip it over my head, then hold my phone up, angling it so he can see what it is I'm wearing.

When I'm satisfied with the photo, before I can think about what I'm doing, I send it with two words attached: *Even me.*

That night, the Serpents win for the first time since they've been on the road, and for the second time, I fall asleep wearing Lawson's jersey.

Chapter 12

LAWSON

It's official—Coach is done.

After touching down in Seattle last night, we got the call from the general manager. Apparently, it's been in the works for a while now, since before Christmas break even, and given what's transpired this season, it's not entirely surprising. You can't be hanging out in the Super Sixteen at the beginning of the season, then take the nosedive we did and not expect a coaching change to be made.

The worst part is, it's not all on Coach, and every person on the team knows it. Sure, he's responsible for us, but we're the ones out there on the ice playing. We're the ones not pulling our weight. Unfortunately, though, sometimes a change like this has to be made to spark some life in a team, and hopefully this shift will light a fire right under our asses.

Thanks to that losing streak, we're several spots out of the Playoffs right now, but if we can somehow come back after the All-Star break and win, win, win, there's a small chance we could pull off a miracle and snag a wild card spot.

That break we so badly need starts *now*. I roll out of bed later in the day, having taken advantage of the time off to sleep in, something I haven't done since before training camp started, then I rush around my apartment getting ready.

I'm picking up Daisy from the clinic, and eager as I am to see her, I'm even more excited to see Rory. I can't believe she heard all that shit last night with Hayes, the fucking idiot. He kept sending me looks all throughout dinner, making sexual gestures with silverware and toying with me when it came to Hutch. For a split second, I wished I were on Buffalo's team so I could take a run at him and lay him out like he deserved.

I think what surprised me even more than her hearing it was that she didn't seem fazed by it at all, like maybe she wasn't entirely uninterested in the idea of me being into her. I mean, she obviously knows since I kissed her, but that was weeks ago, and nothing has happened since. Maybe guys kiss her all the time.

I clench my fists at the thought. Fuck, I hope guys *don't* kiss her all the time. I want to be the only one kissing her as badly as I *want* to kiss her, which is saying something because I really, really want to kiss her.

I pull on a sweater, then grab my phone, keys, and wallet and race downstairs.

"Lucas!"

I turn to find Paige coming out of her apartment. "Hey, how are you?"

"Good, good. Listen, I'm so sorry to ask you this, but I need to be at the restaurant for my shift in twenty minutes and Jaden left his clarinet at home. Is there any way you could run it by the school for me?"

"Uh…" Fuck. I don't want to say no because I don't want to let Paige down, but I also really, really want to see Rory. Going nearly two weeks without her is far, far too long.

"Oh, gosh. What am I doing asking you that? That's too much. I'm sorry. I—"

"No, stop. It's not too much. I'm happy to do it," I tell her, crossing the hall and grabbing the instrument from her already full hands.

"Really?" She beams up at me. "Ugh, I don't know what I did to deserve to live next to a great guy like you, but I'm so thankful for it."

The tips of my ears burn hot at her words. "It's no problem, Paige, really."

She gives me a look that says I'm full of shit, but I ignore it.

"Need help carrying anything down to your car?"

She worries her lip between her teeth for a moment before forcing a smile. "No, no. You go on. I've got to lock up, then I'm heading straight to work."

Now it's *my* turn to give her that same look. She's not going down to her car because it means her car isn't running. Again.

But, like me, she ignores the stare, ducking her head and eyes away. I make a mental note to call my financial guy and look into a way to get them a new car. It's bullshit they keep having to take it to a mechanic, especially when I can do something to help.

I lift the clarinet. "Well, I'd better get going and get this to Jaden."

"Thank you again."

"Sure. That's what neighbors are for, right?"

"Right." She eyes me skeptically as I back away.

I'm to the elevator, already pressing the button when she calls my name.

"Lucas?"

"Hmm?" I ask, peeking over my shoulder as the car arrives.

Her eyes are narrowed on me. "Don't."

It's one word, a warning.

One I don't plan on heeding.

"Sorry, Paige, can't hear you!" I step in, pressing the *close door* button repeatedly. "Elevator's too noisy!"

The doors shut, but not before I hear her yell, "Dammit, Lucas!"

I laugh as I pull out my phone and call my financial advisor.

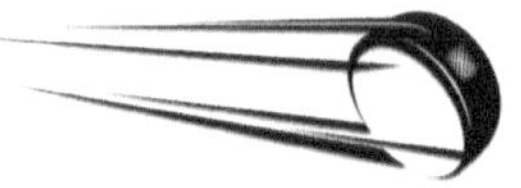

It's past three by the time I finally make it to the clinic, and I feel like an ass because I promised Rory I'd be here well before noon. Luckily, Paige had the foresight to call the school and let them know I was on my way, so all they had to do was call Jaden to the office so I could hand off the instrument. He was so stoked to see me at his school that it turned into me having lunch with him, which then turned into a tour to meet all his favorite teachers, which, as it turns out, is all of them. It was way more than I bargained for, but I'm pretty sure Jaden is now the coolest kid in school, so it totally makes it worth it.

I pull open the door to Seattle's top veterinary clinic with two hot coffees clutched in my hand, ready to apologize, when I come face to face with the last person I expected to see here.

"Auden."

Her jaw drops. "Lawson. What are you doing here?"

"Oh, uh…I'm, uh…"

I scramble to find words, any words at all. Anything that doesn't make this seem like it's more than just me coming to pick up Daisy. Which technically, it's not, but it also kind of is. I've been talking to Rory every day while I've been gone. Whether she wants to admit it or not, we've become friends.

"Auden, you forgot your…"

Rory stops in the middle of the waiting room, a coat clutched tight in her hands. Her light green eyes dart from me to her twin and back again, the panic in them clear as day. I only hope Auden can't see that.

"Lawson, you're finally here for Daisy, huh?"

"Wait. Daisy's here?" Auden looks at her sister. "Where is she?"

"Under my desk."

"What? I was just in your office. I didn't see her."

Rory shrugs. "Well, she's under there."

"Why?"

"Because I've been watching her?"

"Since when?" Auden crosses her arms over her chest like she can't believe her sister didn't tell her this.

"Since before their road trip. It's not that big of a deal. We do it all the time."

Casey, the vet tech, looks up from what she's doing, her eyes making contact with mine because she knows damn well Rory does not, in fact, do this all the time. I'm a special case.

But Auden doesn't know this, so when she puts her hand on her chest and says, "Aww, that's sweet of you," it's a relief.

She's not going to question it, and I'm glad. The last thing I want to explain is what I'm doing here and how often Rory has been watching Daisy for me. That would mean I'd also have to explain all the time we've been spending together, and I'd rather not get into that now.

"You know," Auden says, walking back over to her sister, "you may act like you have a black heart, but you really don't. You can't keep all that bottled up inside forever, you know. Let it out, especially on hard days like these."

Hard days like these?

Auden grabs her coat from her sister, then pauses. "Aw, screw it." She throws her arms around Rory, dragging her in for a hug, and she fights every minute of it.

Her eyes connect with mine, and all I can think is, *You didn't fight it when it was me hugging you, Wednesday.* I'd bet my left nut she'd flip me off right now if she could.

Auden finally releases her, then pats her shoulder before turning on her heel. She stops beside me.

"I sincerely hope one of those is for her as a thank-you. It's been a long day, and she could use it."

Okay, that's twice now Auden's mentioned something along those lines. I want to ask what happened, but not her. I want to ask Rory.

But I don't. Not yet.

Instead, I nod. "One is."

"Good." She tosses me a wink. "Maybe you're not as bad as Hutch makes you out to be."

"He loves me, but not as much as Keller loves me."

Auden laughs. "Sure, something like that."

She gives her sister a wave, then disappears out the door.

I immediately cross the waiting area to Rory, who turns and heads down the hallway. I follow closely behind her, not caring if this is allowed or not. I'm too eager to find out what's been going on today.

I expect a protest when I nudge her office door shut behind me, but I don't get it. She's already falling into the chair behind her desk, her head dropping into her hands. I set down the coffee I bought her on her desk, then take a seat across from her. We sit in silence like that for several moments, Daisy eventually crawling out from under the desk and running over to me.

"Hey, there's my little good girl," I whisper as I raise the Labrador into my arms, burying my nose in her soft fur. She smells like puppy still, and I love it. "Were you good for your momma?"

Rory groans, but it's not a normal groan. Something's wrong. She lifts her head, and that's when I see it—her eyes are rimmed red. She's crying, or she's about to cry. Either way, it has me rising from my chair and moving around to the other side of the desk.

"What are you—"

But I don't let her finish. I spin her chair around, then drop to my knees, setting Daisy down before I wrap the overworked veterinarian in my arms and hug her. And, like the last time, she doesn't fight me on it.

No, she *leans* into it. Hell, she even hugs me back, her arms coming around me and holding on to me for dear life as her body begins to shake with quiet sobs.

Oh, she's crying all right. She's *really* crying, and fuck, I hate every second of it. It's not like it's the first time I've experienced a woman crying. My mother was left by my father. There were many nights I spent awake with her, even when she didn't know I could hear her crying from the other room. When I would go to her, she'd pretend everything was okay, feed me ice cream, then usher me back off to bed, all while wiping away tears.

So I'm not afraid of what's happening now, not in the least, but I am surprised by it. Rory is always so... Well, there's a reason I call her Wednesday. If she's breaking down like this, it must mean something went really, really wrong today.

I give her time, letting her get it all out. And she does, clinging to me as the sobs rack her body and the tears flow freely down her cheeks and onto my shoulder. I rub her back the whole time, offering nothing but comfort as she works through it.

When she finally calms down, she inches away. She's snotty and warm and blotchy and definitely looks like she's been crying, yet she's never been more beautiful than right now. She shoves her hair out of her face, and I watch as embarrassment passes over her features.

"Hey…" I say softly.

She tries to look away, but I don't let her, gripping her chin and forcing her to face me.

"Hey," I repeat. "It's okay."

"It's not." She sniffles. "It's not okay. That was extremely unprofessional and not to mention gross. I hate…" She shudders. "Feelings. I hate having feelings."

I chuckle. "Feelings are normal."

"No. No they are not. I hate them."

"Okay, well, hate them all you want. That's fine. I just…" I tuck a strand of hair behind her ear. "What happened?"

She sniffles again, then exhales heavily. "It's… I

had to put a cat down today, and it looked so much like Hades, all big and fluffy and gray, and it...I don't know. It sort of crashed into me. It's dumb, I know that, but it was hard." Her tear-filled eyes find mine. "I didn't expect it to be so hard, you know?"

Fuck. I never even thought about that side of what she does. I mean, it's obvious, but I like to trick my brain with happy thoughts when it comes to veterinary offices. All the puppies and kitties and sweet little animals that come through here, not the older, broken-down ones that are struggling in their last days. I never, ever want to think of that, and knowing Rory has to deal with that so often... It's no wonder she tries to bury all her emotions.

"I'm sorry," I tell her. "I know that's not helpful and probably doesn't mean shit, but I'm sorry. Truly."

She gives me a sad smile. "It's helpful, Lucas. More than you know."

Lucas.

My heart stutters at the sound of my name. It's dumb, I know that. It's my name for fuck's sake—I hear it all the time. But somehow, just now, it sounded like so much more than my name. And the fact that she trusted *me* to cry in front of...that means something too. What? I don't know, but I know it's something big I can't quite put my finger on.

Rory blows out another breath, then groans,

shaking her body like she's trying to shake off everything she's feeling.

"I've got to get back to work. I need…" She scoots the chair away and starts fiddling with things on her desk as I rise to my feet. "There's so much I have to do, like…I need to—"

"A break."

"What?" she asks without looking at me, too busy lifting the calendar pad that covers part of her desk, searching for I don't even know what.

I grab her chair once more, spinning it my way.

"Lawson, I—"

I drop my hands onto the armrests of her chair, leaning down until we're nearly touching. To her credit, she doesn't shrink back. She meets my hard stare, not backing down.

"You need a break."

Her shoulders sag. "What? What are you even talking about?" Her words sound tired, but not an *I'm tired of you* kind of tired. It's more the *I am tired down to my bones* kind of tired.

"I'm talking about you taking a break, getting out of here, out of the office—and not just for an afternoon or a day. I'm talking about taking a legit break, an overnight-or-two kind of break."

She's already shaking her head before I'm even finished. "I can't, Lawson. I can't do that. I—"

"Can. You can. And you will."

"You can't just *command* me to take a break."

"No, but I can throw you over my shoulder and carry you out of here and make you take one."

"I…" She scoffs, crossing her arms over her chest. "You wouldn't."

"Oh, Rory…" I inch closer, casting her in shadow as she stares up at me with wide eyes. "I so would."

She gulps, and her breaths start to sound a little uneven. "You're nuts."

"And so are you if you think you can keep working like this and not fall apart."

She opens her mouth to argue but quickly snaps it shut. I'm right. She knows I'm right. There's no way this is sustainable. She just fell apart because a cat that looked like her own had to be put down. She's only one minor incident away from a full breakdown, and I feel partly to blame. She's been not only working around the clock to take care of the clinic, but Daisy too. I owe this to her.

"What am I supposed to do for a break?" she asks after several charged seconds.

"Come with me."

Her brows pull together. "With you? Where? And why?"

"Yes, with me. And where? Well, it's a surprise.

Why? Because of all the other reasons we've already been over."

"Those aren't reasons to come with *you*. I don't even like you."

I sigh. "I'm on vacation too, Rory, and I'm planning on leaving for a few days." I am. In fact, I was going to go home and finally see my mom, but seeing Rory like this…I can't leave her. "No funny business. No ulterior motive. Just a nice, relaxing weekend spent out of the city and getting some fresh air, some mountain air. You know, out there where the sky is bright and goes on uninterrupted for miles and miles and mi—"

"I'm in!"

I grin. I knew I'd get her with that. "Really?"

"Yes. Really." She sighs, slouching back into the chair, staring off into space. "You're right. I need a break away from here. Dr. Helms, Casey…they can handle things while I'm gone."

"They can."

"And my patients will be fine. Totally fine."

"They will."

"I can do this," she says, more to herself than to me. "I can do this."

"You can. You will."

She looks up at me. "I'll go with you…on one condition."

I narrow my eyes skeptically but nod. "Okay…"

"I'm bringing my cat."

I laugh. "Deal. You can bring your cat."

"Yes!" She fist-pumps the air.

"But, Wednesday?"

"Yes?"

"Bring my jersey too."

Chapter 13

RORY

I'm supposed to be giving Petey his monthly anal gland expression right now, but instead, I'm sitting in a swanky BMW next to Lucas Lawson of all people. It's Friday morning and we're twisting through the mountain roads, inching closer and closer to our surprise destination by the minute. I have no clue what I've agreed to for the weekend, but I'm completely on board, even if it does mean he's taking me out to the middle of the woods to murder me. At least I won't have to go back into work after this.

Aw, who am I kidding? I'd miss my patients far too much for that.

"This is a really nice car," I tell him, running my hands over the leather seats again like I've been doing for the last hour.

"Thanks. I have three more like it back in the parking garage."

"What? Seriously?"

"No." He laughs. "You've seen my apartment—do you really think I'd have three of the same car?"

"Maybe? I don't know. You're not what I assumed you'd be at all."

It's true. He's far from what I had in my mind the first time I met him. Right away I knew he wasn't the kind of guy I'd ever want to hang around. He oozed jock vibes, and not in the good way.

But the real Lawson… Well, he's definitely not just a jock. He's something so much more.

"Hmm. I'm not sure how to take that."

"It's a good thing," I tell him.

He slides his gray eyes over to me momentarily before looking back at the road. It's something he's been doing the entire drive. It's almost like he can't believe I'm here.

Hell, I can't believe I'm here either.

Obviously, I didn't tell Auden about this, but when I did tell Casey, the shock on her face was immediate. It was quickly replaced by a high five and telling me to get the hell out of there before she called security on me. I, of course, reminded her we don't *have* security and finished handing off my patients to Dr. Helms.

"Anyway," Lawson continues, "I'm not like other

guys in the league who come in and see the big dollar signs they throw our way, then turn right around and spend every last penny. I pay my bills, live in a modest apartment, splurged on a car, and take the rest of my money and invest it so when my hockey career is over, I'm not penniless. We're heading to one of my investment properties now."

"You have…*investment properties?*"

He laughs. "Yeah, I do. Does that surprise you?"

"Oh, I'm sorry. Do I need to repeat my previous question with even more shock shoved into my words?"

He grins. "No."

He shakes his head, adjusting his grip on the steering wheel. I never knew watching a guy drive was something I was into, but I'm slowly starting to realize there are a lot of things Lawson does that I shouldn't find attractive yet do.

"But yes, I do have several properties. I actually have a business degree."

"*What?*"

"Okay, that's the second time you've used a tone that's a mix of disbelief and complete shock. Watch it because I *will* turn this car around." He glances into the backseat where Daisy is in her crate next to Hades in his crate. "Won't I, Daisy?" She makes a noise, then huffs. Lawson pitches his thumb back at her. "See? She understands."

"I'm sorry. Sorry. It's just…I wasn't quite expecting that. I can't really picture you in college."

"I went online."

"Like while you were playing hockey?"

"Yeah?" He phrases it as a question, but it's more of a question like *Why is this surprising?* "A lot of guys do it. It's hard as hell, but it's worth it when you get out of the league and don't know what to do. At least you'll have something to fall back on."

It's smart. Really damn smart. Smarter than I expected Lawson to be, that's for sure.

"I'm sorry. I thought… Well, let's just say you present yourself in a different light, but now I'm wondering if you're doing that on purpose so people don't expect much out of you or because you're like an actual good person and don't want the attention to be on that. You just want to do good and be good and *pretend* to be a bad boy."

"Oh, trust me, Rory—I'm a bad boy where it counts."

He tosses me a wink, and it's as cheesy as that line he fed me during The Balcony Thing—yet my body throbs at the gesture.

Even through that, I don't miss how he's deflecting again, like he did on our phone call when I asked him about Jaden. It makes me believe that, despite the stereotypical jock, meathead persona he puts out, it's far from the man he really is.

I like the man he really is. A lot.

We chat about random things the rest of the drive, from the weather to the last thing we binged—a horror anthology for me and some spy action show for him—and our families. He tells me more about his mother, regaling me with stories from her time working at the bar, and he asks me what it was like growing up with a pro athlete for a father. When I tell him my father didn't force the game of hockey on me, he seems surprised.

"I always hear the worst stories from guys in the league who have a parent that played sports. It's always a competition or they've been pushed so hard their entire lives that they know literally nothing else but the sport. It's wild."

"That's just sad."

"It is. Reminds me of what Dan Scott did to Nathan."

"Dan Scott? As in Dan Scott from *One Tree Hill* Dan Scott?"

His cheeks pinken. "Uh, yeah. That one."

"*You* watch *One Tree Hill*?"

"A few times. It's one of my mother's favorite shows." He glances over at me. "What?"

I shake my head, not even bothering to try to hide

my surprise. "Nothing. Just another mark in the Ways Lawson Continues to Surprise Me column."

"You're keeping lists about me?"

"Sure. There's the Ways Lawson is a Total Asshole list. The Ways Lawson Resembles a Human list. The Places I Could Hide Lawson's Body list, which is not to be confused with the Ways I Could Murder Lawson list. And of course, there's the one I just mentioned."

"That's quite a lot of lists. I'm surprised there's no Ways Lawson Continues to Turn Me On list." He grins wolfishly. "Unless there is."

"No," I answer quickly. *Too* quickly.

I glower at him before he turns back to the road, still grinning. Lawson flicks on the blinker, then pulls into a small store just off the side of the road.

"What are we doing here?"

"Groceries. This is the closest store to the cabin."

I try not to panic at that. As much as I never thought I'd live in a big city, I sure have become quite accustomed to having everything so close. Now, we're going to be in the middle of nowhere, and anything could go wrong.

Like, for example, Lawson could kiss me again, and I'd be stuck with him for a whole weekend trying to resist kissing him again. It sounds like torture if you ask me.

We pile out of the SUV, leaving it running for

Daisy and Hades, then make our way inside. It's a cute little shop stocked with all the essentials. There's even a deli counter off in the corner, which I did not at all expect.

"Lawson!" the guy working there yells as soon as we walk through the door. "Haven't seen you around here in months."

"Hey, Willy. How are you?"

"Good, good. Been watching the season, kid. That's been…" The older, burly man whistles. "It's rough."

"Yeah, yeah. I know. That's why I'm coming out here. Bit of a reset, you know? Hoping the fresh air and mountain view can get me back on track."

"Ah, it can. It definitely can. That stuff is magic, I'm telling you."

"I hope so. I could use some magic right about now."

Willy's eyes drift over to me. "And who is this?"

"Hi, I'm Rory. It's nice to meet you."

"Bringing a girl, huh? You haven't done that since…"

"I know," Lawson says, his eyes finding mine.

He's brought other women up here?

Be serious, Rory. Of course he has.

Right. It makes sense. I'm not stupid. I know I'm not special. This is probably normal for him. He might do things that make him seem human, but he's still the same playboy and this still means nothing to him.

"Well, not much has changed since you've been here. We got a few new sodas, but that's about it."

"Thanks, Willy. We'll be out of your hair in no time."

Lawson grabs a basket, then hands it to me before snatching up another. "Cabin's stocked with all the cooking essentials, so we can make anything. I can take care of dinner if you want to oversee snacks and drinks?"

"All right." I head off in the opposite direction of him.

It's stupid, I know that, but I can't shake the idea of him bringing other women here. This was supposed to be a weekend away, for me to finally relax; now, all I'll be able to think about is which surface is safe to touch and did he properly disinfect it after he was done.

I toss a few things into my basket, crackers and some different cheeses and a couple of bags of chips and pretzels. I grab some pieces of fruit from the tiny selection, then fill the rest of the basket with wine. Lots and lots of wine. Before I'm about to head to the front counter, I grab a six-pack of beer for Lawson, then I meet him up front.

Even though I try to fight him on it, Lawson insists on paying.

"I grabbed us steaks and potatoes for dinner, some chicken breasts, a few things for breakfast, and I figured we could do sandwiches for lunch," he explains as he hands over his black credit card to Willy.

"All right," I say again, looking anywhere but at him.

Get a grip, Rory.

I inhale and exhale a few times, waving goodbye to Willy before heading off with our four bags of groceries, Lawson carrying all of them. We pile back into the SUV, and I try my hardest not to be turned on by Lawson putting his arm on the back of my headrest and turning around to reverse. He has a perfectly good backup camera he could be using. Does he know how hot that move is and is just doing this to torture me?

He comes to a stop before pulling out onto the road, but it's not a normal stop. His gaze is trained fully on me and not at all looking for oncoming traffic.

"Rory?"

"Hmm?"

He doesn't continue. He waits for me to look at him first.

I suck in a breath, then turn toward him. Those damn eyes that are impossibly gray meet my own, and I briefly wonder if there will ever be a time when I look into them and don't feel like my breath is being stolen from my lungs.

"He was talking about my mom."

Relief floods me, and it's dumb. I have no right to be feeling this way, to be worried I'm not the first person Lawson has brought here.

"I've never brought anyone else here," he continues. "Just you and just her. I don't share this place with people who don't matter."

Then he pulls back out onto the road, and we finish the drive in silence.

Down a gravel road I wouldn't have seen if it weren't for the small mailbox at the end of the lane sits the cabin. It's not really a cabin, though, at least not what *my* version of a cabin is.

This isn't some one-room shack in the middle of nowhere. It's a huge, two-story sprawling work of art tucked into the trees. There are a few feet of snow piled up around it, making it look extra cozy and inviting, and it's all ours for the weekend.

"This is incredible," I say as we step out of the vehicle. "And so not at all what I was expecting."

He chuckles. "Yeah, my mom said the same thing. I had to practically drag her back out to the car kicking and screaming because she didn't want to leave."

"Your mom might be onto something. I'm not so sure I'm going to want to leave either."

"Come on. It's even better on the inside."

Better than this picture-perfect scene? I doubt it.

Lawson tosses my bag over one shoulder and his over the other, then grabs Hades and Daisy. He looks silly standing there loaded down with our things, but when I offer to help, he refuses, saying he'll come back out for the groceries. Normally I'd argue, but I'm too eager to see the inside of this cabin he promises is better than this view.

"I had the neighbors plow the driveway for us, but I don't know if they salted the porch, so watch your step," he tells me as we make our way up the stairs.

We make it up without any issues…at least until we hit the door.

"Oh fuck," Lawson mutters.

"What's wrong?"

"I, uh… My…" His cheeks are flushed, and I have a feeling it's not just because of the cold. "The keys. They're, uh, in my pocket."

"Oh."

"Yeah. Could you…"

He trails off, not finishing his sentence, but we both know what it is he's going to ask.

I shouldn't. I really, really shouldn't. And yet…

"Sure."

I reach out, trying not to pay attention to how shaky my hands are. Funny, because I perform surgeries on animals and am known for having steady hands. When it comes to Lawson, though, it's a different story. I hook my fingers into his pocket—*of course* he's wearing the world's tightest jeans—and ease inside, fishing for the keys. I guess in the short walk from the car to the door, they've managed to fall deep down, because I can't feel them to save my life.

I reach down farther, sliding my fingers deeper and deeper, but there's still nothing except the heat and hardness of his sculpted thighs. I know hockey players use the hell out of their legs, which means they're probably fairly strong, but *holy hell*. I was not expecting them to be like *this*.

"Uh, Rory..."

"Yes?"

"I meant my coat pocket."

"Oh!" I yank my hand out, my cheeks burning hot at this point, then reach into his leather jacket and pull out the keys. I smack at his chest. "You ass! Why didn't you tell me that?"

He shrugs with a grin. "I just figured you wanted to feel me up."

"I hate you," I tell him, spinning around and unlocking the door.

He laughs lowly at my back. "You wish you did, Rory. You wish you did."

I push the door open and am surprised to find several lights on inside and that it's warm when I step in. I half expected to freeze for a bit until it warmed up and am delighted I won't have to.

"I had the neighbor get the fireplace going too so Hades and Daisy don't freeze to death."

"Your neighbor sounds extraordinarily nice."

"He is, but that's because he uses the place all the time in exchange for regular maintenance on it during the season. Obviously, in the winter I don't get to spend as much time here as I'd like, so I let Jeff and his family use the place."

He says it like it's nothing to let your neighbors come into your home and do their own thing when in reality there's no way most of the population would ever entertain the idea. Not Lawson though. I want to think it's his small-town mentality shining through, but I don't think so. I think he's just genuinely a good guy.

I toe off my snow-covered boots, then grab the pets from Lawson's arms so he can take his shoes off. I set them on the floor, then open the crates. Daisy darts out instantly…then goes straight to Lawson, scratching at his legs for attention.

Hades, on the other hand, doesn't have much interest in anything. He certainly didn't miss me in the two hours we spent in the car, and it shows. I leave the door open and let him be. He'll come out and explore whenever he feels like it.

I pad farther into the cabin, and though I hate to admit it, Lawson was right. The view from the outside was great, but it's nothing compared to the inside. The space is modern with stainless steel appliances in the kitchen and sleek furniture, but it still has a rustic cabin feel to it with high ceilings and your typical lodge décor of flannel blankets on the back of the leather couch and old photographs adorning the walls.

The real eyecatcher is the wall of windows on the other side that give the most incredible view of the tree line and mountain off in the distance. The sight is something straight out of a movie, and I gravitate toward it, pressing my nose against the cold glass, clearly not caring about smudges.

"This is… *Wow.*"

"I told you," Lawson says, coming to stand behind me. The heat radiating off him negates the iciness of the window. "It's breathtaking, isn't it?"

"It truly is. I've lived in the PNW for a long time now, but I've never seen a view like this."

"Then you really need to get out more."

"Says the guy who's always on the road."

"Hey, when I have downtime, I spend it out

exploring. I hiked over a hundred miles during the summer."

"Seriously?" I ask, finally tearing my eyes away from the picturesque view in front of me, letting them linger only momentarily on the hot tub I intend to take full advantage of while I'm here.

"Yep. I have to keep in shape somehow." He pats his stomach, which I *know* is perfectly cut. "Plus, it keeps me out of trouble."

"I thought you liked trouble, Lawless." He cringes, and I laugh. "Only you could get away with not one but two ridiculous names."

He shrugs. "It's a gift."

"Hmm. Something like that." I turn back to look out the window. "So, what are we going to do first? Skinny-dipping in the hot tub, right?" His jaw drops in his reflection and I laugh, turning around to pat his shoulder. "I'm kidding, Lawson. I'm not skinny-dipping with you. I brought a bathing suit."

I walk past him, grabbing my bag and heading for the stairs to find my bedroom.

"Oh, and, Lawson?" I call down where he's standing frozen by the window.

"Yeah?"

"It's a two-piece."

Chapter 14

LAWSON

"It's a two-piece."

Those words have been bouncing around in my head for the few hours Rory's been curled up in a chair near the fireplace, flipping slowly through a book. There's some woman in a red dress stepping onto a gift box on the cover, the title something about gifting her to a best friend, which is surprising. I didn't peg her as a romance reader at all. Horror for sure, maybe a murder mystery or two, but definitely not romance.

I tried reading for a bit but couldn't get into the book, or maybe it was just Rory distracting me with the little noises she kept making. She'd giggle at something on one page, then gasp at another, making a soft *hmmph* when she didn't like something. I even caught her rubbing her thighs together a few times, and I can only assume it was when she was reading a naughty scene.

The urge to peek over her shoulder and see what had her wiggling in her seat was so damn strong, but I managed to suppress it, instead busying myself with stoking the fire and bringing in more wood. Now, I'm about to start on dinner. I wasn't sure what she likes, so I kept it simple with steak and a side. It's not the only thing I know how to cook, but it is delicious.

I cue up some music on my phone, some soft lo-fi in the background, then work on feeding us. I've just laid our steaks down in the pan when she finally comes up for air.

"That smells heavenly," she says, padding into the kitchen. "Anything I can help with?"

"Maybe grab the plates?" I point to a cabinet. "I guess I should have asked how you like your steak. Any preference?"

She scrunches up her nose. "I'm not really a steak person."

I pause. Fuck. I didn't even think about that.

She bursts out a laugh. "I'm kidding. I love steak. The bloodier the better, please."

Oh, thank fuck.

"A woman after my own heart," I tell her, dropping some extra butter on top of each slab of meat.

She circles the island, pulling open the cabinet and pushing up on her tiptoes to reach for the plates. It's pointless. She's still too short to reach them.

Mind you, when I bought this place, I had only myself in mind. I didn't care that someone smaller than me couldn't reach the cabinets because this was supposed to be my home away from home as long as I'm in Washington. But seeing Rory here, watching her read in that big leather chair or trying to reach something in the cabinet, I suddenly want to rip everything out and start over, build a place for me and for someone else too.

The thought slams into me, nearly knocking me over. Is that what I really want? A place built with two people in mind? Since when? And with who?

My eyes slide over to the petite woman who is now using the counter to launch herself higher in hopes of reaching the dish. She still misses, and I laugh, which causes her to shoot daggers my way over her shoulder before turning back to the task at hand.

I cross the kitchen toward her, standing maybe a little close as I reach above her, grabbing the plates with ease. Her back is pressed against my front as she slowly lowers to her heels, her ass rolling over my cock, which has been straining against my jeans since I picked her up from her apartment earlier. Hell, I feel like it's been straining even longer than that, maybe since I first met her last year in the bar of The Sinclair hotel. All I know is that she's under my fucking skin. I feel like I could burst at any second, and it's taking everything I have not to.

"Here." I hand her the plates.

She takes them from me, but I don't let go.

I can't. If I let go, I'll have to move, and if I move, I just might die if I'm not touching her anymore. It's a precarious situation I've found myself in, made even more stressful when she presses back on me, and I don't mean a shift backward or a slip or that she's lost her balance.

No.

Rory actively presses her ass against me, and my cock eats up the attention. *I* eat it up too. I grip the counter, my arms caging her in. She lets out the tiniest of gasps, and it's official—we're dancing, skirting right around all the things we want to do but can't seem to find the courage to make happen.

Like how I want nothing more than to press my lips to her exposed neck. Grind my aching dick against her more. Sink to my knees and see just how sweet she tastes.

But I do none of that.

It's not just because I have dinner cooking and it's about thirty seconds away from rare to medium rare. No, I don't because I want Rory to be the one to fold. I've already kissed her once. Now, she's going to be the one to come to me. I'm one hell of an opponent in the face-off circle, and this is one draw I'm not going to lose.

For now, I push away from the counter and turn my attention back to dinner.

It takes Rory a full minute to move from her spot by the counter, and I know without a doubt that by the time this weekend is over, I'll have won.

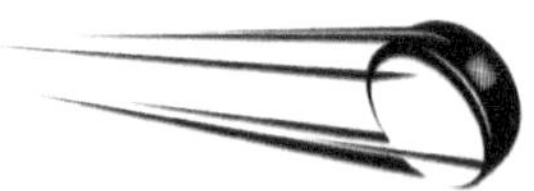

"Oh, gosh. I can't eat any more. I'm too full." Rory pushes her plate away from her, then rests her head on the countertop. I'm impressed. There are only two small bites of steak left and none of her potato. For someone so small, she sure can pack it away.

"And to think I have a pie cooking in the oven for dessert."

"Pie?" She perks up, and so does Daisy, who has been sitting right at my feet through the entire meal, hoping for scraps she's not going to get. "What kind of pie?"

I laugh. "I was kidding. There's no pie."

"Asshole."

"But if you do want dessert, I might have snuck a half gallon of ice cream into our grocery haul."

She considers it for a moment before shrugging. "Maybe later."

She hops off her stool, grabs her plate, and reaches for mine. I snatch it away before she can take it.

"What the hell? Give me your plate, Lawson."

"Absolutely not."

A dark look crosses her face. "Give it to me."

"No. You're a guest in my home. You're not doing my dishes."

She sighs. "You've been doing stuff all day—keeping the fire warm, refilling my hot chocolate, and then you cooked dinner. Let me do this one thing. *Please.*"

She noticed I refilled her hot chocolate? She was so wrapped up in her book, she didn't even budge each time I brought a fresh cup over. I guess she was paying more attention than I thought.

"Fine," I relent, handing my plate over to her. "But I'm drying."

"Ha. Funny. No." She nods toward the small bar over in the corner of the living room. "Make us drinks or something. Relax."

I roll my eyes but do as she says, pushing off the stool. "Any requests?" I ask over my shoulder. "I have pretty much everything."

"Surprise me. I'm easy."

My steps falter, and by the sound of it, hers do too. The house goes eerily quiet for only a moment before her loud laugh breaks the tension. I smile, shaking my head as I sidle up to the bar. I pour us each a glass of my favorite bourbon—which I only keep here because if I kept it at home, I know I'd reach for it far more often than I should—then carry them back over to the island.

Rory's elbow-deep in the sink, scrubbing the plates and pan I used to cook the steaks. I hate sitting here doing nothing, but I'd be lying if I said I wasn't enjoying the view. With every scrub, her tits sway. She even drops a few tufts of soap on her shirt, and it soaks through almost instantly, causing the black of her bra to poke through her white top.

It's as enticing as it is painful to watch, and before I know it, my bourbon is gone. I'm in desperate need of another drink, but I'm too fucking scared to stand. There's no way she's not going to notice the bulge in my sweats.

"So, you said this is an investment property?" she asks, drawing my attention from her nipples straining against her shirt.

"Yep." Oh fuck. My voice is all gravelly, and based on the way she peeks up at me, she doesn't miss it. I clear my throat. "Yes. Why?"

"I was just wondering…if it's an investment

property, what do you do with it when you're not here? Rent it out?"

"Not yet, but I will when I'm no longer playing with the Serpents."

She whips her head my way, and if I didn't know any better, I'd say she doesn't like the idea of me not being in Seattle anymore. This time it's her who makes a throat-clearing sound as she moves her attention back to the sink.

"Right. When you move on to something else." She nods. "That's smart, actually. You get to use it now, then make money off it later."

"Yep. That's the plan. Something to keep making me money later when I've hung up my skates."

"When do you think that'll be?"

"Geez, I'm only twenty-six, so…maybe in like twenty years?"

She blanches, and I laugh.

"I'm kidding. Kind of. I love hockey and I'll keep playing as long as I possibly can, but if you mean when I think I'll be done with the Serpents, I don't know. Whenever the city gets tired of me, I guess."

"They won't." She tenses, like she automatically regrets the words, then relaxes. "I mean, I *assume* not. This city loves the people who love it. If you give them your all, you're golden."

"Good to know."

Rory finishes up the dishes, then grabs a towel to start drying them. It's killing me to not be helping her, but I still don't trust myself to get up. I'll be too damn tempted to touch her again, so I'll sit right here until I'm certain I won't do just that.

When she's finished, she wipes her forehead, and I try not to notice how her shirt rides up, or how cute she looks with her cheeks red from the heat of the water…or how adorable it is when she picks up the bourbon I poured her and crinkles her nose when she sniffs it. To my surprise, she tosses it all back in one go.

"Ahh." She wipes her lips. "That was awful."

I laugh. "It's my favorite bourbon."

"Well, you have shitty taste," she says matter-of-factly.

I let my eyes roam over her, tracing every single inch of her that's visible. "No, Rory, I don't think I have bad taste at all."

There's no mistaking the double meaning of my words, and she knows it too. The ruddiness of her cheeks deepens about two shades. She looks nervous, self-conscious even. And it's cute as hell.

"Another drink?" I offer, reaching for her empty glass.

"Uh, no. I'm good. I actually think I may turn in. I never get to go to bed this early."

"Oh." I don't know what I thought she would say,

but I certainly didn't expect that. "Yeah, okay. That sounds like a good idea."

She looks momentarily disappointed I've agreed, but she hides it fast and well. "Cool." She rocks back on her heels, looking unsure. "So…good night?"

"Good night, Wednesday."

She looks like she wants to say something but thinks better of it. She pads past me and up the stairs. I don't move again until I hear her door *snick* shut.

I pour myself another glass of bourbon, tossing it back in one shot like Rory did, then make sure the fire is out before turning down the lights and making my way upstairs to my room. I flop down on my bed and can't help the sigh that leaves me. Between the drive and trying to contain myself around Rory, it's been a long, long day.

I close my eyes, letting the quiet of the house roll over me. It's part of the reason I love being out here. I love the fast-paced-city vibe, but sometimes it gets overwhelming, and I like coming out here to reset and clear my mind.

That's not possible tonight, though. Not with Rory down the hall. Rory with her dark hair. Rory with her mouth that doesn't know how to not be sassy. Rory with her piercing green eyes. Rory with her lush, soft lips and her full tits.

For the hundredth time today, my cock hardens,

and this time I don't want to ignore it, so I don't. I slip my hand into my black sweatpants, past my underwear, and wrap my fist around myself. The contact isn't nearly enough, but it'll have to do for now.

I jack myself slowly, not in any hurry.

It's wrong, so fucking wrong, but the whole time, I think of the raven-haired beauty down the hall. I think of her washing the dishes, splashing just a bit too much water on herself. She's wet and her nipples are hard on her chest, and she looks at me, shrugging before she pulls her shirt over her head. It's a dumb fantasy, but it's the best I have.

I tighten my grip and pick up my pace, my impending orgasm building and building. My breaths are coming in sharper, my heart racing harder, and I sink my teeth into my bottom lip as I barrel toward relief.

"Fuck," I mutter.

Faster. Harder.

I'm so close. So. Fucking. Close. I just need a little more…just a bit…

That's when I hear it, a sound that can't be mistaken.

Footsteps.

Rory's up, moving through the house like I've conjured her with my dirty thoughts.

I look over at the door, the one I didn't close all the

way. Though it's too dark for me to see her standing there, I know she is. I can *feel* it.

Maybe that's why I do it. Maybe it's not.

Either way, I roll my thumb over the head of my cock on the next upstroke, and I look right out that door as I whisper, "*Rory.*"

And I come all over my hand.

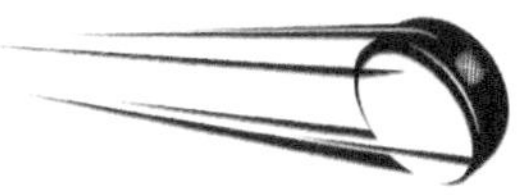

I try my best to act normal the next morning. I sleep in until nine, grab a shower during which I definitely *do not* stroke my cock thinking of Rory, and then make my way downstairs.

To my surprise, Rory is already awake. She's back in the chair, her nose stuck in another book and a blanket draped over her lap. Hades is lying on top of her, shooting death glares my way. Daisy sits beside them on the floor, playing quietly with one of her toys I brought along.

"Good morning."

She startles at my intrusion, peeking at me over her book. Hades doesn't move, having already been alert to me being in the room.

Rory holds my stare, and it's a hard one, like she's

trying to prove she's not afraid to look me in the eye after last night. "Good morning."

"Coffee?"

She looks to the cup I missed sitting on the table. "I already made some. There's a cup or two left in the pot."

I nod, making my way into the kitchen. "Breakfast, then?"

"Uh…sure. That sounds nice."

"Pancakes okay?"

"Perfect."

I pull out the ingredients and get the pan warming up before pouring myself a cup of joe. I rest against the counter, watching her. She's back to reading her book, or at least pretending to. Her eyes haven't moved in a solid minute. She's just staring at the page and holding her breath, clearly waiting for me to say something.

I don't want to save her though. Not at all.

"Sleep well?" I ask, lifting my cup to my lips.

"Like a baby," she answers, not bothering to look at me this time.

Fine, Rory. We'll play this the hard way.

"Did you end up eating some of that ice cream?"

Finally, she glances my way again, and her eyes narrow. "Yes."

"And did you enjoy it?"

She swallows roughly, then turns her attention back to her book. "It was fine."

But the truth is, it was more than fine. She gives herself away with every heavy breath she takes and the flush that creeps into her cheeks, with how her eyes darken to a color I haven't seen from her since I kissed her in my apartment all those weeks ago.

Fine is an understatement. Rory liked what she saw just as much as I liked her watching.

I smirk, pushing off the counter and getting to work on breakfast. We eat in silence, and that's how we spend most of the day too, skirting around one another but still teasing and tempting. The tension in the air is palpable, and it has me feeling on edge the entire day.

At lunch, Rory takes extra care to suck mayonnaise off her fingers after we finish our sandwiches. Then later, when she's returned to her spot on the chair, she gives an excessive, extended stretch, making sure her shirt rides up just enough to give me a glimpse of the smooth skin beneath. When the sun dips below the horizon, she disappears upstairs, only to come bounding down ten minutes later in nothing but a small, emerald bikini that matches her eyes.

"I'm going to take advantage of the clear night and go enjoy the stars in the hot tub," she announces, flouncing past me where I've been parked on the couch watching some nature documentary on TV.

I let my eyes follow her as she slips out the back door, not bothering to even throw me a backward glance. She turns on the hot tub, then sets her towel on the ledge before throwing a leg over the side and sliding down into the water. She tosses her head back, releasing a sigh.

Oh, she knows what she's doing. She knows *exactly* what she's doing, and I'll be damned if it's not working. I rush upstairs, quickly exchanging my sweats and t-shirt for a pair of swim trunks before I run back down.

"Stay," I tell Daisy quietly as I push open the door to the balcony.

If Rory is surprised by my presence, she doesn't show it, her head still back, eyes trained on the sky. The water sloshes a bit as I settle down across from her. I relax into the warmth, skimming my hands over the surface of the water as I watch her watch the night sky. I'm not sure how much time passes before she finally acknowledges me.

"This really is something else," she says quietly, like she's trying not to disturb the world around her. "I don't think I've ever seen something so beautiful in my life."

"Me either," I say, but I'm not talking about the stars. Not at all.

Rory drops her head, turning her eyes my way. "How come you invited me here?"

"Because I like you."

"Why?"

"Because I do."

"Right, but *why*? Most people find me abrasive or rude or unemotional."

"You're all of those things." Her shoulders deflate at my words. "But," I continue, "I like those things. They make you *you*, and I like that. I like the authenticity of it. This hockey world is full of a lot of fake people, but you're not one of them. I like that."

"Most people don't. They're unnerved by it."

"Oh, Rory. You unnerve me all the time, but I like the challenge of it."

"Is that all I am to you? A challenge?"

"No. In fact, I think *I'm* a challenge to you."

Her brows pull together. "How so?"

"Well, I'm guessing I'm not at all the kind of guy you're usually drawn to."

"Someone thinks highly of himself."

I ignore her because we both know her words are bullshit. "I think it's a challenge for you to keep your hands off me, for you to deny yourself what you truly want."

"And what is it I truly want, Lawson?"

"Me."

I say it so simply, so earnestly. We both know it's true.

"Please. You wouldn't know how to handle me."

"I'd rock your world and we both know it."

"For what?" She arches a brow. "Thirty whole seconds?"

"Hey, thirty seconds is a long time."

She snorts out a laugh. "Is that what your ex-girlfriend told you?"

"No. I've never had a girlfriend." I point to myself. "Hockey player. Have you ever been in a five-on-three for that long? Thirty seconds can feel like a lifetime."

"Oh, I'm sure it can on the ice, but off it? No."

"I doubt that."

"Please." She lifts her chin higher. "I doubt you could do anything in thirty seconds."

"Is that a challenge?"

She rolls her eyes, turning away and lifting herself out of the hot tub. "I don't want to embarrass you."

Fuck, she's being such a brat right now, and I love it. I love it when she's mean like this, when she digs in deep and brings her claws out. Is that wrong? Does that make me sick? Probably, but I don't care. Not when I have an opening like this.

"Rory."

"Hmm?" She grabs her towel, patting her legs with it. Her nipples are already hard from the cold night air, straining against her barely there bathing suit.

"Rory," I say again, but she ignores me this time, and I can't fucking take it another second.

I hop out of the tub, then march across the deck to her. I don't stop, not when she takes two steps back, nor when she takes another. I prowl toward her until her back hits the railing.

"What are you..." But she never finishes the question.

I lift my arms, blocking her in so she can't run anymore. A soft gasp slips from her lips, her eyes widening, but it's not terror I see in them. Far from it, actually. It's *hunger*. Her chest is heaving now, her breaths so fast and sharp her tits are brushing against my chest with every choppy inhale and exhale. It's such a simple touch, an unconscious one, yet I love every single fucking minute of it.

I lean down, my lips mere inches from hers. Her eyes flick to my mouth, then, slowly—so fucking slowly—she drags them back to my gray stare.

"I said, is that a challenge?"

I can see a myriad of answers spinning around in her head, can see her considering just what it is she wants to say.

Then finally, she opens her mouth. "Yes."

"Oh, Rory. Wrong answer."

And I drop to my knees.

Chapter 15

I've seen a lot of great views in my lifetime. I've watched the Christmas tree get lit in Rockefeller Center; the sun rising over the Atlantic Ocean on New Year's Day, signifying a new beginning; Vermont in the fall with leaves the most gorgeous shades of oranges and reds. I've been up and down the California and Oregon coastlines. I've been to Paris to see the Eiffel Tower sparkle at night, and I've even seen the Colosseum—*twice*.

But this? Seeing Lucas Lawson on his knees for me? It's better than all those combined.

"What are you—"

My question is cut off as Lawson rips my towel from my hands, tossing it to the side. I should be cold. My skin should be pebbled in goose bumps and I should be running inside to escape the frigid February air, but I'm not cold. Far from it. My body is an inferno, and Lawson is doing nothing but stoking the fire.

He starts at my ankles, grazing his fingertips ever so lightly across my skin as he works his touch up, up, up until he's palming my thighs. I should stop him. I should tell him this is a bad idea and we should walk away while we still can.

But none of those words come, and truthfully, I don't want them to.

He inches higher, splaying his hands over my thighs, his thumbs brushing at the edges of my bathing suit. All it would take is one move, one small push to the side, and I'd be exposed to him.

I've never anticipated a move more.

He drags his eyes up to mine, lifting his brow in a warning that says, *Last chance,* and I give him a look back that says, *Do your worst.* He doesn't waste a second, rising to the challenge and pushing my swimsuit to the side. Just like that, I'm bared to him, and the lowest, most delightful sound leaves his chest as he gets his first look at me.

"Fucking hell, Rory. You're…" He brushes his thumb against me, and I shudder at the simple touch. "Your cunt is so fucking wet for me, baby."

I am. So, so wet. I should be embarrassed, should be mortified, but I can't find it in me, especially not when Lawson is looking at me like I'm a trophy he's been waiting his whole life to win.

"Last chance to stop me, Rory. Once I get a taste of you, there's no turning back."

I say nothing. He grins, and it's the last thing I see before his mouth is on me and I'm tossing my head back on a relieved sigh. I knew it would feel good having Lawson between my legs, but I never imagined it would be so good I'm seeing stars.

No, wait—that's the actual night sky.

I want to close my eyes, want to relish this moment, but I can't. It feels too fucking good, so good I can't even move. All I can do is stand there while he rolls his tongue over me again and again, licking and sucking at my needy pussy like he's branding me as his. When he pulls back, an involuntary whimper leaves me, and he laughs.

"Look at you," he says lowly. "What a fucking sight: your pussy exposed for anyone to see, your head thrown back, your legs shaking like you're about to come. It's only been ten seconds, Rory, and you're already close."

Ten seconds? Is that really all it's been?

"Shut up," I say, but there's no nastiness in my tone, just pure fucking lust.

He lets out a sinister laugh, sinking a single finger into me. "There's only one way to get me to do that..."

"What?"

"Ask." He pumps in and out slowly, teasing and torturing me. If I moved *just so*, I could sink down on it more and he'd hit that sweet spot, but I don't. I'm too scared he might stop.

"W-What?" I ask, disgusted by the tremble in my voice.

"Ask."

Of course that's what he wants: for me to admit I want this, as if his glistening chin isn't enough proof.

"Ask," he instructs again, pumping harder, just barely brushing against where I want him.

Fuck, fuck, fuck, I chant in my head. Then finally, "Make me come, Lawson. Eat my pussy and make me come. *Please.*"

He grins wickedly. "Your wish, Rory…"

He sweeps his tongue across me, and I fucking break. Just like that, I come apart, bucking against him, eager for more. It's wild and heedless and the most senseless thing I've ever done, being eaten out on a deck in the middle of fucking winter in nothing but a bathing suit, but I don't care.

I don't care because it's the best orgasm of my life…and he's going for another. Lawson doesn't let up. He continues to eat at me, sucking my clit into his mouth just long enough to bring me to the brink, then letting up in time to inch me away from the edge.

It's cruel, but I love every minute of it. I alternate between watching him lick at me and watching the stars, loving the weightless feeling that settles over me as my second orgasm crashes through me.

Only then does Lawson give me a reprieve, kissing my swollen pussy and my thighs. He replaces my suit, then makes his way up my body, pressing kisses over every inch of me on his way. He stops to suck a nipple into his mouth, teasing it through my swim top before moving on to the next. He kisses up, capturing my mouth with his, the taste of me exploding onto my tongue. I like it, me mixed with him, and he does too, not stopping until I'm breathless and nothing but putty in his arms.

I wrap my legs around him when he swoops me up, moaning into his mouth as his cock brushes against my still sensitive clit. He carries us inside and doesn't stop moving until we're upstairs and walking into what I assume is his room. Light bathes the space as he settles me onto my feet, where he keeps kissing me until I'm practically pawing at him, needing more. He laughs into me, and I groan, which only eggs him on.

"Someone's a little needy, no?" he says against my neck where he's alternating between nipping and sucking at me, no doubt leaving behind marks I'll have to cover up on Monday.

"*Someone* is feeling a little full of themselves." I press tighter against him, which really doesn't help my case.

"That's because *someone* won the challenge, and that someone is me."

"It was longer than thirty seconds."

He laughs. "Not a chance, Wednesday. Not a fucking chance."

"Fine." I push away from him, dropping to my knees. "Let's see how long *you* last."

I peel his wet trunks down until his cock springs free, and *my god* what a beautiful cock it is. I never thought I'd say that, but it's true. Just long and thick enough, the head an angry red as it reaches out my way, begging for my touch.

I'm not one to deny. I lean forward, running my tongue over it, delighted by the saltiness I taste.

He hisses, drawing out a long, painful "*Fuuuuuuuck*" before he grips my head, his fingers crashing through my hair and tugging me to him. I let him, but only because I'm as eager for this as he is.

"That's it, Rory," he says in a low growl. "Suck my cock like you mean it. Like the good girl you are."

Good girl.

It's the two words I've been dying to hear, and just as I thought they would, they hit right between my legs, making my already eager pussy desperate for more of Lawson.

I pull him back deeper, sucking him harder.

"Fuck, baby." He lets out a string of curse words. "So good. You're doing so fucking good."

Okay, so *maybe* when he said those words before, they did have some sort of effect on me, because when he says them this time, my entire body begins to hum. His words of encouragement spur me on, and I swallow him down, alternating pressure until he's bucking into my mouth, fucking my throat.

I love it. God, do I love it. Even as tears begin to prick my eyes and even as they fall, running down my cheeks, I still love it. My pussy is throbbing, *aching* at this point. I want to touch it so badly, but I also want to savor the ache. It only makes release that much sweeter.

Suddenly, he pulls me off his cock, hauling me to my feet.

"What the—"

He presses a hard kiss to my swollen lips, not caring that I just had them wrapped around his dick.

I'm breathless when he releases me. "You stopped me. Why'd you stop me?"

"Because, baby, I want the first time I come to be in this tight little pussy of yours."

"But I thought—"

"Time's up. I can't wait any longer." He gives me a

dark, hungry look. "Later. Now, get on the bed and spread your legs. I want to see what's mine."

I don't bother arguing with him about his *mine* comment. I can't. Not when he's staring at me like that.

I scramble to follow his instructions, bouncing onto the mattress and turning on my back in the center. I shimmy out of my wet bottoms, then toss them aside. I lift my knees, feet planted, and let my legs drop wide.

I'll be damned if the hunger in his eyes isn't even more prevalent than it was out on the deck as he gets his first true look at me in something other than dim lighting. He grips his cock, almost unconsciously like he can't help himself, and strokes himself as he moves closer.

"Do you have any idea what you do to me, Rory?" Another stroke. "Anything at all? Do you have any fucking clue how wild you drive me with that smartass mouth of yours? The way you make me wish I could paddle your ass until you're no longer able to smart off, only to let you up so we can start all over again?"

His words make me shake. Not because I'm scared, but because I want that too. So fucking bad.

"Yeah, you like the idea of that, don't you, baby?"

I nod. "So much."

"I knew you would." He jacks himself again. "And I promise to do just that, but later. Right now, I need to feel what your pretty, pretty cunt feels like squeezing my cock. I'll save the spankings for another time."

With his swim trunks now tossed aside, he settles one knee on the bed, then another, inching toward me like a predator. He dips down, running his tongue along my pussy, followed by the scratchy beard he's been growing since we got here. It hurts and yet it feels so, so delightful.

He crawls up my body, fitting himself between my legs, his hot and heavy cock dragging along my slick center. He kisses my chest, pulling my top aside and exposing my tits. He lashes my nipples with his tongue, using his teeth to administer just the right amount of pain. It has me bucking against him, seeking the one thing I want more than anything else—*him.*

"Needy," he says into my neck.

"Well, I wouldn't be if you would just fuck me already."

He laughs, moving from my neck to below my ear, hitting a spot I didn't realize could feel so good. "Is that what you want, Rory? For me to fuck you?"

"Yes!"

He glides his cock against me, rocking back and forth. "You want to feel how good it is when I stretch your pussy around my cock? When I take you hard and without restraint?"

"Y-Yes…" I practically moan, his movements

getting rougher with each pass, the sensation rocketing through my clit.

He kisses my jaw, my chin, each corner of my lips, but never fully on the mouth, just like how he moves his cock down, the head of it teasing my hole before he pulls away. He does this again and again, rocking into me but never fully entering. He's just fucking me with the tip as he kisses me, and it's *agonizing*, almost unbearable. I'm going to break if he doesn't do something soon.

"Tell me…" he whispers against me.

Another rock. Another inch toward bliss.

"Do you want me to fuck you and fill you up with my cum, baby?"

"God, *yes*. Yes, yes, *yes*."

Then, as he promised, he's stretching me around him, sliding his beautiful, beautiful cock inside of me, pushing until he's buried as far as he can go, and oh, is he far. I've never been so full in my life. It's nearly overwhelming, the size of him, but I love it. I love it, and I want more of it. I want him to move so badly, possibly more than I've ever wanted anything in my life.

Like he can read my mind, he does. He thrusts into me slowly, so excruciatingly slow it's almost worse than when he wasn't moving at all.

"Lawson…*please.*"

He laughs, but it quickly turns into a groan, and not a good one.

"Fuck, shit, fuck," he mutters.

He tries to pull out and away, but I stop him, digging my heels into his ass and sinking my nails into his back, keeping him pressed against me.

"What? What's wrong?"

"Condom. I need to grab one," he says, but he's still moving inside me with slow and gentle thrusts. I'm not even sure he realizes he's doing it, but I do, and it feels so, *so* good. I don't want to stop.

"I have an IUD," I tell him, my eyes rolling back in my head a bit. "I haven't been with anyone in over a year."

He looks relieved. "I've never gone without, and I'm tested regularly. Do you trust me?"

I get what he's really asking: *Are you sure?*

"I trust you."

I do. I wholeheartedly do. Lawson would never risk anything happening to me.

"Thank fuck."

Then he fucks me as he said he would—hard and without restraint. My orgasm barrels into me fast. I'm coming around him before I realize what's happening, but Lawson doesn't stop. He can't. He's too far gone, sitting back and setting my leg up on his shoulder, pounding into me so hard I'm nearly seeing stars again. He watches where our bodies meet, where his cock is stretching me impossibly wide and I'm taking his thrusts like a punishment. It's glorious and magnificent and so many other words I can't think of because all I can do is *feel*, and all I feel is him.

Lawson, Lawson, Lawson.

"So damn beautiful," he says, his voice full of awe as he watches us. "You're taking me so well. So fucking good." His thumb lands on my clit. "But I need one more, Rory."

I shake my head. "I can't. No more."

"*One* more." He smacks my tortured pussy, and it stings in the most wonderful way. "Don't force me to make it two."

"I…"

The words die on my tongue, my world turning upside down when he circles my clit again and again and another orgasm races in out of nowhere. My body tenses, then trembles with the release. I feel languid, like I've been drugged or something of that sort, but I know I haven't. It's all him. It's all us. It's all *this*.

Man do I want more of *this*.

Lawson fucks into me harder and faster, pumping until he spills inside me. Only then do his harsh and hasty thrusts slow as his orgasm comes to an end. With shaking arms, he settles back down onto me, his body sticky with sweat, but it's okay because mine is too. He drops his mouth against mine, kissing me slow and lazy, such a striking difference to how he just fucked me, then slowly slides out.

I miss him the moment he goes, wishing I could fall asleep and stay this way for the whole night. The thought startles me, and I try to tamp it down, try to wad it up and throw it away, but I can't. It's already been thought. It's already there, right in the back of my mind—how easily I could get used to this.

Lawson rolls to the side, landing on his back, his breaths coming in sharp.

"That was…"

For the first time, I think he may be speechless.

"Yeah," I say, apparently just as incapable of forming full sentences.

I lie there for far too long, not wanting to let this blissful moment go, but my doctor brain kicks into gear and I leap off the bed, heading for the bathroom that's connected to his room. I do my business, then wash my hands, trying to ignore the mirror in front of me because I look an utter mess. My boobs are hanging out of my swim top, my hair is a knotted nest, my skin is blotchy from coming so many times, and there are little marks all over my body from Lawson's beard and teeth.

I look ridiculous, yet I've never felt so satisfied in

my life, and it's all because of Lawson. That's scarier than I care to admit.

I discard my swimsuit, flip off the bathroom light, and make my way back into the bedroom. Lawson's turned off the overhead light, trading it for the bedside lamps instead. He's stripped the bed of the old, messy sheet and replaced it with a new flannel one. He's sitting on top of it —still naked—and looking at me with a wary expression.

"Hey," he whispers finally, his voice thick and low.

"Hi," I say back just as quietly.

"Are you, uh, good?"

I nod. "I am. So good."

That perks him up. "Yeah?"

Another nod as I pad closer to him. "Yeah."

"Good." He reaches out, hooking his hands around my legs and drawing me to him until I'm straddling his lap. His cock stirs to life against me. "I'm glad. Though, I do have to tell you something…"

My heart races. "What?"

"You lost."

My brows cinch together. "What?"

"You. Lost." He grins. "The challenge. I won— both times."

I bark out a laugh, shaking my head at his ridiculousness. "Is that so?"

"Yep." He puffs his chest out, clearly feeling proud.

"Well, I want a rematch."

"Any time, Wednesday. Any time."

"What about now?" I ask, grinding down on him like I'm in heat or something. I've never been so horny, especially not after coming consecutively like that, something I've only ever achieved with my vibrator. I've worked myself up a few times and managed to squeeze out two orgasms, but that was it before I was tapped. It was nothing like tonight, and yet, I still want more, more of Lawson, which terrifies me to no end.

He laughs, leaning forward to pepper my neck in kisses. "Now, huh?"

I nod.

"Well, now *does* sound like a good idea, but…"

"But?"

"Do you know what sounds better?"

I pull back. "Than orgasms? Uh, nothing."

His body shakes with laughter again. "No. *Sleep.*"

He spins me around him, dropping me on the other side of the bed. Somehow, he manages to get the cover pulled over us in record time, and before I know what's happening, I'm snuggled up in the warmth, tucked safely into Lawson's side.

His hand snakes down and he palms my ass cheek, tugging me even closer. I writhe against him, trying to sit up to straddle him again to get this going once more, but he holds me down with one hand.

"But…" I protest.

"No." He shakes his head. "Sleep."

It's…weird. I'm not used to sleeping with someone else. All my escapades in the past ended with me bolting immediately afterward. I didn't stick around, and they never wanted me to either.

That's exactly how I imagined it would be with Lawson: we'd fuck and go our separate ways, sleeping in our own beds tonight, but apparently, he has a different idea…and I'm not sure how to feel about the fact that I don't hate it as much as I thought I would.

"Why?"

"Because I have plans for you tomorrow, and you're going to need your energy." He presses a kiss to my forehead. "Now, sleep."

"Fine," I grumble, snuggling closer to him, another new thing since I typically hate touch like this. I don't cuddle. It's not my thing in the least.

Yet, like so many other things when it comes to Lawson, I'm relishing it in a way that surprises me.

He gives another soft laugh. "Good night, Rory," he murmurs.

"Night, Lucas."

I close my eyes, and I swear, I've never fallen asleep faster in my life.

Chapter 16

LAWSON

When I brought Rory to the cabin, my intention wasn't sex. Sure, I wasn't going to turn it down if it happened, but I was content with this thing between us playing out at whatever pace she needed.

As such, the last thing I expected was to be waking up to Rory's lips wrapped around my cock, but here I am anyway. I tangle my fingers through her hair, and she peeks up at me, her green eyes meeting my sleepy gaze.

She pops off just long enough to say, "Hi."

"Hi." She giggles around my dick, already back to sucking me. "Not that I'm complaining, but what are you doing?"

She pulls back again. "Finishing what I started."

"Well," I say, lifting my other arm up and under my head, giving me a better angle to watch her from.

"If you're going to do that, make sure you do a good job this time."

Her eyes ignite with the desire to please me, and she eagerly takes me back in. It's truly a gorgeous sight. Feels even better too, her mouth wet and warm and applying just enough pressure. She takes her time, licking me like she's cherishing me. Her tongue swirls over my swollen head, then she moves forward, pulling my cock right to the back of her throat.

To her credit, she doesn't gag. Instead, she holds eye contact with me, constricting her throat in the most delectable way. I bite down on my lip, trying to keep from coming right then and there, and she grins around me, finally giving me some reprieve, dragging the tip of her tongue along my cock.

"I think I've decided how I want this to go," she says, her lips brushing against me with every word.

I quirk a brow. "Is that so?"

"It is." She nods, closing her lips around just the tip of me, sucking lightly, and it feels entirely too fucking good. I'm already so goddamn close it's embarrassing. "I want you to fuck my throat like you did my pussy."

I inhale a sharp breath.

"Rory…"

She shakes her head. "No. No trying to talk me out of it. It's what I want."

"Are you sure?"

She nods again, her mouth brushing against me. "I'm sure."

I eye her carefully, wanting to be certain she understands what she's asking for.

Her stare doesn't waver from mine. She wants this.

And fuck, I want it too. So damn badly.

"Then get on the bed, Rory. Feet to the headboard, head hanging off."

She scrambles to follow my directions as I move out of her way, letting her get into position. She looks incredible like that, looking up at me with her dark hair hanging like a curtain.

"Like this?" she asks, her eyes full of uncertainty I'm not used to from her.

"Just like that." I walk toward her, situating myself until I'm hanging over her, my heavy cock brushing against her lips. "Open wide and relax for me, baby. I want to see how good that throat feels."

Like the good girl she is, she opens, and I slowly slide my cock into her mouth, working my length in and out, letting her adjust to the new angle. I'm unsurprised when she reaches for me, her nails digging into my thighs as she pulls me closer. She's eager to please, and I'm just as eager for her to please me.

"If it gets to be too much, I want you to tap me three times. Understood?"

She nods, and the movement has me cursing,

which makes *her* laugh and me curse again. It's a vicious cycle, but I love every second of it.

I start slow, fucking into her. Her nails dig deeper, but she doesn't tap, not even when I pick up my pace, sliding my cock deeper and deeper until she gags against me. I let up, giving her a moment to breathe, then do it again. I do it over and over, bringing us both to the edge, then backing away before we can slip over it. She presses her thighs together like she's dying for friction.

"You want to touch that pretty pussy?" I ask, my cock lodged in the back of her throat.

She nods, her eyes watering with unshed tears.

"Do it," I tell her. "I want to watch."

And she does, wasting no time dropping her legs wide and sliding her fingers between them. It's fucking magnificent watching her fingers glide through her wetness, *hearing* how slick she is for me as she pumps two inside of her in time with my thrusts. She drags them back out, drawing quick circles around her clit.

I know the second she comes, letting out a muffled scream around my cock, and it's only then that I finally pull out.

"W-What... What are you..."

She's gasping for air as I lie down next to her, moving her around like a doll until she's situated on top of me, my cock brushing at her entrance. She's facing away from me when I enter her, and she throws her head back on a groan.

"Oh fuck. Fuck, fuck, *fuck*," she sings as I buck up into her violently.

She continues to moan as she bounces on my cock, taking everything I give her and loving every second of it. She's stunning right now, her head back as she rides me, and she feels even better, gripping me like she's going to lose me at any second. It's almost too much to watch her because I'm so fucking close it nearly hurts.

I want just one more thing…

Without warning, I pull her off me, hauling her up until she's sitting on my face.

"What the… *Ohhhh.*"

She groans as I fit her thighs around my head and plunge my tongue into her already dripping cunt. She tastes sweet, but a little like me, especially from our adventures last night. I love it. I love how we taste mixed together like this. If this were the only thing I could have in my mouth for the rest of my life, I'd be good with that.

I lick and suck at her, drawing her clit into my mouth as she grinds against me. The second I slip a finger into her greedy pussy, she's shaking around me, her orgasm racing through her as she throbs against my tongue. I come too—messily and all over myself, spurting ropes of cum everywhere as she continues to shudder against me.

She sags a bit, her breaths coming in sharp. She sits there a moment, getting her bearings, then with shaking legs, she pushes off, sitting on her knees beside me. She runs a single finger through the mess I've made, gathering a bit of the evidence of what just happened, then brings it to her mouth, sucking her finger clean before grinning at me.

"Good morning," she says innocently, and I laugh.

Yeah, good morning indeed.

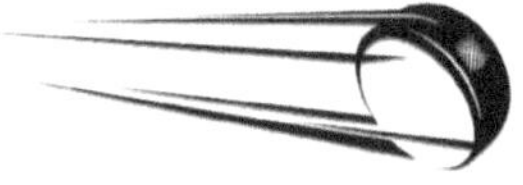

"So does that mean you're not coming home?"

"Not this time, Mom. I'm sorry."

"Oh, don't worry about me," she says, her usual cheerful self. No matter how much my mom's sacrificed for me over the years, all the late nights and long weekends, the smile on her face has never faltered, and me telling her I won't be home for the All-Star break is nothing different. "I'll be fine. I've been binge-watching *Grey's Anatomy* again, which we all know has like eighty seasons, so I have plenty to do anyway."

"I promise to make it up to you over the summer. Maybe I can spend a week there, and you can spend a week here and I'll finally get to show you all the sights."

"Yeah, maybe," she says, though we both know it's not likely to happen. My mother isn't big on travel. She'd much rather stay in our small town and enjoy the little things in life. It's a miracle I got her to go away for Christmas, but she needed the break. She spends too much time at that damn bar.

Just like someone else I know.

I let my eyes drift upstairs to where Rory is. The shower is still running, but I'm sure it'll go off at any moment, which means I'd better wrap up this call before my mother starts asking too many questions I can't answer and Rory comes downstairs to hear it all.

"So, kiddo." Always with the kiddo, no matter how old I am. "Who's the girl?"

I freeze, the egg I'm about to crack suspended in the air. "What?"

My mother laughs one of those laughs only parents do, the all-knowing kind that makes you feel like you're a five-year-old who has been caught sneaking cookies before dinner.

"Come on, Lucas. You're my son. I know you. There's a reason you're not coming home right now, so I assume it's a girl. Who is she?"

I hold my breath, hoping maybe if she can't hear

my breathing, she'll think the call got disconnected and hang up, but I'm not so lucky.

"Are you going to tell me or am I going to have to get it out of Loretta? I mean, that *is* how I found out I'm a grandmother to Daisy and all."

Curse my mother and my brother's mother for being so damn close, and curse Jacob too, just because. I knock my head against the cabinet in front of me a few times, blowing out a lengthy breath before resuming my task of cracking eggs for breakfast.

"She's…a friend."

It's not entirely a lie. Rory is a friend. But she's also a little bit more than that.

"A girlfriend?"

I laugh, but only because I know Rory would hate being called that.

"Oh. I get it," my mom says. "She's a *friend* friend."

I pinch my nose. "Mother…"

"What? I'm curious, is all. I want to see my baby boy happy."

"I *am* happy."

And I mean that. I'm happy. I've *been* happy…I think. I honestly can't tell anymore because this happy I'm feeling now is entirely different than the happy I was feeling before—before Rory.

"She's my teammate's girlfriend's twin sister."

"Oooh. That sounds a bit scandalous because it

sounds like you're also kind of in love with your teammate's girlfriend," she says, going into full romance movie mode.

"I'm not in love with anyone, Mom." At least I don't *think* I am. "And I am not in love with Hutch's girlfriend. They might look a little alike, but they couldn't be more opposite."

"Well, boo." She blows on her tongue. "But I guess also yay, because that could have made playing together very, very awkward."

"Tell me about it."

"So, if you're not in love, why are you going away for a weekend together?"

I peek back upstairs, the shower still going, and while the coast is clear, I tell my mother what happened with Rory and why I whisked her away for the weekend. When I'm finished, she sighs gleefully, and I can just picture her kicking her feet, her hand over her chest.

"Oh, my sweet boy. You're a good man, you know that?"

I grunt, uncomfortable with her praise. "Stop."

"No. I'm serious, Lucas. You *are* a good guy. You never let people see all the amazing things you do, so they miss out on seeing you for who you truly are. It makes me sad. I wish you'd share that part of you with more people."

I could tell her she's wrong and she's just saying all that because she's my mother, but she also may be a tiny bit right. I'm bad about letting people assume the worst of me because I'm a jock, probably because I do love playing into it often. But there is a side of me that wants to find someone who accepts *all* those different facets of me.

My eyes drift back to the second floor, where the shower's just shut off, and I can't help but think of Rory. I'm not even picturing her naked or wet or anything like that. All I'm thinking of is how *she* accepts me. Even when I'm annoying or crass or do something to piss her off, she still doesn't push me away and lets me in.

Maybe… Maybe Rory could be that person I share all of me with.

I table that thought for later, the sounds of drawers opening pulling me from my own head.

"I hear you, Mom," I say into the phone. "And I love you, but I gotta go. I'm making breakfast and I'm about to burn the bacon."

"Now *that* would be a travesty."

We exchange I love yous and I promise to call her later in the week, then we hang up. I'm just about done frying the bacon when Rory comes padding down the stairs in nothing but my jersey.

She brought it.

If I thought she looked good in it before—that night in my apartment and in the picture she sent me —I was wrong. Seeing her like this? Her hair wet after a shower, her face dewy and red from coming so much, and her legs wobbling…it's ten times better than before.

She trips a little on the last step, her legs tired and nearly giving out. I smirk, thinking, *I did that.*

"Knock it off," she grumbles, taking a seat at the counter. "I'm sore."

"Too sore for the plans I have for you today?"

"No." Her answer is quick, and it has me laughing as I plate our eggs and hash browns. "Who was that on the phone?"

"My mother." I grab the bacon next, making sure to hand a tiny piece down to a begging Daisy.

"Oh?"

She sounds…scared. Is Rory worried what my mother would think about me having her here?

"Don't worry, I didn't tell her all the debauched things I'm doing to you."

She cringes. "I sure hope not."

"But she did say hi."

She lets out a squeak, and I laugh, grabbing the toast from the toaster and slathering on some butter before sliding our plates onto the counter.

"She doesn't care what I do, Rory, or who I'm

doing it with. Just that I'm happy." I reach into the fridge to retrieve some orange juice and pour us each a glass.

"And are you?" she asks from behind me, and there's no mistaking the mix of hope and trepidation in her words.

I put the jug of juice back in the fridge before grabbing the glasses and carrying them over to the counter. I give her one and keep the other, then slide onto my stool.

"Yes," I tell her truthfully. "I'm very happy."

She smiles at that, and I have to grip my fork tightly to keep from reaching over and kissing her, which would definitely lead to more, which would be unfortunate because I just made breakfast.

"Eat," I instruct. "Your food is getting cold."

She wastes no time digging in, shoving a forkful of eggs into her mouth while moaning. It's distracting, even though it shouldn't be after last night and this morning, and it has me watching her the entire meal. It's all her own fault, her creamy thighs on display, the jersey inching up higher and higher, giving me a peek at a dark shadow but never fully showing anything off.

Is she even wearing panties? If I were to reach over right now, would I feel her bare pussy against my hand? Would she be wet? Would she let me have *her* for breakfast?

I try to block out the thoughts as we eat mostly in silence, only making a few comments about the weather. Once we're finished, she tries to grab my plate to do the dishes again, but I refuse, forcing her to sit in the chair while I clean up. She glowers at me the whole time I work, but I ignore her.

"So," she finally says, "I have to confess something."

"That's fine. I think we might be beyond secrets anyway."

She huffs out a laugh. "Yeah, I'd say." She takes another sip of her coffee before saying, "I saw you."

I pause, only for a moment, before I continue scrubbing. I know exactly what she's talking about without her clarifying, but she does anyway.

"I saw you masturbating."

I almost wish my ears *would* turn red, wish I would feel *some* sort of embarrassment about being caught, but I don't. Not even a little bit.

"You did?" I ask casually.

"Did you say my name on purpose? Because you knew I was watching?"

I finish the last plate, then set it on the drying mat I have spread out on the countertop. I dry off my hands and round the counter. I grab her chair, angling her my way and tipping her head back until she's forced to look at me. I trace my thumb—the same one that traced her clit last night—over her supple bottom lip. Her breath catches as she stares up at me with wide, curious eyes.

"No, Rory. I didn't say your name because I knew you were watching."

She sucks in a breath.

"I said your name because it was *you* I was thinking of long before you came out of your room." I pinch the jersey between the fingers of my free hand. "Just like it was *you* I thought of the last time I stroked my cock, imagining you in nothing but this."

"You've… You've pictured me before?"

"So many times," I confess. "Too many times. It's my favorite fantasy, the one that's been haunting me since I first met you and you basically told me what a loser I am."

She grimaces. "I was pretty mean, wasn't I?"

"Yes, but I liked it. In fact, I liked it a little *too* much, and I had to talk my dick down because we were in public."

"No you didn't."

"Yes, I did, Rory. If I hadn't, it would have been hard, just like this." I grab her hand, bringing it to my erect cock. I close my hand over hers, squeezing myself with both our palms. "I don't know why, but that mouth of yours does that to me. It makes me feel things I haven't felt before…makes me want things I've never wanted."

As I say the words, I realize I mean them, and even more than that…I realize maybe this isn't purely about sexual attraction. Because, yeah, I'm attracted to her. It's something I made obvious the first moment I met her. It's something more than that though, something…pure.

I like Rory. A lot.

"I…" She rolls her tongue over her lips, but she doesn't say anything else.

She's struggling to admit she might feel something for me too, and that's fine. She'll get there, but I won't press it. Instead, I'll spend my time worshipping her in ways that show her just how serious I am about liking her.

And I'll start now.

I let her hand go, and she keeps hold of me, stroking my cock through my sweatpants while I drop my attention to her exposed thighs, the urge to know if she's naked under this intensifying by the second. I finger the edge of the dark green jersey, lifting it only the slightest bit, not enough to bare her secrets.

"Tell me, Rory…are you naked under my jersey?"

She smiles up at me coyly, lifting a shoulder. "I don't know. You tell me."

"I think you are," I say, gripping the material more firmly, tugging her closer.

Her grip tightens on my cock, and she knows exactly what she's doing right now, teasing me the way she is.

"I think you like prancing around here with nothing but my name and number on your back," I continue, dropping my lips against hers, nipping at them roughly before moving my assault to her jaw.

She arches into my touch, bringing her legs up and letting the tops of her thighs brush against my knuckles.

"You like tempting me, huh? Being *mean*. Don't you, Wednesday?"

"Maybe," she murmurs, inching her hand up to my waistband. She just barely dips it inside, but I snatch her wrist up. She pouts up at me, and I laugh.

"You might like being mean, but so do I. Get up. Hands on the counter."

She rises, spinning so she's gripping the dark countertop. She arches her back, causing the jersey to ride up *just* to the point that I still can't see a thing.

She peers at me over her shoulder. "Come on, Lawson. Take a peek. You know you want to."

And fuck me, I do. I really, really do.

I sink to my knees, loving the soft mewling sounds that leave her. I grip her waist, inching the Serpents sweater higher and higher until I'm blessed with the loveliest sight. She's naked under there all right, and she's already dripping wet. Her arousal sticks to her legs, the insides of her thighs glistening as she presses her ass back toward me.

I might like being a little mean, but I'm not going to deny myself what I want—*her*. I waste no time gripping her hips, bowing her ass out toward me more, giving me access to my new favorite place.

I love being on the ice. Love the feel of it, the cool wind whipping around me. I love the exhilaration that flows through me every time I put my skates on. But this? Rory bared to me like she is? I love this far more.

I bury my tongue inside her, and she cries out.

"Oh hell..." she groans, pushing back for more, and I oblige.

She bucks against me rowdily, and I fucking love it. Her hand lands on my head, pulling me toward her like she can't get enough, but that wasn't part of this deal. I pull away and laugh when she lets out a frustrated growl.

"Lawson..." she objects.

"Hands on the counter, Rory. Keep them there."

She whines but follows my directions. Only when she's gripping the counter once more do I continue my assault, swiping my tongue over every inch of her pussy, making sure no spot is untouched. I pull her overused clit into my mouth, sucking hard and loving every crude word that falls from her lips at the move.

"Fuck, fuck, shit, fuck. Mother…*oh fuck!*"

She comes apart on my tongue for the second time this morning, and I pull away with a grin, loving the shake to her legs. She tries to move, but I grip her hips before she can go far.

"Did I say we were done?"

Another whimper. "Please…I can't…"

I land a hard whack to her ass cheek, and she cries out. It's a sound of pure passion, not an ounce of pain mixed in.

"You can," I tell her before landing another blow.

Another cry, a soft tremble, and she presses back like she wants more. I hit her again. Then again. Her legs are shaking, sweat rolling down her forehead as she lies against the cool counter, giving up trying to hold herself up on her arms. I massage her red cheeks, working away the sting I'm sure she's feeling.

"You love this, don't you?"

She bites her bottom lip, nodding. "Yes."

I spread my hands over her ass, working out the tension that's building there. With each squeeze, I pull her cheeks apart a little more, giving myself a small look at her hole, and I don't miss how she arcs into each pass.

"I think I might know something you'll like

more…"

Then I spread her wide, flattening my tongue against her puckered hole, and she sighs in relief, like this is what she's been wanting all along.

"Lucas…" she moans, and hearing my name on her lips spurs me on.

I eat at her, over and over and over again. I have no idea how long I keep my face buried in her ass, but it's long enough that my cock is literally leaking against my sweatpants. If I don't come soon, I'm going to make another mess all over myself when really, I want to come in her again.

I force myself to stop, completely agreeing with the angry rumble that works its way through her chest. I pick up her leg, setting her knee on the stool, then pull my pants down just enough to free myself and slam into her pussy without warning.

"*Yesssss*," she cries out, bucking against me. "Yes, Lawson."

"Lucas," I tell her. "When I'm inside you, it's Lucas."

"Lucas," she calls out again, and it's my undoing.

I thrust into her hard and fast, not chasing her orgasm this time but my own. It doesn't matter; her already tight cunt squeezes me even tighter as she comes around me. It's just as good as it was last night, maybe even better, and it's enough to have me emptying myself inside her, feeding her every last drop of my cum.

I continue to slow-fuck her until I have nothing left to give, then I slip out, tugging her off the counter and hauling her into my arms. I carry her up the stairs, and this time I do step into the shower with her, where I slide inside her again.

We fall into bed afterward, and there's no doubt in my mind that this is the best All-Star break of my lifetime. For the first time ever, I'm dreading going back to hockey.

Chapter 17

I'll be the first to admit I've been in a bit of a haze since coming home from the cabin, and I'll be the first to admit I didn't *want* to leave the cabin at all. *Me!* The certified workaholic who readily dishes out advice to my sister to take a break but never takes one herself.

Can I be blamed? Especially when Lawson was so good at coaxing orgasm after orgasm out of me? I swear I've never had such a sex-fueled weekend where it actually hurt to walk, and yet, I truly believe if he waltzed into this office right now, I could go again. *That's* how much I enjoyed myself this weekend.

Even though most of the time was spent with Lawson giving my body the workout of its life, I can't remember the last time I felt so relaxed. I'm sure it largely has to do with the orgasms, but I'm also sure a lot of it has to do with Lawson himself. When we weren't finding new ways to reach big heights, we were either soaking in the hot tub enjoying the mountain view or curled up on the couch with something playing in the background. It was peaceful and easily the most I've allowed myself to unwind in a long, long time. It made coming into the office today harder than I'd care to admit.

"Dr. Sinclair?"

I jump at the intrusion, nearly knocking over the coffee sitting on my desk. I whip my head up, surprised to find Casey standing at my office door. "Yes?"

"Uh, sorry. I didn't mean to scare you. I called your name a few times…"

She did?

"Sorry. I'm a bit…distracted." I set my pen down, the same one I've been using to trace a circle repeatedly. I rock back in my desk chair. "What'd you need?"

"Just letting you know Mr. Duhaime is here."

I scrunch my brows together. "Did he not come in last week? With Dr. Helms?"

"No. He insisted on waiting for you, said you're his favorite."

It's a sweet sentiment, really, but I also don't really feel like having to talk him off whatever ledge he's teetering on regarding Petey's health today.

"All right. Tell him I'll be with him in just a moment."

"Sure thing, Doc. Will do."

Only she doesn't make a move to leave. Instead, she stands there, eying me closely.

I lift a brow. "Yes, Casey?"

"Oh, uh…I was just wondering…did you have a nice weekend away? You seem…different. Lighter. *Happy*."

In all my years working here, I've never, not once had *anyone* describe me as being *happy*. Sure, there have been occasions when I've come close to that, but I've never truly been *walk around with a smile on my face* kind of pleased.

I guess a weekend with Lawson will do that to a person.

"It was a good vacation."

She smiles. "Good. I'm glad. You deserve a good *vacation*."

That might be what she says, but it's not what she means, and it's obvious.

You deserve someone who makes you happy.

She gives me one last grin before flouncing away, leaving me sitting there with the true meaning of her words hanging over me. I told Auden she deserved Hutch, and I meant it. After everything she gave to her company and all the things she gave up, she earned the happiness she found with him, even when it was against her contract with the Serpents. Is that how she'd see this thing with Lawson too?

Even though I went away with him this weekend, I didn't tell her. When she was in my office on Thursday, she asked again about me spending the All-Star break with her and Hutch in Banff, but I told her no, said I had to work. At the time, I intended to do just that, but then Lawson came swooping in, whisking me away on a weekend I'll never forget, and I *still* haven't told my sister, not even when she called me from her own vacation.

I felt awful not telling her what was really happening, but I still can't find the point in doing so. Sure, I had a really good time with Lawson, and yeah, I wouldn't mind a repeat of it. But this thing we're doing, all this sex…it's just that: *sex*. It's not more. It can't be…can it?

Maybe.

The tiny voice in my head rattles me, and I try to silence it, mentally kicking and punching at it, trying to get it to go away, but it won't. It's the same voice that's been there since Lawson kissed me. The same voice I've tried so, so hard to ignore. The same voice I will *still* ignore because it's wrong. So damn wrong.

This thing we're doing is temporary. That's all it

can be, because I'll be damned if I do something stupid like go and fall in love with him.

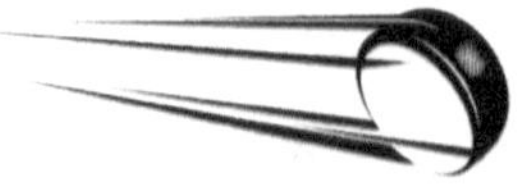

My phone rattles against my desk, and I ignore it. It's eight o'clock the next evening, and I'm sitting in my usual spot: my office chair. Everyone's gone home for the night, even Casey, so it's just me here trying to catch up on all I missed.

Truthfully, there isn't much work to do. My team covered the majority of it, and this is just me being a nitpicky boss. This is also me avoiding going home alone, something I don't want to do for the first time in a very long time.

I...I miss Lawson.

Or maybe I just miss naked Lawson. I can't really tell.

All I know is the idea of going home and heating something up in the microwave while I watch a shitty horror movie does absolutely nothing for me. It's not what I want. What I want is a little more complicated than that.

My phone buzzes again, and this time, I look at it. I snatch it up embarrassingly fast, putting it to my ear. I manage to catch myself before I do something absurd like greet him with a giggle, and I blow out a steadying breath.

"Yes?"

"Wednesday!" he says in his typical loud greeting.

My lips twitch with a grin. "Lawson."

"How are you?"

"Fine…"

We've texted a few times since he dropped me back off at my place with a lengthy kiss, but we haven't actually spoken. I think we're both still trying to come down from what transpired between us.

"Why'd you call, Lawson?" I ask after he's quiet for a few moments.

"Oh. Right." He shuffles around. "Well, I, uh, I could use your help with Daisy."

My senses are on high alert, and I sit up straight. "What's wrong? What happened?"

"Oh, nothing. She just misses you."

"Lawson…" I groan, rubbing at my temples. "Don't scare me like that. I thought something was wrong."

"It is. Her little heart is breaking because she hasn't seen you in two days. She misses her mom."

I don't even bother trying to correct him this time. It's obviously a fruitless endeavor.

"You're so annoying."

"Yeah, I know, but you like that about me."

"I do not."

Do too, that annoying little voice says.

"What are you doing?" he asks.

"Uh…" I rack my brain for a good lie. "I'm at home."

"Really? What are you doing?"

"Watching *Dateline*. Some lady killed her husband for being the most annoying person on the planet. She poisoned him. It was brutal."

"Wow, that sounds intense."

"Eh, not really. He deserved it."

"For being annoying?"

"*So* annoying."

"What kind of super annoying stuff did he do? Wait, let me guess—he cooked her breakfast?"

"Maybe a few times."

"Uh-huh," he says, and there's another shuffle on his end of the line. "He gave her orgasms?"

"Geez, I sure hope so."

"And he definitely showed up at her work with dinner, didn't he?"

"Uh…no? I don't know." What? What is he on about?

"He did. He definitely did."

Then I hear it—the faintest of tapping.

"What the…" I mutter, more to myself than to Lawson.

I rise from my chair, the wheels squeaking across the floor, then make my way out of my office. It's not completely dark in here—I'm not an idiot—but it's still dim, several of the lights turned off, including in the front lobby.

It doesn't matter. There is no mistaking the outline at the front door, and since I just spent the entire weekend wrapped up in it, I'd know that body anywhere.

Lawson.

I practically run to the door, unlocking it as I shove my phone into my pocket. I pull it open and he and Daisy barrel inside, shaking off the February rain.

"What are you doing here?"

He shoots me a grin. "I told you already—Daisy missed you."

I drop to my haunches, opening my arms for the sweet puppy. "Did you miss me, girl? Did you?"

She wags her tail but doesn't move. I tip my head, looking up at Lawson for an answer.

"We've been working on some leash training. She's doing pretty good." He looks down at the coffee-colored Lab. "Go ahead," he tells her.

She springs into action, jumping into my arms and knocking me back with her weight. I swear, she's grown another three inches since I saw her only two days ago. She's getting big fast, and I love seeing how much she's growing, not just in weight or height, but smarts too. She's going to be a good companion.

Daisy licks at me, letting me know she missed me too, and Lawson tugs on her leash.

"All right, that's enough. *I'll* be the only one kissing Rory, thank you very much."

It takes two more tries, but Daisy eventually listens to her owner, letting up enough for me to catch my breath. Lawson reaches down with his other hand, and I take his offering. He pulls me up so effortlessly it makes me dizzy—or maybe that's just Lawson himself.

He catches me when I sway a bit. "Whoa. You okay?" he asks, concern lacing his features.

"Yeah, sorry. It's probably because I haven't eaten anything since…" I glance up at the clock. "Well, I guess since breakfast."

"And you had a massive, sprawling meal, right? A pancake stack ten high, a pound of bacon, and half a dozen eggs?"

I recoil. "Gross, no. I had a banana."

"Rory…" My name comes out a growl, and the sound goes straight between my legs.

Turns out, two days without him is far too many, and my body knows it as well as I do. I clench my thighs together, ignoring the zing as Lawson turns and grabs two bags, holding them up to me.

"Lucky for you, I brought food."

As if on cue, my stomach rumbles loud enough for both of us to hear. We laugh, and I lead him and Daisy back to my office.

Lawson sets the dog free as I clear off a spot on my desk. I take my seat behind it, and he sits opposite, digging into the two bags he brought. He pulls out container after container of Chinese food from one bag, then sandwiches from Bernie's from the other. It all has my mouth watering, and I don't know where to start.

"This is entirely too much."

He shrugs, opening a container of what looks like black pepper chicken and broccoli, then pops open another one full of rice. "I like leftovers."

"Which one am I supposed to eat?"

"Whichever you want. I'll eat what you don't. I'm not picky. I wasn't sure what you'd want, so I got options."

I give him a look as I grab for a sandwich, surprised to find it's buffalo chicken and blue cheese.

He remembered.

And when I peep in the bag, sure enough, there are two bags of the sweet-and-spicy barbecue chips. I swear, I could lean over this desk and kiss him right now, but I don't. I'm too hungry to start something I sure as hell won't want to stop.

We talk about our day as we eat. Lawson tells me

about taking Daisy to the dog park and how she met two other Labradors. I tell him about some of my patients that came in, one who brought in her bird because it wouldn't stop saying *Fuck* and another whose cat ended up being pregnant even though they swore they got her spayed. When we get to the end of our meal, Lawson smiles at me from the other side of the desk.

"What?" I ask, feeling a little self-conscious with all his attention on me.

It's silly, given what's transpired between us, but it's true. It's one thing to have a whirlwind weekend away with him, but it's another to have him here in my office, acting all domestic by bringing me dinner and eating with me.

It's…strange, but I don't hate it. Not at all.

"Is it weird to say I missed you?"

"Yes."

His face falls, and I laugh. "But I might have missed you too."

He perks back up. "Really?"

I nod. "Yes, really—but *only* the parts of you that brought me to orgasm, and that's it."

"Ah. That makes much more sense." He shakes his head, his eyes shining with amusement. "You look different today."

I pull my brows together, those words sounding eerily similar to what Casey told me when I got back.

"I do?"

"Yeah, but good different. Like you're…well, a little less Wednesday. Not so many dark clouds and all that."

I grin at his words. Only Lawson could say something like that and it make total sense, and only he could say something like that and it send a jolt of panic through me. I try my best to cram it down and shrug it off.

"I'm happy to be back at work is all."

His perpetual smile slips ever so slightly, but I don't miss it. I also don't acknowledge it.

"So, have you talked to Hutch about this weekend at all?"

He rears his head back. "Uh, no. Why would I?"

"I don't know." I lift my shoulders. "I figured you guys talk, so…"

"We don't sit around gossiping, if that's what you're wondering."

I send him a look that says I don't believe him, and the small twitch of his lips tells me I'm not entirely wrong to think that.

"Well, good," I finally say after several beats.

"Have you told Auden?" he asks.

"I haven't."

"Hmm."

It's all he says as he holds my stare, the same one that declares, *And I don't plan to.* His intimidatingly gray eyes narrow slightly, but after a few moments, he nods once, the message clearly heard—we keep this between us. Only us.

I work for another half hour, then lock up. Instead of going home, I head the opposite way—to Lawson's, where I let him show me just how much he missed me.

Twice.

Chapter 18

LAWSON

We're back on the ice after the much-needed break, and I'm feeling better than I have in a long time. I am one hundred percent, without a doubt certain it has to do with Rory. She's been at my apartment nearly every night since I went to the clinic, and we've been spending all those nights tucked away in my bed and exploring each other in all the ways we didn't get to at the cabin. It's been amazing. *She's* been amazing, and I can't imagine it getting any better than this.

"Fuck, man. How am I tired already?"

"It's because you're old," I tell Locke.

He reaches out with his stick, whacking me on the legs. Gear or not, it fucking stings, but I deserved it, so I let it slide.

"All right, Lawsy. Let's see what you got," our new head coach, Owen Smith, hollers at me.

I take off at full speed toward the puck, drag it to me, then shift left, right, and left again, inching closer to Fox. When I'm a few feet away, I wind back and shoot, and the puck soars over his glove hand.

"Nice," Coach Smith says. "But don't be afraid to come in with even more speed. These new kids coming in are quick. Push more with your legs. You're still young. You got the stamina."

He's right, I do. Just ask Rory.

I want to say that, but I can't, because apparently, we're not telling anyone at all what we're doing. To a certain degree, I get it. I really do. Her sister is dating my captain. It's a little weird, a tough situation because obviously, if something goes south with us, it will make things awkward.

But my problem with that is I don't intend for things to go south at all. I like Rory. Like *really* like her. The kind of like you don't just get over or move on from easily. I know I'm not supposed to be worried about this kind of stuff right now, not during the season when we're gunning for a Cup, but I can't help it. Rory blazed into my life when I least expected it, and I'm not ready to give that up yet—Cup or not.

Coach Smith lifts his dark brows, his lips that are almost hidden by his beard dipping into a deeper and deeper frown with every second I don't answer him.

"Noted, Coach," I finally say.

He nods, satisfied with that, then blows his whistle. "Fox, swap with Dasher. Next!"

Thomas skates up to the puck one of our assistant coaches has dropped onto the ice, and I head to the other end, tagging up with Hayes and a couple of the other guys, Fox right behind me.

"Can't believe I'm stuck with this old man again," Hayes says grumpily, looking over at the new coach with fire in his eyes. "Thought I was done with the Comets when I got sent out here."

"Don't worry, Hayes, I can't escape them either," I tell him, patting his shoulder. I've come to accept that with Greer being on the Comets, they'll be in my life for a long, long time.

"This is his first coaching gig, right?" Fox asks, eying the new guy warily.

"Second." Keller skates in after his shot, which Dasher caught. "Ish. He did video before this."

"He was an incredible player. I have no doubts in his coaching ability," Locke says to us, clearly impressed by the guy.

I don't blame him. Owen "Apple" Smith had a decorated career, racking up assists like they were going out of style, earning him his nickname that people still call him by even though he's been out of the league a few years now. He was good on the ice, and something in my gut tells me he'll be just as good behind the bench too.

Hutch nods. "What Locke said."

They exchange a quick look, and I don't miss the surprise that flutters over Locke's features. Shit's been a little off with them since all that drama went down with Auden, but it seems they're coming around to each other again.

I'm glad. The last thing we need is for them to keep up their weird pissing match and cost us more games. We need everyone focused on hockey right now, not on other things.

I should really tell myself this too, but I don't. Glass houses and all that.

"Well, if you two are on board, I'm in too," says our starting goalie, giving us his usual grin. Lots of people say *I'm* happy, but it's nothing compared to Fox. He's perpetually positive, even when you don't want him to be.

"Hmm," Keller grunts, and it's not at all surprising he has nothing meaningful to add to the conversation. Dude's too grumpy for his own good.

I look to Hayes, but his attention is on the bleachers, where a few new faces are sitting. I see Auden, which I'm not shocked by, and a few other players' wives, but what truly sticks out to me is one person I wasn't at all expecting to see—Rory.

How the hell did I miss her before?

Like she can feel my gaze on her, she turns her head my way, a soft grin tugging at her lips. Fuck me if I don't want to rip off my helmet, march my way up those steps, and haul her against me, kissing her until we're both senseless, skates and all.

But I can't. I really, really fucking can't.

In fact, I need to look away. *Now.* I need anything to distract me, distract the team—especially since Hayes is now giving me a knowing look. I snap at him, then point toward the bleachers.

His eyes tighten for a short second before he peeks over there and says, "Um, Auden?"

I can't decide if he's dumb or just playing along.

"No, the woman next to her."

"Rory."

His lips twitch. Okay, not dumb—just a jackass.

I glower at him. "No, you idiot. The bombshell redhead that just walked in."

"Ah, her. She's—"

"*Mine.*"

We spin on our skates, Coach Smith now standing close. His big arms are crossed over his chest and his dark brows are slashes above his eyes.

"She's mine," he says again, looking past us and to the bleachers.

She must feel our attention, lifting her hand and waving. Coach Smith smiles, but only barely, and it makes *me* smile because I know that smile. It's the smile you make when you're into someone, and I am into someone. Big-time.

"Duly noted," I say, turning away before anyone can question why I'm grinning like a loon.

"Back to skating, boys," Coach commands.

"Yes, Coach Smith," the team says in unison, and most of the group skates away.

Not me though. I linger, flicking my eyes back up to the bleachers. I skip right over the redhead, training my attention on the only woman I want to see.

Once again, she looks over at me, and this time, her smile is much bigger than before. If I'm not mistaken, it's the smile you make when you're into someone—big-time.

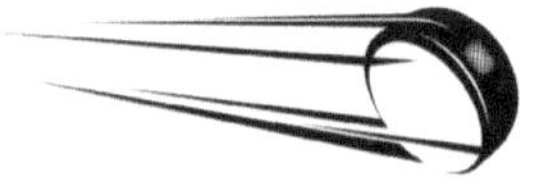

We call it quits on practice about fifteen minutes later. As much as I should hit the stationary bike, especially after being off the ice for a week, I don't. I'm in too big of a rush, hoping like hell to catch just a glimpse of Rory before she leaves because I'm *that* eager to see her, even though I just did last night.

I rinse off quickly in the shower, then grab my shit and practically run from the locker room. I skid to a stop just down the hall when I spot Auden and Hutch making out like two teenagers. It's not them I'm watching, though.

It's Rory.

She's gagging, looking at them with nothing but disgust, and I don't know why, but it turns my stomach sour. Is she really that opposed to something like what they have? Better question: am I suddenly *looking* for something like that?

I shake off the thought, making my way down the hall. Rory spies me before Hutch and Auden do, and her eyes dart between my teammate and her sister. She's scared I'm going to say or do something to out us, and I wish she'd give me a bit more credit than that. Sure, I'm a little annoyed she's wanting to hide this like she is, but I'm not a dick. I'll respect her wishes.

For now.

"Coach Smith seems to be fitting in," Auden says to Hutch. "And his fiancée is really nice."

"And totally smoking hot," I say as I walk up, because it's the kind of thing I would *normally* say. Pretenses, right?

I slide my eyes over to Rory and give her that same smirk I did the first time I met her. It's the smirk I've always reserved for picking up women, the smirk I know she hates.

"Is this what you do now?" I ask her. "Stalk our practices? Because if so, I'm going to have to talk the new coach into doing a *shirts vs skins* game. I call skins." I bounce my brows up and down.

Because I know her so well, I see it the moment it happens—she goes full Wednesday, and I eagerly await every second of tongue-lashing that's coming.

"Really? You'll take your shirt off? Dreams really do come true," Rory says, her voice dripping with sarcasm. "I'd especially love to see you dragged across the ice with no gear." She bats her lashes, somehow still looking sweet when she does it, despite her words. She looks to her sister. "I'll be in the car, Auden."

Then she turns on her heel, marching down the hall without so much as a goodbye, and I'm stuck standing here with my cock stirring to life in my pants like a fucking weirdo, enjoying the sparring entirely too much.

"She's so mean," I mutter before I realize I'm saying it.

Panic races through me, because even I heard the desire in my words. I will myself to act cool and unaffected, even though every cell in my body is itching for me to track her down and show her how much I love that mouth of hers.

"And she so wants me," I tack on smugly.

Hutch laughs, his heavy hand landing twice on my back. "Keep dreaming, buddy. Keep dreaming."

"Sorry, Lawsy," his girlfriend says, "but I'm with Hutch. Rory doesn't want anyone. She's probably more committed to staying single than you are."

Oh, don't I know it.

But that's not how Other Me would respond. So, I force myself to say, "Who said anything about not staying single?"

I go to jiggle my brows, but the gesture has Hutch stepping toward me, and, joking around or not, I know when to bounce before it gets too violent.

I hold my hands up, backing away. "What's that, Hayes?" I call out, even though he most certainly didn't say a word to me. I don't even know where he is. "You need me? Coming!"

I turn, darting back down the hall, pulling my phone from my pocket on the way. I hit the last number I called, pressing the phone to my ear as I step outside, heading for my BMW. It rings only once.

"That was entirely too close."

"Why didn't you tell me you'd be here?"

"Uh, surprise?" she says.

"I'd say."

"It wasn't my idea." She rushes to defend herself, like she's worried I wouldn't like her being here. She's wrong. I *love* having her here. Hell, I want her at all my practices, especially since the second I saw her there, I started pushing myself harder and faster. I played not just for me, but for her too. Besides, it's kind of nice to be watched sometimes, and Rory was definitely watching.

"Auden dragged me here. She's like obsessed with Hutch or something."

I'm obsessed with you.

"Well, I'd hope so. He is her boyfriend. He's only been begging her to move in with him since Christmas."

"What? Has he really?"

"Auden didn't tell you?"

"No," she says quietly, and I know right away it bothers her that her sister didn't mention such a big thing to her. But, if we're being fair, she has no right to feel that way, not with her hiding *our* big thing from Auden.

She must come to that same conclusion because she says, "But that's fine. Uh, good for them."

"Yeah. Good for them."

I pull open my trunk, toss my workout bag inside before shutting it again, and climb in behind the wheel. I don't start the car up yet, waiting for Rory to say something else. The silence is stretching, teetering on awkward, and I hate it so damn much. We don't do awkward. Not even after she caught me masturbating, when we skipped right past discomfort and straight to moving on.

Which is why I find myself saying, "So, did you enjoy the show?"

It works. The tension breaks, and Rory laughs.

"You mean did I like watching you get yelled at, beat into the boards, and shoved around? Uh, yeah. It was the highlight of my day."

I actually believe her, and I somehow find comfort in that. We may flirt, we may fight, and we may fuck, but no matter what, she's still Rory, and it's my favorite thing about her.

"Crap, Auden's coming with Hutch. I have to go."

"Okay. Will I see you later?"

"I don't know."

"What?" I try to keep the growl out of my voice, but the word comes out sharp anyway. What does she mean? I leave tomorrow on a four-game road trip; it's my last chance to see her.

"Rory?"

"I…I just…"

"Just say whatever it is you're going to say."

I brace myself. This is it. She's calling it quits on us already. I'm already working out a speech to convince her otherwise when she huffs like she's disgusted and frustrated with herself.

"Are you really into her?"

That's her hang-up? I chuckle, loving a little too much how jealous she sounds right now. "Don't worry, Wednesday, the only person I'm into is you."

"Really?"

"Yes, really. Now, let's try this again. Will I see you later?"

She sighs, and I hear the smile in it. "Yes, Lucas. You'll see me later."

"Good. You've got a key, so just let yourself in."

"And where will you be?"

"Well, that's for me to know and you to find out."

"Are you playing some weird sex game, Lawson?"

"Noooo." And really, I'm not. I just like teasing her.

"Whatever. I gotta go. Bye."

She hangs up, and I laugh because it's so *her*. I don't know how I got into this with her, but all I know is I never want to look back. With Rory, all I want is forward, and quite possibly a future.

Chapter 19

SERPENTS SINGLES GROUP CHAT

Hayes: All right, I'll say it: Getting rid of Coach was the best thing we've done all season.

Keller: A-fucking-men.

Lawson: Wow, Keller. Weird way to come out to us.

Lawson: We see you and we support you, man. Love is love. I made out with a guy once. Didn't hate it. Got a tingle in my pants and everything, but it ultimately wasn't for me. He was too rough. So, it's cool. Sexuality is a spectrum. You do you. Or him. Or her. Or them. Whatever.

Hutch: Lawson?

Lawson: Yeah?

Hutch: Shut the fuck up.

Lawson: Wow. Rude. I was just trying to be supportive.

Lawson: Oh. Shit. I read that wrong.

Lawson: Sorry, didn't have my glasses on. We're all good now. Proceed.

Hayes: Well, that was…enlightening.

Locke: Very much so.

Fox: I… Wow.

Lawson: Anyway, as Hayes was saying…

Hayes: I was just going to let you take the floor on this one.

Lawson: Fine.

Lawson: Getting rid of Coach was the best thing we've done all season.

Hayes: Dude, that is LITERALLY what I said!

Lawson: Dude, I'm trying to get the conversation going again.

Fox: He really is amazing.

Lawson: THANK YOU, FOXY.

Fox: No disrespect to our previous head coach, but there's something about Coach Smith that feels...right.

Hayes: Yeah, I know what you mean.

Locke: Agreed. He's a damn good coach.

Locke: And I'm not just saying that because we're on a streak. It's not that. It's more.

Hutch: He's THERE. Not checked out, ya know?

Fox: Yes! That!

Keller: Think he'll get pissed at me for getting too many PIMs? Fucking hate that. Let me do my thing out there.

Lawson: You totally just popped a boner, didn't you? Swear you get off on fighting.

Keller: Shut up, Lawson.

Lawson: Ooooh. I'm right, aren't I?

Keller: No. You're an idiot.

Lawson: That's not what your mom said last night.

Fox: Fucking hell. Do we ALWAYS have to bring in the mom jokes?

Lawson: Yes.

Keller: Yes.

Locke: I really wish we could go just one conversation without it happening. It's weird.

Lawson: You're only saying that because you're as old as our moms.

Locke: For the ten thousandth time, I am not that old!

Lawson: Suuuuuure. Whatever you say.

Hayes: I *did* watch him strike up a conversation about canes with some old man at the coffee shop the other day.

Locke: That was ONE TIME!

Locke: And HE started it. It's called not being rude. You'd know that if you had any manners.

Hayes: Sorry. My mom never taught me. Lawson, think your mom could?

Lawson: Watch it.

Keller: What? Don't like it when it's about your mom?

Hutch: Let's leave ALL moms out of it.

Hayes: What if she's a hot mom though? Do we need to leave her out of it?

Hutch: ALL MOMS.

Hayes: Even that one with the tits the size of watermelons?

Lawson: Boooooo! Have some fucking class, new kid.

Fox: Yeah, man, don't be gross.

Locke: Not cool.

Keller: You know you fucked up when you have Lawson booing you. He's as depraved as they come.

Lawson: GASP! HOW DARE YOU!

Lawson: Wait, no, you're right. I am just a little, but only where it counts. *smirking devil face emoji*

Keller: Talking an awful big game for someone who hasn't been bragging about hitting new pussy for months. Dry spell, buddy?

Lawson: Shut up.

Fox: Wow. That was…kind of weak, Lawson. I expected a better response.

Hayes: Me too. I'm disappointed.

Locke: Even I'm a little sad that's where that's ending.

Hutch: Not me. You all need to shut up. You're blowing up my phone and annoying the crap out of me.

Lawson: Aw, oopsie. Sorry, Captain.

Hayes: Yeah, oops. Sorry, Captain.

Fox: Sorry, Captain.

Keller: Sorry, Captain.

Locke: Sorry, Captain.

Hutch: Fucking hell, Locke. You too?

Locke: Sorry. Couldn't help it.

Hutch: All right. That's enough. Mandatory pre-game naps for everyone. Rest up so we can beat Chicago tonight.

Lawson: Aye aye, Captain.

Hayes: Aye aye, Captain.

Fox: Aye aye, Captain.

Keller: Aye aye, Captain.

Hutch: What, Locke? Nothing to say this time?

Locke: Sorry, Captain.

Lawson: LOLOLOLOLOL

Hutch: I'm turning off my phone.

Lawson: WAIT.

Lawson: For real though…love IS love.
Ya know, just in case.

Hutch: Fuck's sake, Lawson.

Hayes: Ughhh.

Fox: Dude, just stop.

Locke: Jesus, Lawsy.

Keller: Please, I am begging you,
delete my number.

Chapter 20

RORY

The Serpents are on fire. After the All-Star break, they came out of the gate hot and are quickly working their way back to where they were before the losing streak. For me, that means Lawson has been gone for a week, and I'm slowly starting to feel like I'm losing it. After being around him so much lately, it's weird not having him here, not smelling leather and cedar, not hearing his laugh.

Okay, fine. I still hear his laugh because we talk every day, but still. It's not the same as him being here. When he's gone, he's a little less annoying, which I find completely unnerving. When he's gone, I don't find myself feeling like I need to bury myself in work as much, which is just strange. When he's gone, those Wednesday-like tendencies, as he likes to say, make an appearance a little more often.

And when he's gone…there's a part of me—a so-very-tiny one—that wishes he weren't. I've maybe gotten a little too used to him, and I try not to overthink that too much as I shuffle some files around on my desk, looking for one in particular.

The Serpents calendar went live a week after the shoot, and not only did they sell out of their first print run in an hour, all the animals featured were adopted within a week and the shelter raked in nearly fifteen grand in donations. Incredible what a few pictures of hot hockey players holding animals can accomplish, isn't it?

I pull file after file out, but none of them are what I want. On a hunch, I grab the folder we use for closed-out bills and open it. To my surprise, it looks incredibly similar to what I'm after, but also not. Something's off.

I march down the hall to the admin station, right to the person who signed the bottom of each page.

"Casey? What are these?"

She stands, taking the stack of papers from my outstretched hand. She flicks through them quickly before giving them back.

"They look like bills."

I grind my teeth. "Well, yeah, I know that. But I don't know *why* they exist and *why* they're all made out to Lucas Lawson."

"Oh." Casey shuffles her feet, twisting her lips this

way and that. It's annoying as hell, and I'm quickly losing my already thin patience.

"Out with it," I demand, arching my brow and folding my arms over my chest, trying my best to ignore how tight and painful my boobs are with my period right around the corner.

"Well, uh, Mr. Lawson called back in January and asked if the animals from the shoot had gotten adopted. I told him yes, then he offered to pay all the bills. I informed him you were planning to take care of it personally, but—surprise, surprise—he wouldn't take no for an answer and insisted we bill him for everything. So, every time a patient's come in, we've billed his account."

I'm stunned. Lawson has been paying for these bills the whole time and hasn't said a word to me about it? Why? Why wouldn't he bring that up? Why would he not tell me?

It's annoying. Completely maddening. So damn frustrating that I just want to…I want to…

Kiss him.

Ugh, god? What is wrong with me? Why, why, why? Why is stupid Lawson in my head so much? And why is he such a nice guy when he wasn't supposed to be? As great as it is, I find it equally irritating. It makes me feel things toward him that I really, *really* don't want to feel.

"Thank you for telling me." My words to Casey are clipped before I spin around and march back to my office.

I shut the door behind me, pulling up my recent calls as I settle down into my desk. It rings three times before he picks up. It's dark, the room nearly black, but I can still make him out on the screen.

"Wednesday?" he answers groggily. "What's wrong? Everything okay?"

"Why didn't you tell me you were paying vet bills that aren't yours?"

"Shit," he mutters. There's a loud scratching noise as he shuffles around the bed, then there's a click, and suddenly he's bathed in light. "I guess you found out about that, huh?"

The phone is jostled a bit as he moves around, disappearing off camera before coming back with his black-rimmed glasses on his nose. He must finally register the pinched expression on my face because he sighs, rubbing his hand through his already messy dark hair. He looks good, too good, which annoys me further.

"Uh, considering this is *my business*, yes, I found out about it."

"I was going to tell you…"

"Were you?" I squint at him.

"Yes. Maybe. I don't know." He's picking at

something on the blanket, not really looking at me. "I, uh, guess I was hoping you wouldn't find out because I knew you'd be mad."

"I'm not mad you did it, only mad you didn't tell me." And even then, I'm not really mad. More like... surprised.

Though, at this point, I shouldn't be, not after all the other things I've seen Lawson do for people. He's played into that jock stereotype so well it's hard to remember that's not who he truly is.

"Do you hate me?" he asks quietly, looking so sad I can't help but laugh.

"No, Lawson. I don't hate you. I...don't think I *can* hate you. Which is incredibly annoying, by the way."

He grins. "See? I knew you liked me all along."

"You wish," I say, though I'm really starting to believe he may not be entirely off the mark.

I look at the paid bills again and let out a choked gasp when I see how much he's spent on these animals that aren't his.

"Lawson..." I shake my head. "This is too much. You're doing too much."

"No, I'm not. Besides, I know you. You were going to cover all that yourself. That would mean *you* were spending too much too."

"So?"

"So let me do this. You're always so busy taking care of everyone else. Let me take care of you."

Let me take care of you.

I don't know what it is about his words, but they hit something deep inside my chest. Something I haven't felt before. Something so fucking strong I physically have to choke back the sob that's suddenly lodged in my throat. I swallow it down the best I can, looking into the camera as Lawson yawns.

That's when it hits me.

"Oh, god. You were taking your pre-game nap, weren't you?"

He nods, lifting his hand to rub the back of his neck. "I was. We're playing Minnesota tonight."

"Then why'd you answer? You should be sleeping."

"Because you called."

He says it so simply, so genuinely, and I fucking break. Everything inside of me splinters open, all the hurt and the pain and the long nights and early mornings…it all comes crashing down on me, and I can't seem to see straight anymore.

"Rory?" he says softly. "Everything okay?"

I blink back the tears stinging in my eyes. "Oh, yeah. I'm good. Totally fine."

He furrows his brow, his gray gaze somehow just as penetrating from thousands of miles away as it is when he's standing right in front of me. This is the first time I want to hide from it, though.

So, I do.

"Hey, I need to go. I have to…patient," I tell him, looking anywhere but at his piercing stare.

"Oh. Okay." He leans forward. "I guess I'll see you tomorrow night, then?"

Right. Tomorrow. When he comes home. Tomorrow, when I'll have to face this all-too-knowing stare in person.

"Yep. Sounds good," I reply, not meaning a word of it.

"Okay…" But he doesn't hang up. He keeps staring and studying, and I hate that he can tell something is off with me almost as much as I hate the fact that something *is* off with me. I just wish I knew how to fix whatever it is.

Maybe it's just my impending period and I'm being overly sensitive. Though I've never been one to be like that in the past, I'm certain that's all this is. It has to be.

"Are you sure everything is okay?" he asks again.

I sigh. "Yes, Lawson. I'm fine. I'll see you tomorrow."

He opens his mouth to say something, but I don't hear it. I'm already hitting the red button and tossing my phone to the side, suddenly feeling very, very worn out. *It's just my period,* I tell myself, and it's all I *will* tell myself, even though it's not as true as I wish it were.

No, the truth knocking right at my heart is far scarier than that.

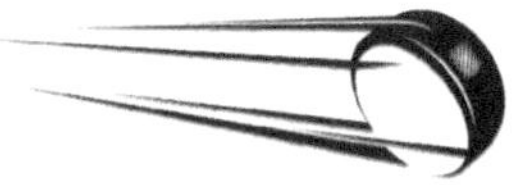

As a rule, I save calling in to work for true emergencies or sickness. I'm not talking a little sniffle or a tummy ache. I just wear a mask or pop some Tums if I need to, but I'll still go in. I have to be glued to a toilet with it coming out of everywhere or someone has to be seriously injured for me to use a sick day.

But today, even though none of those things are happening, I called out. I woke up feeling like I'd been run over and left for dead. One trip to the bathroom later, I knew why—my period has arrived, and it's a fucking doozy.

I've been cozied up in bed all day, the mid-February chill seeping in through my windows despite having my heat cranked all the way up *and* having a heating pad on my lower stomach. I rub my fuzzy-sock-clad feet together, trying my best not to throw my remote at the TV as Lucas Scott lies out of his ass to Brooke Davis, the *real* main character, if you ask me. I've been on a *One Tree Hill* binge since the cabin, and I figured since I was staying home today, I may as well hang out with old friends.

But, truthfully, it's not hitting like it normally does. I'm too grumpy to even enjoy the sparks flying between Haley and Nathan like I usually do. He's an idiot, and it reminds me entirely too much of Lawson, who I really don't want to think about right now.

I'm not mad at him or anything. I'm just…*ugh*, I don't even know what I am. After our conversation yesterday, I had the strangest feeling following me around. I couldn't put my finger on what was bothering me then, just like I can't now. Something's definitely off with me, and I don't just mean the fact that I've gone through almost half a pack of tampons today. It's something else entirely, and the rock sinking in my stomach tells me it has to do with the man I can't stop thinking about no matter how hard I try.

I'm getting ready to start another episode when there's a knock at my door. Daisy, who has been staying with me again while Lawson is on the road and who seems to have finally found her voice, barks at the sudden intrusion.

"Shh," I tell her, ruffling her ears. "It's probably just a package."

I click play on the show, and not even ten seconds into it, another knock sounds. With a huff, I push out of bed and make my way to the front door. I wrench it open, not caring one bit that I look like death or that I'm not wearing a bra, and I come face to face with a grinning Lawson.

"What are you…"

Another bark from Daisy.

Oh, right. Her.

"Wednesday…" he says, but it's missing his usual excitement. Instead, he sounds worried, the smile that was plastered on his face slipping into a frown. "Are you okay?"

"Yeah, I'm fine. Just…tired."

"I went by the clinic to see if you wanted to grab some lunch, but they said you called out. Naturally, I didn't believe them, so I had to come see for myself. And pick up my little angel, of course."

Said angel shoves through my legs, eager to see her owner, who bends and tucks her into his arms, cooing at her.

"How's my girl doing? Were you good? You were, weren't you? Yeah." He nuzzles his nose against her, and she swipes her tongue rapidly over his face, which is in desperate need of a shave.

I cross my arms over my chest. "Did you two need a minute?"

He laughs, turning his attention to me. The second he does, that elation in his eyes dims, and he's back to frowning. "Uh, no. You don't look so hot."

"That's because my uterus is being a real bitch right now, so you'll have to excuse me if I'm not my usual sunshiny self."

To his credit, he doesn't seem the least bit uncomfortable about me mentioning menstruation, which only further annoys me because *of course* he's not uncomfortable like most guys would be.

His lips twitch with amusement. "So, are you going to invite me in?"

"No."

His brows come together. "O…kay." He tips his head. "Did I do something wrong?"

"No. I'm just on my period, and if you come in, you're going to want sex, and I can't give it to you, so there's really no point in you coming in here."

He works his jaw back and forth, nodding only once. "Okay," he says in a clipped tone.

I should probably worry about that, but I don't really have it in me, not right now when all I want to do is crawl back in bed and bury myself under the covers and forget that Lawson makes my heart race wildly.

"Here," I tell him, snatching up Daisy's bag of supplies and handing them over. "I'm crawling back in bed. Welcome home, Lawson."

"I…" He shakes his head, thinking better of saying whatever it was he was just going to say, and slings the bag over his shoulder, tucking the dog closer to his body. Then, without another word, he turns on his heel and…leaves.

He leaves!

It's what I wanted, but it still grates on every last nerve I have. I slam my door, hoping like hell he hears it, then march back to my bedroom and dive right back into my pile of warmth. I hit play on the remote, turning the volume up entirely too high.

I'm being a brat, I know that. But I'm just so…*ugh!*

I missed him. I missed him *so damn much*, and then he comes over here and leaves me like it's nothing. Yes, I know I asked for it, but still. Lawson is never one to back down from a challenge, and he chooses this one time to do so?

"Screw him," I mutter, sliding down farther into the bundle of blankets.

The episode plays out and I start up another, my eyes growing heavier by the second. I'm nearly asleep when something startles me awake. I sit up, straining to listen, and I hear it again.

It's knocking.

He's back.

I spring out of bed, my legs getting caught up in the mess of sheets and comforters, and I nearly fall flat on my face before I make it out of my room. I race to the front door and pull it open, my breathing just a little labored. Like a wish come true, there he is, standing on the other side of the door.

"Lawson."

His lips pull up into a smile. "There's my Wednesday."

And I leap into his arms. He catches me with ease, squeezing me tightly like he never wants to let me go. He buries his face in my neck, inhaling me before placing soft kisses against my skin.

"Mmm. I missed you," he says as I slide back down his body and to my feet.

"I know."

His chest rumbles against me, and he pulls away, looking down at me. "It's okay, I know you missed me too."

"You wish."

He chuckles, pecking a tiny kiss to my nose. "I do, Rory. I really do."

I try not to read too much into his words. Instead, I press up on my tiptoes, kissing him hard and fast. I must take him by surprise, because it's a couple of seconds before he registers what's happening, then suddenly, he's kissing me back, and it's just as good as I remembered.

Our mouths move together in a frenzy, tongues twisting and hands roaming over every inch we can reach. It's good, *so damn good*, and I'm certain there is no way there's another person out there as good at kissing as Lawson is because he doesn't just *kiss me*—he claims me, marks me as his and his alone. It's overwhelming and not enough all at once.

I'm ready to throw my legs around his waist again or drop to my knees for him—I can't decide which—when he pulls away, ending the kiss.

"No, no, no," I whine.

He laughs, pulling away more. "As much as I missed you—and in case you didn't believe me the first time, I really fucking did—I'm not here for that."

I wrinkle my brows. "Then what are you here for?"

He gives me a look that says, *Really? You have to ask?*

He sighs lightly. "You, Rory. I'm here for you."

Then he raises his arms, and I realize he's carrying a bag. I never even registered it swinging against me when he was kissing me, too wrapped up in his touch and his scent and…well, just *him*.

I step back into my apartment, waving him in. I close the door, then lead him back to my bedroom, and he stops at my doorway while I crawl back into my cocoon. He looks so hot leaning against my doorjamb in those jeans that are just tight enough on his strong legs, a simple heather-gray hoodie, and a hat with the Serpents logo twisted backward on his head.

"I brought some supplies," he tells me, shaking the reusable bag that's bursting at the seams.

"Supplies?"

"Yep. Tampons and pads, a few different kinds since I didn't know what you like. Some chocolate—dark, milk, and white." My mouth waters at that. "Some chocolate chip ice cream, a thing of brownie bites, rice crispy treats, chocolate-covered pretzels, a two-liter of Sprite, hot chocolate with extra marshmallows, some cheap leftover Valentine's Day candy, *and* two bags of sweet-and-spicy barbecue chips plucked straight from my pantry."

I gasp. "You're sharing your chips with me?"

He grins. "I'm sharing my chips with you, Wednesday."

"All right, fine. You can stay."

He laughs, pushing off the doorjamb and sauntering into the room. He toes off his shoes before climbing into bed next to me and setting the bag of goodies between us.

He peers into it like a kid pressing his nose against an ice cream shop window. "What do you want first?"

"The tampons."

Again, no discomfort at that. He just reaches in, pulls out a couple boxes, and hands them my way. I take them from him.

"Be right back," I say, jumping from my bed once more and heading for the bathroom.

I do my business, and when I come back out, Lawson's now tucked under the blanket that's usually draped across the back of the couch, and various snacks are laid out in a row between him and where I was sitting. There's also a fresh glass of water and what looks like a cup of Sprite sitting on my bedside table with two aspirin next to it. I notice the bed is absent of the ice cream, which means he must have stuck that in the freezer.

Emotion catches in my throat. It's all just so…*sweet*. And thoughtful. *He's* thoughtful. Full of surprises too. He could have easily gone home and ignored me the rest of the night, letting me sleep off my crabbiness, but no. He came back because, despite the words coming out of my mouth, Lawson *knew* what I really wanted—him.

He smiles over at me. "Well, are you coming? I'm pretty sure this is the episode where Naley kiss for the first time and she finds out he doesn't entirely suck. It's one of my favorites."

It's one of my favorites too.

I wiggle back into my nest, yanking the blankets up nearly to my chin, then reach for a bag of chips. I rip it open, popping one into my mouth as I hit play. We don't talk for a long time, both of us munching on the snacks he brought.

I'm the first to break the silence. "Hey, Lawson?"

"Yes, Rory?" he asks, rolling his head my way, the light from the television shining off his eyes.

"I'm…I'm sorry I was a jerk earlier."

"It's okay. I get it."

"But do you?"

"Well, no." He laughs lightly. "I don't *really* get it, but I've watched my mom go through this enough to sort of understand."

"Ah. So *that's* where you learned about the supplies."

"A little. Some of it was picking it up through the years. Just because I'm not a uterus-carrying member of society doesn't mean I shouldn't understand how it all works. Besides, I like taking care of you. So when I saw you obviously weren't feeling well, I wanted to do something to cheer you up, especially since I had to miss Valentine's Day." He grins down at me, and it's almost bashful. "Did it work?"

Let me take care of you.

His words from yesterday barrel through me again, and just like before, they stir up all kinds of things I don't have a clue what to do with. So, I don't.

I nod. "It worked."

A full smile now. "Good. I'm glad."

"I hate Valentine's Day, so I'm glad you weren't here."

"*You* hate Valentine's Day? I am so completely shocked."

I stick my tongue out at him and his sarcasm, and he shakes his head, a smile still plastered to his face.

"Watch the show. Relax. Maybe if you're lucky, I'll make out with you again later." He winks, then turns back to the TV.

A loud laugh rips from my chest, and it feels good. So, so good. I don't think I've laughed so hard since he left for his road trip, and honestly, I missed it. Just like I missed him.

"Lawson?"

"Hmm?" he asks, slipping another piece of chocolate into his mouth but not looking over at me.

"I did."

"Hmm?" he says again, pulling his gaze from the happenings of Tree Hill long enough to capture my stare with his own. "You did what?"

"Miss you." I swallow densely. "I missed you."

A slow grin inches across his face, that same glow to his eyes as before reigniting.

"I know you did, Wednesday," he says. "I know you did."

Chapter 21

LAWSON

I'm walking with an extra pep in my step, and nothing is going to take that away, not even Paige, who was not very pleased to find a new car sitting in her parking spot. But, after some coaxing, she gave in and accepted the gift.

I know it's a bit excessive, but there's no way I can sit by and see her suffer like she's been and see how damn hard she works and *not* help. She'll forgive me eventually, and in the meantime, at least she'll have reliable transportation for her and Jaden. I walk into the arena whistling, earning me a sharp glare from Keller, who I flip off as I continue on my merry way.

"What's got you in a good mood?" he calls after me.

"It's definitely not having to look at your ugly mug." I take a sip of my coffee from The Coffee Spot.

He grunts. "Don't worry. Feeling is mutual there."

"Aw, Kells, I doubt that, buddy."

"Fuck off, Lawsy."

I laugh, walking away because *nope* not even Keller is going to ruin today for me. Today, Rory is coming to the game, and I'm so fucking excited for it.

I've played in front of so many people—my mother, my father, my grandparents, and even Wayne Gretzky himself—but none of that compares to playing in front of Rory. Sure, I've done it before, but it was just that: before. Now, it means something entirely different. She's going to be in those stands tonight, and she's going to be there cheering *me* on.

I make my way into the locker room, careful to walk around the team logo on the floor, and head for my stall. I strip off my suit, hanging it up, then pull on a pair of gym shorts and a Serpents t-shirt before going out to meet the other guys in the hall for a little warmup.

We kick a soccer ball around, getting loose and having a couple laughs. After, we disperse, going our separate ways to do our own pre-game rituals. I dress in half my gear, then work on taping my stick.

Fox spritzes water into the air, tracking the droplets with his eyes to get them ready to follow the puck. Keller, Hutch, and Locke sit around and say nothing for the most part, each off in his own head.

But me? I'm practically vibrating with excitement, screaming inside. I'm ready as fuck to get out there.

The countdown for warmups hits the two-minute mark, and we begin lining up in the hallway, the boys buzzing and ready now. We hit the ice. Keller smacks the stack of pucks down, and while I'd usually grab one and be off to the races, I don't this time.

I'm too damn busy looking for Rory.

I don't have to look hard—she's sitting right across from the benches, a bored expression on her face, but I know her too well to believe she's actually bored, especially not when her eyes are giving her away. She's fucking thrilled to be here, a smile playing at her lips when our gazes connect.

I so badly want to skate over to her to tell her riding my face this morning wasn't nearly enough and insist on a second round, but I can't. We're way too exposed here, and she's still determined to keep what we're doing hush-hush.

I won't lie, it's a little frustrating hiding it, especially when it makes me so damn happy, but I keep reminding myself that she needs time. Besides, even if she won't admit it, Rory likes me. I know I give her a good dicking, but there's no way that's the only reason she sticks around. We have too much fun outside the bedroom for that.

We've had a few more nights together like the one

last week when she was on her period. Nights where we just sit in her bed and watch TV. Nights where we don't fuck at all. Nights where we act an awful lot like a real couple. As much as I *love* fucking Rory—and I really, really do—I think it's those nights I like the most.

"Who are you staring at so hard?"

I startle, so lost in my own world I didn't even see Hutch's big body coming toward me.

"Uh…"

"Yeah, Lawsy. Who *are* you staring at so hard?" Hayes asks, smirking at me as he lifts and lowers his brows as he skates by.

Fucking fucker. I want to flip him off so badly, but I can't, not out here in the open where too many cameras are trained on us. Later, though, I'll hit him right where it hurts.

Hutch shakes his head. "Kid is fucking strange."

Just then, Rory throws her head back, her body shaking with laughter at something Auden or her friend has said, and everything else around me fades away. It doesn't matter that I'm about to play a game. It doesn't matter that people are flying around me at high speeds or that pucks are soaring this way and that. None of it matters except her.

She's gorgeous under the arena lights, the green-and-black-and-gold Serpents jersey shimmering every time she moves. Her hair is piled up in a messy bun. She's wearing a pair of leggings and not a stitch of makeup. She's not here to look pretty or fancy or whatever. She's here to watch hockey.

She's here for me. Feeling my stare, she peeks over at me, giving me the softest of smiles before turning back to her sister like she didn't just completely melt me where I stand.

I'm doomed. So fucking doomed. Getting giddy over a smile… When did that happen? When did she burrow so deep inside of me? When did she become so fucking important? When did I…

Oh shit.

Realization smacks into me out of nowhere, and once the thought hits, I can't make it go away.

When did I fall in love with her?

Truth be told, I've been thinking about it for a while now. The thought crossed my mind back at the cabin, but I wrote it off as good sex. The nagging feeling kept up even when we got back to Seattle, and it's only gotten louder, more aggressive as the days move closer to March.

I love her. Holy shit, do I love her.

I think it should surprise me more, but it doesn't. It doesn't, and I'm not quite sure what to do with that. Am I supposed to tell her? Surely, I can't. It'll send her running for the hills, won't it? She doesn't even want to tell anyone we're dating. There's no way she's going to be okay with me falling in love with her.

But then again…who cares? If I don't tell her, it's going to eat me up inside. More than that, she's going to believe *I* don't care about what's happening between us when the opposite couldn't be truer. I love Aurora Sinclair, and dammit, I want her to know.

"Lawsy?"

For the second time tonight, Hutch surprises me with his presence. So wrapped up in Rory, I forgot he was even standing there.

"Hmm?" I turn to look over at Hutch, who is now staring at me with crumpled brows.

He said something. Shit, what did he say?

Slowly, Hutch looks from me to where I was just staring, then back at me again, his brows inching even closer together somehow.

Fuck, fuck, fuck. Way to be obvious, Lawson.

I do my best to remain calm, pasting on a megawatt grin I pray Hutch won't be able to tell is as fake as half my teeth.

"Yeah, man, kid's fucking awesome for sure," I tell him.

Then, like a total fucking chickenshit, I skate away, not daring to cast another glance at Rory. I hang out on the other side of the ice, even though I never do that for warmups, just to stay far away from my captain.

It's fruitless, though. He watches me the entire time. Even when our time is up and we're heading back to the locker room, he's watching. As I sit in my cubby, stripping off my helmet to clean the visor, he's watching. And even as Coach Smith walks into the room, commanding our attention in that way only a head coach can, he's still watching.

I ignore him, turning my attention to where Coach is standing with his hands resting on his hips to address the team.

"We're playing some damn good hockey, boys," he says.

Someone—I think Dulak—puts his fingers in his mouth and whistles loudly.

"We still got some things to work on," Coach Smith continues. "We're giving up a few too many easy zone entries. Let's pinch them off at the blue line a little more, make them work for it. We cut our turnovers in half last game, but I want to cut them more, okay? No more breakaways they can capitalize on. And finally, Foxy..."

All eyes snap to our goalie, even Hutch's.

"Yes, Coach?"

"Lead us out."

Fox smiles, the rest of the team whooping loudly.

"Let's go win us a fucking hockey game, boys," Coach concludes.

"Heard!" the room yells, clapping twice before we rise to our feet, making our way from the locker room.

I can still feel Hutch's gaze on my back, even as I make my way down the tunnel, as we take the ice, throughout both anthems. Even when the puck drops, he still. Fucking. Stares.

Finally, during one of my rests, I chance a look over at him, and his eyes trace from me to Rory again. I snap my attention back to the game. We battle hard all night, scoring one in the first, only for Edmonton to come back and score twice in the second. By the third, we tie it up, and with thirty seconds left, I head out for my last shift of regulation.

"Give 'em hell, Lawsy!" Locke calls as my skates hit the ice, and I take off like a track star.

"Mine, mine," I yell, and Keller whips the puck to me.

It hits my stick and I push with everything I have. Edmonton's tired. They're leaving their top line out there when they've already been out for over a minute, trying to end this before it can go to overtime.

I speed into their zone, dangling between two players in white, then racing toward the net. I shoot, and even though it's a dirty shot, Dulak is there to clean up my mess, tipping the puck right past the goalie. The home crowd explodes, the music blasting through the speakers as the goal horn goes off, and it's glorious. There are ten seconds left on the clock, and we just took the lead.

The team cheers, then we get right back out there for the puck drop. Hutch wins the draw back, flipping the puck to Dulak, who hangs on to it as the clock races down to zero. We celebrate our win, lining up to give our goalie a hug.

Because I just can't help it, I look over to where Rory is, my breath catching in my lungs as she stands against the glass, her eyes locked on me and the biggest fucking smile on her face.

My place? I mouth.

She bites her bottom lip, nodding, and I grin, moving forward in line.

A hand lands on my shoulder, and I know who it is before I even look. Hutch leans down into me.

"Is that something I need to be concerned about?" he asks lowly, so quiet nobody else can hear us, especially not over the loud cheers.

"What?" I ask, trying to play innocent.

But just as I figured it would be, it's pointless. Hutch isn't dumb. He spent months hiding a relationship with Auden. He knows a secret being kept when he sees it.

He sneers at me menacingly. "Want to try that again?"

I sigh, stepping up to Foxy, bumping my helmet against his. "Nice game, bud."

"Thanks, man," he says, that bright grin of his in place as usual.

Hutch is next, offering his own words of encouragement to our goaltender. I make my way toward the center of the ice, waiting for everyone else, and my captain follows me, still waiting on an answer, so I turn to him.

"No, Hutch, you don't need to be concerned about it."

"You sure?" he presses. "Because that's Rory, Auden's sister, and if anything happens to her…"

He doesn't need to finish his threat. I read him loud and clear.

"Chill, Hutch. It's all good."

"All good?" he growls. "That's not reassuring, Lawson. Not when you're you."

"Yeah, well, this time I mean it. It's all good. *We're* all good."

He squints at me, trying to figure out if I'm being serious or not.

"Look, man," I say. "I'm not…I'm not going to hurt Rory. If anything, it's the opposite."

"So you're going to protect her?"

"Yes. With everything I have."

His brows do that thing where they pull in together again. "Why would you… I don't understand…"

He gives another glance toward Rory, who appears mildly concerned as she watches our interaction. I try to tell her with my eyes that everything's good, but I'm not sure she gets the memo, Auden pulling her attention away.

"No," Hutch says. "No, no, no." He's fitting the pieces together, everything clicking into place for him. "No fucking way."

"Yes fucking way," I tell him.

"When?"

"Does it matter?"

He blows out a breath. "I…I guess not." He shakes his head. "I just… Fuck! I don't want anything to happen, you know? I don't want her getting hurt. I don't…"

"I promise, you have nothing to worry about."

"You can't say that for sure. You—"

"I love her, Hutch. I love her."

He stands before me, his mouth slightly ajar, his eyes shining with disbelief at what he's hearing right now.

Then, ever so slowly, he grins. "Oh, you are so out of the fucking club now."

I blow out a relieved breath, chuckling. "Only if you go first."

One final horn goes off, signaling the official end of the game, and we all lift our sticks in the air, saluting the crowd.

Hutch sends me one last shocked look, still shaking his head. "I can't believe it. You, out of all people."

"I know, man. Trust me, I know."

"Does *she* know?"

"I… No. Not yet."

He nods. "Tell her. She might not be ready, and that's okay, but you should tell her."

"You think?"

"Yeah. If there's anything I wish I would have done differently with Auden, it's that I should have told her a hell of a lot sooner how I felt. Could have saved us both the heartbreak."

He's right, and I remember what a miserable fuck he was when everything happened. I don't want to feel like that, not if I can help it.

"And who knows, man—she might just feel the same."

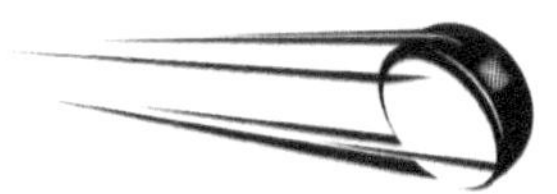

"Oh fuck. I'm gonna come."

"That's it, baby. Ride my cock. Ride it like it belongs to you because it does. It's yours, Rory. Only yours."

"Mine," she agrees in a sex-fueled daze, her head thrown back as she rides me reverse cowgirl, my cock impossibly deep inside of her pussy. She stretches forward, hands on my thighs as she gives me the most beautiful view of her hole I haven't yet taken, the one I'm dying to.

"I can't wait to fuck you here," I tell her, collecting some of the mess we made and pressing my wet thumb against her tight hole.

She moans, wiggling back, searching for more. "Yes. Please. I haven't…"

"No? Never?"

"Never."

"You mean I get this virgin ass to myself?"

"Yours. Only yours," she promises as I pound up into her, my thumb still playing against her asshole.

With a few more hard thrusts, she falls apart, squeezing a release right out of me. Gulping in heavy breaths, she falls back against me, my cock still nestled inside of her as I grab her chin, turning her face to capture her lips.

I kiss her slowly and softly as I come down from my high, reaching around to pinch at her nipples, which has her wiggling in my lap. I love it. I love this moment. I love her.

Tell her.

Hutch's words echo in my head. I should. I should tell her.

"Everything okay?" she asks, twisting around until she's facing me.

"Hmm? Oh, yeah. Everything's fine. Why?"

She shrugs. "I don't know. You looked like something was on your mind."

"I…"

"Yes?"

I chicken out and shake my head. "Nothing."

Another shrug. "Okay."

She presses a kiss to my nose, then swings off my lap, grabbing the sheet that we somehow managed to toss on the floor and wrapping it around her.

"Are you hiding in the blanket?"

"No. I'm just cold."

"Are you lying?"

She giggles. "Maybe."

"Come on, Rory. I've seen every part of you. There's no reason to hide."

"Yeah, well, tell that to all the salt I consumed via the helmet of nachos I had during your game."

I laugh, shaking my head. "God, I love you."

She stills, and so do I. The room, though it felt so fucking hot a moment ago, goes cold. I don't know how long we stay like that, neither of us making a move, but it's too long. So long that she begins to laugh uncomfortably.

"Ha, ha, ha. Funny. Good one, Lawson."

She shoots me a wobbly grin, pulling the blanket off the floor so she doesn't trip as she heads toward the bathroom.

"It wasn't a joke."

She pauses mid-stride, turning back to me. "What?"

I clear my throat. "It wasn't a joke, Rory."

Her brows arch. "What are you…"

"I love you, Rory."

And just like that, it's out there, right in the open, hovering between us in the room like a heavy cloud.

Ten seconds go by.

Twenty.

Thirty.

Then finally, she whispers, "You can't say that to me, Lawson."

I lean forward off the headboard. "Why not?"

"Because we just had sex! You just came inside of me, and you said *that* and you can't. It's not right." She clutches the sheet tighter, hiding herself as if I didn't just have my cock buried inside her or my thumb pressing against her ass as I promised to fuck it moments ago.

"So?"

"So? So!" She huffs. "I don't… You can't! It's not real."

"Bullshit it's not."

"We just had sex, Lawson, then you blurt out you love me. You cannot tell me that's real."

I laugh, but there's no humor to it because I don't find her words funny at all. She can't be serious right now. She cannot stand there and tell me she didn't see this coming.

And yet…

"You were supposed to be easy," she says. "*This* was supposed to be easy."

"It is easy."

"It's not." She shakes her head, her sexed-up hair whipping around her. "It's not, and you know it."

But I don't know it because for me it *is* easy. Loving her is so simple too; it's like skating or breathing. It's effortless. It's natural.

"You were supposed to be like me. You were supposed to not want *that*."

"I didn't. I didn't want that at all. Hell, I've been carrying that club all on my own for two years now, and yet I still fucking fell in love with you."

"Club?"

I wave my hand, not wanting to get into it right now. "It doesn't matter. What matters is, I *didn't* want this, not at all, but it happened and I'm not going to run away from it. I've spent my entire life watching my mother do that because she got hurt by my father. I'm not going to let that same thing happen to me. So, I'm going to accept it. I'm going to own it." I look her right in the eyes. "I love you."

"You can't say that," she repeats, almost frantically this time.

"I can."

"Fine. Then you can't say it because I don't want you to, because I don't believe in…"

"Love? Is that the word you're afraid to say?"

She glares at me. "Shut up."

"No." Now *I'm* annoyed. I shove out of the bed, only unlike her, I don't bother to cover myself up.

Her eyes dart down to my cock that's still half hard, then she averts her gaze like she's suddenly embarrassed by the idea of seeing me naked. That's not it, though. Not at all. She's embarrassed all right, but only by her feelings for me.

Rory can tell herself she doesn't believe in love all she wants, but I know that's not true. I've seen it firsthand in the way she takes care of her sister. How she's always there for Daisy. How she works herself to the bone for her patients. Or how, even when she's dead on her feet, she still stays up late to watch my games.

I've especially seen it all over her face when she falls apart underneath me or on top of me or from my fingers or my tongue, and it's not that whole blissed-out kind of love. It's real. Rory loves me—she just won't fucking admit it to herself.

"I won't *shut up*, Rory. I love you, and you're going to hear it."

"Lawson…" she begs, backing away.

I chase her, matching her move for move until she's backed against the wall with nowhere to go.

"No. You don't get to *Lawson* me. You don't get to dictate whether I've fallen in love with you or not. That's not your choice. It's mine."

"But I don't *want* you to be in love with me. That's not what this was supposed to be. This… You… You're *you*! You don't do love either."

"If you'd have said those words to me last year, I would have readily agreed with you. Probably would have said something along the lines of *ew* or *gross* or *not in this lifetime*. But that was before, Rory. That was before."

"Before?"

"*You*. That was before *you*. And now…"

"Don't," she begs, but I don't listen.

"Now I know. It's not *ew* or *gross* and it's certainly

not in the next lifetime. It's in this one and it's real, so fucking real that it tears me up inside. *You* tear me up inside, twisting me around in ways I can't even begin to understand, ways I don't even really *want* to understand because it doesn't matter. It doesn't change the truth. I love you, Aurora Sinclair."

"Lawson…" She drops her head. "I can't. I just… can't."

"That's okay, Rory. Really. You know why?"

She sniffles, shaking her head. I notch my finger under her chin, tipping her head back and forcing her to look up at me. Her green eyes are shining with unshed tears, and she looks so fucking scared that it hurts.

"Because, baby…" I brush away the lone tear that streaks down her cheek. "Even if you're not ready to say it, I am, and I can't go another minute without telling you. It doesn't matter how long it takes you to say it back—or if you never do—it's okay. I'm still going to be loving you."

"That's so stupid," she says, and I laugh.

"It may be stupid, but it's true."

"This wasn't supposed to… You weren't supposed to…"

She doesn't finish either sentence, but she doesn't have to. I know what she's trying to say all the same.

I shrug. "They don't call me Lawless for nothing."

A laugh bubbles out of her, and it's the second-sweetest sound I've heard all night. I wrap her in my arms, tugging her close, and she lets me. She lets me hold her. She lets me love her, and that's really all I can ask.

We crawl back into bed, where I tell her again how much I love her, this time with my cock and my mouth and my hands all over her body. I tell her until we're both drifting off to sleep, and just before I close my eyes, I press a kiss to her head and tell her once more.

"I love you, Rory."

She sighs contentedly. "I…"

But she doesn't say it back, and I keep my promise—I keep on loving her, even if she's not ready yet. I know, without a doubt, one day she will be, and I'm willing to wait.

Chapter 22

RORY

I've been hiding from Lawson for four days now, and he's let me.

He's still checked in with me daily, calling and texting and even going so far as to send me gifts. When I told him I couldn't get away from the office and wouldn't be coming over the night after The Three Words Thing, he had Bernie's delivered with *extra* sweet-and-spicy barbecue chips. Then the next night when I claimed I had a headache, he dropped a bag full of Tylenol, electrolyte-filled drinks, and Beecher's mac and cheese off at my door. I know it was him because there was a note attached that read:

Wednesday,

Why is Seattle so obsessed with mac and cheese?
I swear it's on every menu around here and not
just for kids. So weird.
Anyway, hope your headache goes away soon. I
miss you.

Love,
Lawson

I cried, which *did* give me an actual headache.

Next I told him I couldn't come over because it was hair-washing day. He let that one slide, and just an hour ago when he asked if he could see me tonight, I said I was going out with Auden.

He responded with, *Have fun, baby. I love you.*

I cried for the second time. Not once, even when I've obviously been lying, has he called me out on it. He knows I need time, and he's giving it to me.

There's a part of me that wishes he wouldn't, wishes he'd barge in here and *demand* I love him back, but he won't, and it's so sweet and also so infuriating at the same time. Him pressuring me would make this so much easier. It would make me hate him again. But he won't, so I can't.

All I can do is sit here in my bed for the fourth night in a row, watching cat videos on YouTube while Hades sends me death glares.

"What?" I say to him. "You try having the guy you're just having sex with go and fall in love with you."

He pushes onto his feet, jumping off the couch and wandering away, leaving me to sort this out myself just like Lawson's doing.

"Ugh!" I toss my head back against the couch, frustrated.

Why did he have to up and do something stupid like fall for me? I thought we had an understanding between us, thought we both knew the score. We were having incredible sex and having fun hanging out—feelings were *not* to be involved. Why did he have to break the rules?

Oh, right. Because he's *Lawless*.

I roll my eyes, but there's really no spite in the gesture. If anything, I smile when I do it, thinking about his stupid nickname and his stupid face and his stupid perfect body and his stupid, stupid heart that apparently has *feelings* for me.

When did this happen? When did we go so wrong? And why did he have to tell me? We could have gone on pretending like nothing was wrong. We could be having sex *right now*. We could have…

Ugh. I don't even know what else we could have done, because truthfully, I think deep down somewhere, I knew this was coming. It started with the tiniest of things. The quick glances. The hidden smiles. The nicknames. The inside jokes only we thought were funny. The games. The pushing and the pulling. The cabin. After the cabin. After the cabin *again*. And again…and again.

No matter how many times I tell myself it's not true, every time I let Lawson into my body, I let him into my heart. I tried so fucking hard to block him out, but I couldn't. He's wormed his way in because *of course* he has. It's Lawson. Did I really expect anything less?

But even though he's definitely carved his name into my chest…is that really love? I don't know. I've never been in love before. This is entirely new territory for me, and the only examples I have are from TV shows and movies and my parents, whose love story honestly sucks. Sure, there's Auden, but is she even an expert? Things with her and Hutch are still so new. How would she really know?

As if on cue, my phone shakes against the table, belting out the song that's assigned to my twin.

"Hello?"

"Can we talk?" she asks.

My heart—the same one that's at war with my brain—drops.

This cannot be good.

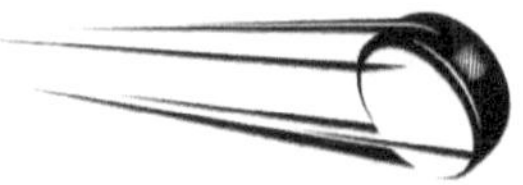

I walk through the doors of The Sinclair Seattle, the hotel that, until a few months ago, my sister owned. This place is her baby. She built it from the ground up, and it stands tall and proud amongst the other buildings of the city. It's a place I've always felt at home, but not tonight, not walking in here after that phone call.

Auden wouldn't say *what* she wanted to talk about, just that she wanted to talk, so here I am. I wave to Betty at the front desk, then make my way into the bar.

Huh. Guess I didn't lie to Lawson about tonight after all.

I push that thought away, focusing on the woman sitting at the bar who looks so similar to me. Looking at her in a pair of leggings and an old, ratty sweater I got her for her birthday many moons ago, you'd never guess her bank account is rocking multiple commas. I take a seat next to her, gesturing to the bartender, Hilda, that I'll take the same thing Auden is drinking— a white wine.

She's barely set the glass down in front of me when Auden finally says, "I have something I need to tell you."

My brows hitch up. "Go on…"

My sister sighs, then spins toward me on her stool, her hazel eyes locking with my own.

"I…I'm moving in with Hutch."

I wait for more, for her to tell me she's knocked up or getting married or something, but nothing else comes.

"Okay," I say.

Her jaw drops. "Okay? *Okay?* That's it?"

I nod. "Yeah, Auden, that's it."

She blows out a long, steadying breath. "Wow. I…I did not expect that."

"I'm sorry?" I chuckle lightly. "I think it's great. You live in a hotel right now, so *not* living in a hotel isn't a bad thing. Besides, you and Hutch are good together. He obviously makes you happy, and that makes him okay in my book. I don't know what else you expected me to say."

"I…" She lifts a shoulder. "I don't know. I figured you'd tell me I'm moving too fast, making a huge mistake, this is the dumbest idea I've ever had—"

"I'm sleeping with Lawson!"

The four words tumble from my lips loudly,

surprising me as much as they surprise Auden if her wide eyes and slackened jaw are any indication. I don't know *why* I say them—maybe because she's sharing such a huge thing and I've been hiding an even bigger thing from her—but they're out there now and I can't take them back.

Honestly, I don't want to. My shoulders are sagging with relief and I'm feeling better than I have in days.

"I… What the fuck?"

I laugh because I don't know what else to do with that response. I puff out a breath. "Yeah."

"You're…" She shakes her head hard, her ponytail slashing back and forth. "How? When? And *why*?"

She says the last word with such disgust, and it makes me smile because it's exactly what I would have said to her if the roles were reversed.

"I don't know. I—"

"Wait. Stop. Start from the beginning. *How?*"

I sigh, then gulp back half of my wine before wiping my mouth with the back of my hand.

"Well, it all started last year…"

For the next thirty minutes, I tell my sister everything. *Finally.* I tell her about Christmas Eve, then Christmas Day. I tell her about the photoshoot and watching Daisy. The kiss. The *way* he kissed me. I tell her The Balcony Thing, where she forces me to pause so she can swoon for a full five minutes. I tell her about my breakdown and the cabin. Well, not *everything* about the cabin, but she gets the idea. Then I tell her about my conscious decision to lie to her about seeing Lawson, and that's when I can tell I start losing her.

"Okay, but why? Why didn't you tell me it was Lawson when I called you out on seeing someone? Why hide it?"

"Because I wasn't seeing him then. We had only kissed once at that point, and it was nothing. It meant nothing. But then after that…"

"After that, it meant something?" she guesses.

"Yeah. Then the All-Star break happened and the cabin and…" I shrug. "That's when things changed."

"Uh, I'd say. He dicked you down good."

"Auden!" I gasp, stunned at her crudeness. That's usually my thing, not hers.

She laughs. "What? Only *you* can say things like that?"

"Yes. No. I don't know." I groan. "Ugh. Why is this happening?"

"What? Our conversation or you sleeping with Lawson? Because I think we definitely covered that already."

"But did we?"

"Well, no. I guess we didn't. So, Aurora, tell me, why *are* you sleeping with Lawson, obvious reasons aside? I mean, he's *Lawson*. He's…well, kind of a moron most days, and a little reckless. You don't get the name Lawless Lawson for nothing."

I shake my head. "But he's not. Yeah, he's loud and annoying and does some really dumb stuff sometimes, but he's more than that. Did you know he hangs out with his neighbor? Name's Jaden and he's twelve. Lawson gives him jerseys and tickets to games and all kinds of stuff. Takes him out on his off days and even knows his schedule. And that's not even the cutest part. He… He bought them a car, Jaden and his mom, Paige—that's her name, by the way. She's single, like his mom was, so Lawson takes care of them. He helps them out, you know. He doesn't live in some fancy place that costs more for one month's rent than most people make in two. It's just your average, everyday apartment. And seeing him with Daisy? It's…something else. He loves her. Like truly loves her. Spoils the ever-loving shit out of her. And he's good with Hades, and you know that cat doesn't like anyone. Hell, he even schemed with Casey and offered to cover all the medical bills for the pets from the calendar shoot. I was going to cover that from the clinic, but Lawson wouldn't allow it. He did it without anyone else knowing, just out of the goodness of his heart. He's just… Sure, he's Lawson, but he's so much more than that too."

Mouth dry, I toss back the rest of my wine, wishing I hadn't driven so I could have another.

Auden sits beside me in silence, her stare burning a hole into me. I don't dare look her way though. I can't, not after that big, rambling speech, especially not when, out of the corner of my eye, I catch a grin curving her lips upward.

"What?" I whisper, like I'm terrified of what her answer might be, and yeah, I guess I am. I know…I just know what she's going to say, and I'm not so certain I can deny it any longer.

I dare a peek at her.

"You love him."

"Shut up," I grumble, and she laughs loudly, jostling my shoulder as I bury my face in my hands, hiding from her, hiding from the truth.

Being the good sister she is, she lets me sit like this for several minutes while I try to get my brain to stop working overtime. All it's doing is spinning, spinning, spinning, and my heart is just thumping.

Thump-thump, thump-thump, thump-thump.

"You know, Rory, it's okay…"

I lift my head, looking over at her. "It's not."

"Why not?"

"Because…feelings!"

She laughs. "Oh, little sis. You and your feelings."

"I hate them," I bite out.

"I know you do," she says. "I know, and I get it. I do. We had the worst example of love growing up. Our parents loved each other, yes, but their love wasn't the forever kind of love. It was fleeting and they tried hard to hold on to those fleeting feelings for too long, damaging us in the wake." She drops her chin to her hand, looking wistfully at the mirror that hangs behind the bar. "You know, I was scared to love Hutch, too."

"Yeah, I remember. Had to convince you pretty hard it was okay to love a forbidden man."

"You did, and you did it so well, so I'm going to tell you the same thing: it's okay to love Lawson, even if you don't *want* to. It's okay to have feelings, even if they are fleeting ones. It's okay to love blindly and recklessly too. You know why? Because we're allowed to love. Just because our parents messed it up, it doesn't mean we will. It doesn't mean every relationship we have is doomed to fail, and it *really* doesn't mean we should spend the rest of our lives pushing people away because we're scared we're going to get hurt. It's not fair to us. And, Rory, we *have* to choose ourselves because that's the greatest love story of all. Choosing ourselves, putting that trust into ourselves, and fighting for what *we* want, even if it doesn't make sense to anyone else. Hell, *especially* if it doesn't make sense to anyone else."

She takes a steadying breath, then looks at me. "Is

that how you feel about Lawson? Like you want him even if it doesn't make sense?"

I nod, then whisper, "Yes."

She gives me another knowing smile. "You're in love with him."

I cringe. "Stop saying that."

"No."

"Why not?"

"Because it's funny, for one. And for two, because as much as you don't want to admit it, it's true."

"No." I shake my head. "No, no, no."

Auden lifts a brow. "Rory?"

"No," I say more forcefully this time. "It's not."

Her brow inches higher, and I groan, looking away, because she's right. I *do* love him. I don't know how, I don't know when, and I really don't know why, but I do. Despite my best efforts, I've fallen in love with Lucas Lawson, and I have no clue where to go from here.

"It's okay," she says softly. "It's okay to love him, and it's okay to let him love you in return."

I nod, swallowing down her words. It's okay. I'm okay. Feelings are okay.

"Feelings are normal."

That's what Lawson said, and maybe he was onto something. Feelings *are* normal, and I have big ones for him. I'm not so sure yet what I'm going to do about them, but I do know I'm not ready to go home yet.

I turn to my sister. "So, what's this thing about a club?"

Auden sighs, dropping her head, her shoulders shaking with laughter. "Oh, boy. We are *so* going to need that second drink."

Chapter 23

The Serpents' winning streak came to an end.

We all knew it would eventually, but I didn't expect for it to sting this badly, though I'm sure a lot of that has to do with the fact that I haven't seen Rory in five days. She's clearly been lying to me to keep me away, and that's fine. Well, it's not really *fine*, but I get it. Sort of.

Even though it's easily the hardest thing I've ever done—including the Cup run I made with St. Louis—I'm trying to respect her wishes and give her the space she needs to figure out what she wants from this. I really hope it means she's thinking about what I said, about me loving her, and not thinking of other ways to bail on me.

Fuck, I really, *really* hope it's not that.

I push off the wall of the elevator as the doors slide

open to the twelfth floor. I carry my heavy feet down the hallway, grinning when I hear footfalls on the other side of my door. Even if this thing with Rory doesn't pan out, at least I know Daisy still loves me. That's how I know I'm pathetic, excited about the idea of my dog loving me more than my sort-of girlfriend.

I give myself a shake and push the key into my lock, twisting it. It doesn't swing up like it normally does once I've unlocked it, which means I must have forgotten to latch it before I left. Good thing Daisy isn't smart enough yet to open the door or else I'd have a real problem on my hands.

I try the lock again, and this time it does what it's supposed to. I push the door open and my adorable chocolate Lab is there immediately, wagging her tail and licking at my suit pants.

"Hey, baby girl." I bend down to pet her. She's growing so fast, already standing tall, about halfway to my knees.

She's also learning quickly. She's well-behaved on the leash, hardly ever barks, minds her manners around other pets, and doesn't cause a mess outside of leaving her toys everywhere. With the help of those tips Rory gave me, she's doing *much* better with her attachment issues to the point that I'm able to leave her home all day without worrying.

"Miss me?" I ask as she licks my palms. "Yeah, I

know you did. How about a treat for being such a good girl today?"

More tail wagging.

I rise to my full height and make my way into the kitchen, reaching into the pantry where I keep her goodies. I pull out a jar, then toss down two pieces of bacon-flavored snacks just because I can. She's been good. She deserves it.

I pull off my suit jacket, set it on the counter, and turn to the fridge for a beer. I snag one, popping off the top and lifting it to my lips.

That's when it hits me.

I spin back around instantly, my eyes going to the bag sitting on the counter—the bag I know.

Rory.

"Rory!" I call out, my feet carrying me forward.

Where to, I don't know, but I guess my brain knows where to go, because I'm led right out to the balcony, where the girl of my dreams stands, gazing up at the stars.

"Wednesday," I say softly, and she turns, giving me a smile I've missed so damn much. How five days can feel like a lifetime, I don't know, but it did.

"Lawson."

One word. It's all it takes.

I cross the small terrace, gathering her into my arms. She doesn't protest, winding her arms around me and holding on to me like I'm holding on to her—like I'm afraid to let go. I bury my nose in her neck, inhaling my favorite combination in the world—pear and flowers—and relishing it.

I missed this.

I missed her.

I missed *us*.

When I finally gather enough courage to loosen my grip, I pull back, but only enough to plant my lips on hers. She giggles against me, but the giggle soon fades to a moan as I slide my tongue into her mouth, tasting her as if I've never tasted her before. She twines her hands into my hair, tugging me to her, her body already reacting to my touch as she starts to writhe against me.

I want to be proud, want to be smug, but I can't. Not if I don't know if this is real or not. Not if I don't know if she's back, if she's mine.

We kiss for so long I almost forget we should probably have a pretty serious conversation, so I kiss her more, delaying it just in case. I don't know which one of us comes up for air first, but eventually we part, breathless and panting.

Rory grins up at me. "Hi."

"Hi, Wednesday."

The grin grows. "How are you?"

I laugh. "How am I? *How am I?* Did you really just ask me that?"

She pulls a face. "Yeah, I guess that's a pretty dumb question."

"I'd say."

She rises up on her tiptoes, giving me a quick kiss before settling back down. "So, how's Daisy been?"

I squeeze my eyes shut, shaking my head. "Rory…I can't."

"Can't what?" she asks, and I peel my eyes back open.

"Can't do this."

Her face falls.

"I mean stand here and pretend I'm not waiting on pins and needles for you to tell me why you're here," I explain.

"Oh. That."

"Yeah. *That*," I echo.

"I mean, is it not obvious?"

"No. Not really."

She looks upward. "You have the best view of Seattle."

I roll my lips together, unimpressed by her answer. She sighs, her hands fisting my shirt over and over again. Only then do I notice the tremor in them, like she's nervous, and that makes *me* nervous. She drags her green eyes from my shirt, which she's been burning a hole into, to my face, her gaze catching on my lips momentarily before she brings them higher.

"I…"

I hold my breath, waiting…*hoping*.

"I've been doing some thinking."

"Okay…"

"I've been thinking that maybe…maybe feelings aren't *such* a bad thing after all."

The smallest amount of hope sparks in my chest, and I try hard not to fan the flame.

She sucks in a deep breath, then, all at once, rushes out, "IloveyouLawson."

I'm about ninety-three percent sure I caught what she said, but I ask anyway.

"What?"

"I love you, Lawson!"

That spark? It ignites.

"You…" I tip my head to the side. "You love me?"

"Yes!" she explodes again. "And I have no fucking clue why." The words come out softly, her eyes dropping back to my chest where her fists are gripping my shirt still. "You're obnoxious ninety-nine percent of the time. You drive me nuts. You're nothing at all like what I thought you were like. You're just so annoying and so…ugh. Good. You're *good*, Lawson. Your heart is pure and even when you're being so *you*, you're still good. You're doing it to lighten the mood. To take the attention off other people not because you want the attention, but because you want to help them out. And you do help out so much. With the calendar, with your teammates, with your neighbors, your mother. *Me.* You're a good man, Lawson. So damn good and I don't deserve to have you love me because I've been mean and awful, but you do, and I can't deny anymore that I feel the same way." She finally looks up at me. "I feel the same way."

I grin down at her. "You love me."

"Shut up," she practically growls.

"Nah. You *loooooove* me."

"I do not. I take it back." She turns, trying to run away, but it's pointless. I grab her arm, twisting her back to me. I grip her waist, holding her steady so she can't run. Not this time.

"Ah, ah, ah." I shake my head. "You're not going anywhere after that. You just blurted out that you love me. There's no running away from it. You love me."

"Stop." She buries her face into my chest to hide the blush, and I press a kiss to the top of her head, hugging her closer.

I let her stay like that as long as she needs, because this time, I know she won't run. Not anymore. She told me she loves me, and for Rory to do that, it means she's not going anywhere. I'm glad, because I really don't want her to go anywhere, not tonight or tomorrow or the next day, not next month or next year or even ten years from now. I want her forever. I want her for always.

I want her as mine.

When she finally does pull away, she looks up at me, and I can't help myself—I have to kiss her again. I lay my lips against hers, this kiss much softer and slower than our last.

"Can I ask you something?" I murmur when our mouths have finally stopped moving against each other.

"Anything."

"That night…the one on my balcony…"

"Which balcony?" She raises her brows.

I laugh. "I guess we do have more than one, huh? I mean here, at my apartment."

"Ah, yes. The night of The Balcony Thing."

"The Balcony Thing?"

"Yes. It's the night you said, *For you, Rory, I'd gather every star in this sky and string them high somewhere only for you, just to see you smile like that again.*"

Now it's my turn to raise my brows. "You remember that?"

"Something *that* cheesy? Of course."

"It wasn't cheesy, was it?"

"No, Lawson. It wasn't cheesy. Not at all." She laughs softly. "What is it you want to ask me?"

"Right." I squeeze her closer. "You saw a shooting star."

"I did…"

"And your mouth moved. I saw it because I was watching you. You made a wish, didn't you?"

"Well, yeah." She shrugs. "It's kind of customary. See a star, make a wish."

"Right. So…"

"What did I wish for?" I nod, and she gasps. "Lawson! You're not supposed to ask people that. It goes against wish rules."

"I know, I know. And I didn't then, but I am asking now…"

Her face transforms into a smile, the kind that says, *Do you really have to ask?*

"You, Lawson," she finally says. "I wished for you. And truthfully, I'd do it all over again."

What I don't tell her is, that night, I saw a shooting star too, and I wished for what's right here in my arms —her.

Chapter 24

RORY

"Remind me again why you *need* ice cream at two o'clock in the afternoon?"

"Whoa, whoa, whoa. This was not *my* idea. All I said was I had a bad morning, and you said, *What flavor?* Now, here we are."

"Oh, right. That is how that went, huh?"

I laugh into the phone. "That's exactly how it went."

"It's because I like spoiling you."

"You do it too much."

"There's no such thing as *too much* when it comes to you, Wednesday."

His words zing right through me. It's been two weeks since I showed up at his apartment and confessed that his feelings for me weren't unrequited. Since then, he's told me no less than five times a day how much he loves me. It's a lot. Entirely too much, no matter what he says.

Yet…I don't think I'll ever tire of it. How could I when this man is moving mountains for me, buying me pints of ice cream in the middle of the day because I had a rough morning here at the clinic?

"You're lucky it's not a game day and I'm already done signing jerseys and pucks for the afternoon. That game-used one better go for some good dough. I have a bet with Keller that my signature will sell for more than his."

"Wait, people *bid* on items signed by you?"

"Yeah, baby, you're dating a hockey player. People are kind of obsessed with me."

"Are they, or are you just obsessed with yourself?"

"Well…"

I grin because we both know the answer is *definitely* the latter. "That's what I thought."

"If it makes you feel any better, I love you more than I love myself. And I love myself *a lot*."

"Thank…you?"

His warm laugh fills my ears. "You're welcome. I— Daisy, no. No. Don't pee on that kid!"

"You have Daisy with you?"

"*That's* your question? Not why is she *peeing* on a kid?"

"Veterinarian, remember? I've seen dogs pee on babies before. This is just another day for me."

Casey appears at my door, nodding along with what I've just said. She knows. She's witnessed it entirely too many times, just like I have.

"God, your resilience is so fucking hot." He lets out a low growl that has me squeezing my thighs together. Sure, I might have woken up next to him this morning and had two incredible orgasms before coming into work, but it doesn't stop me from wishing he were here right now so I could show him just what he does to me. "Have I told you that?"

"Maybe, but feel free to go on."

Casey clears her throat, pulling my attention again. She's lingering, which means she must need me for something. I tip my head her way, silently asking, *What's up?*

"Oh, I thought you'd never ask," Lawson says before taking a deep breath like he's about to spend the next two minutes straight talking without a break. Knowing him, he likely is.

Casey points toward the front and mouths, *Need you.*

"Well, for starters," my boyfriend says, "the sounds you make when I have my tongue between your legs, pushing into your pu—"

"Actually, hold that thought." I cut him off not because I don't want to hear what he has to say—I really, really do—but because this conversation will require my full attention…and maybe some privacy.

"Aw, come on. I was just getting to the good stuff."

I chuckle, mainly because there is no doubt in my mind that Lawson has his bottom lip stuck out right now, like he's put out by me cutting this conversation short.

"I promise we can finish this later when you get here."

"Oooh, office sex. Nice. You know, I've been wondering how hot it would be to bend you over your desk and fuck you senseless."

Oh god. I've certainly thought about it before—who hasn't?—but I can't think about it *now*, not when I need to work. But before I can stop him, he continues.

"Think you could be quiet enough so your employees wouldn't hear you? Or do you care? You definitely didn't when I had you on my cabin balcony."

The urge to say fuck work is so strong I have to grip my desk to hold me in my chair and stop myself from fleeing the office and meeting him wherever he is so he can take me home and we can spend the rest of the day in bed, just me and him and nothing else.

"Lucas…"

He makes another low noise. "I know, I know. I'm riling us both up. I'm terrible."

Only it doesn't *sound* like he thinks he's terrible. He

knows exactly what he's doing, and as much as I hate it because it's so mean, I love it too.

"I'm grabbing your pint now. I'll see you in ten."

"The one with—"

"The cookie center. I know, Wednesday. I love you."

"I love you, too." I surprise myself with how effortlessly the words roll off my tongue, even more with how much I mean them.

After talking with Auden, I felt like a fool. How could I have been so blind before? How could I have not seen it? All the signs were there. Everything pointed at the obvious. Why couldn't I just admit to it?

It took some time—and a lot of self-reflection—but the second I pushed my key into Lawson's door, I knew without a doubt there was no going back, not only because I was there but because I didn't *want* to go back.

I knew he was it for me.

I knew I was ready.

I knew I was madly in love with Lawson.

I *know* I *am* madly in love with him.

A wave of giddiness rolls through me as we end our call because it means I'm one step closer to seeing him again. I just have to figure out what's going on with Casey first.

I put my cell back into my desk drawer, then rise to my feet. "What's up?" I ask, crossing my office.

"There's an older gentleman out there asking for Daisy."

My steps falter. "D-Daisy? As in…"

Casey nods. "Yeah, I thought it was strange too, so I wanted to come get you. Just in case, you know?"

I give myself a mental shake, straightening my shoulders as Casey steps aside to let me through, following behind me as I make my way to the front of the clinic. There's no way he means our Daisy. He can't.

I step into the main lobby. There are patients scattered around, one holding a cat and the other a small poodle, but they aren't what capture my attention.

The small, fragile-looking man stands in the center of the room. He's shorter than me, his back hunched over a beat-up walker that's decorated with stickers and a basket full of what looks to be mail. He sports a flannel shirt and polka-dot bow tie. His jeans, which look like they're two sizes too big, are barely being held on by suspenders, and two stark white tufts of hair stick out of the sides of a bowler hat.

Frankly, he's adorable, and I'm dying to know why he's in my office asking after Daisy. I grin, making my way toward him.

He peeks up at me, his own crooked grin forming. "You the lady owner?"

I fight back a laugh. "Yes, I'm the owner, Rory. Heard you wanted to speak with me. How may I help you today?"

"Rory? Like that smart kid? You know, the one with the mom who talks too fast?"

"Yes, just like Rory from *Gilmore Girls*," I tell him, even though it's not true.

He lights up. "That's it! Man, I love those ladies, but they wear me out the way they talk so fast. That mom…the older one? Well, she ain't really all that old to me. Maybe to a young woman like yourself, but she's still a spring chicken to us truly old folk."

"Emily?"

"Yes, yes." He nods. "Emily. She sure is a looker, ain't she? A firecracker too."

"She is."

He shakes his head, his eyes glazed over like he's remembering bits and pieces from the show. I'm surprised he knows *Gilmore Girls*, but I love that he does. It's endearing, just like the grin that's still plastered to his face.

"Well, it's nice to meet you, Mr…"

"Walter," he provides. "You can call me Walter. None of that mister mumbo jumbo. Makes me sound old."

I suppress my laugh—but only barely. "Nice to meet you, Walter. What brings you in today?"

"Ah, right," he says, lifting one hand off his walker and slicing it through the air slowly like he's cutting through mud. "I came because I found this flier for my dog."

His what?!

Slowly, he reaches down into his basket and produces a sheet of paper, and sure enough, it has a picture of Daisy from several months ago. But that can't be the case. All the signs were there that she was dumped.

Maybe...Maybe I had it wrong.

"Are you sure?"

"I'm sure. This my little Angel."

Angel. I can't help but smile. That's what I've called her so many times over these last few months, all the months I've cared for her and treated her, loved her like she was my own.

She is mine. She's Lawson's.

She's *ours*.

"You see, my hips ain't what they used to be, and she escaped. Ran right out of my house, and I didn't even realize it until the next day. Angel was a gift from my neighbor who moved after the pups were born. Nobody else has moved into the apartment yet, and I can't get around like I used to. I've been looking since she went missing and just happened upon this flier at the post office and well…"

He trails off, his chest heaving, winded from his speech. I wait for him to catch his breath, taking him in more. Not to age shame him, but…well, he's old, too old to be taking care of a young dog like Daisy. He's hardly able to stand here and talk. There's no way he can give her the proper care she needs.

The bell over the door chimes loudly, and as if she knows we're talking about her, Daisy comes bounding over the threshold, darting right past Walter and straight to me.

"Angel!" the old man yells, but Daisy doesn't listen. She's too busy trying to climb up my legs.

"Daisy, down," I instruct. "Down."

She listens, settling back onto her butt and staring up at me, her tongue wagging as she pants with excitement.

"Wednesday," Lawson says, sidestepping Walter and pressing a kiss to my cheek. "I brought your ice cream—cookie center—*and* a slice of cake because I could tell you're stressed and—what's wrong?" He rears his head back, looking down at me, brows wrinkled with concern. "Whose ass am I kicking?"

I nod toward Walter.

Lawson glances over at the old man, then looks back at me. "Uh, look, Rory, I love you *a lot*, but I'm not so sure I'm comfortable throwing hands with an old man. I'm Lawless, but not *that* Lawless."

I laugh, patting his chest. "I don't want you to fight him. He's… Well…" I look down at Daisy, who is staring up at us, then back to Lawson. "This is Walter. He says Daisy is his."

"He what?" Lawson tugs on Daisy's leash, tucking the dog back behind his legs like this little old man is going to snatch her up and sprint away with her. I'd laugh if I wasn't so worried about the same thing.

"It's true. This Daisy of yours is *my* Angel."

He recounts the same story he told me, and as he talks, it becomes clear how Lawson feels about this. He feels terrible for taking Angel/Daisy away from him, but he doesn't want to lose her. It's the same way I feel.

"Angel…" Walter says, bending as much as he can, and Daisy tips her head to the side, her ears perking up.

Lawson loosens his hold on her leash, allowing her more freedom, and sure enough, she inches closer to Walter. Her steps are tentative, but they change the second her nose touches his hand. Then she's licking him like crazy, snuggling closer to him.

And my heart breaks.

It breaks because this *is* Angel, which means Daisy isn't ours. What are we supposed to do? What does this mean? Not just for us, but for Daisy, who has known only us for most of her life.

"Oh, Angel. I've missed you. I've—oh, ow!" Walter grabs his hip with one hand and then his walker with the other.

Lawson springs into action, helping stabilize Walter. The older man groans as he's steered toward a chair, closing his eyes on a soft whine as he settles down. Daisy sits at his feet, looking up at him with worry, much like the way Lawson is staring down at him. He peeks over at me, and I see it all over his face.

There is no way he can take care of Daisy, not like this.

"Are you all right?" Lawson asks Walter. "Can we get you anything?"

Walter waves him off. "Nah, nah. I'm okay, kid. Don't you worry about me. I'm—oh, who am I kidding? I'm not okay. I'm old as dirt." He looks down at Daisy. "You don't want an old fart like me taking care of you. You don't need that. I can hardly get around, and I don't have anyone nearby who can help. Heck, if I could afford it, I'd move into that fancy place they got up the road for old folks like me, and I'd have to give you up anyway. Maybe this just wasn't meant to be."

Daisy knocks her head against his leg, comforting him. He pets her, letting out a long, heavy breath.

I dare a peek over at Lawson, who is watching the

exchange like I am. My boyfriend catches my eye, and I see his wheels turning already.

"Hey, Walter. We didn't get a chance to be properly introduced. I'm—"

"Lucas Lawson. I know who you are, son. You're on a six-game point streak, flying all over that ice and checking left and right. I like your grit."

Lawson smiles. "I like you, Walter. But I—"

Walter holds his hand up. "You don't have to say it. I know it." He looks back down at Daisy. "My little Angel, you're better off with these two, you know that?"

She licks at his hand like she agrees. While it makes me sad for Walter, I agree too. He's in no condition to be taking care of her. Hell, I'm not even sure he's in a condition to be taking care of himself, either.

Walter looks between me and Lawson, then sighs. "How long have you had her?"

Lawson swallows coarsely. "Christmas Eve."

"Christmas E—oh, wow. That was about a week after she took off. I…" He hangs his head, shaking it slowly. "She's yours. She's not mine. Angel…she belongs with you, not with me."

"Walter…" My throat constricts, and my eyes begin to burn. I hate this, but I know it's right.

He looks up at me. "It's all right, doc. Really. I want what's best for her, and it's you. She belongs here." He sighs, then reaches down to run his fingers through Daisy's soft fur again. "I guess this is goodbye, Angel."

I choke back the sob that's lodged in my throat, and Lawson doesn't miss it. He rises, wrapping me in his arms and pressing a kiss to my forehead.

"I'll talk to him. Go take a breather, baby," he whispers before moving his lips to my cheek. "Go."

I nod, not even bothering to argue. I've witnessed a lot of pain during my time as a veterinarian and am usually fairly numb to it, but even I have my limits. Apparently, this is one of them.

I step into the hallway, just out of view of the waiting room as Lawson deals with Walter. I don't know how long I stand there, barely holding back tears, before Lawson finally comes around the corner, Daisy trotting along beside him.

He places his hand on my hip and gives me a gentle push forward toward my office. Once inside, he closes the door, then lets go of Daisy's leash and gathers me into his arms, and just like that, everything feels right in the world again. Yes, I'm still sad for Walter, but having Lawson's arms around me is an instant relief.

"Feelings are normal, Wednesday," he tells me in a low voice. "So, if you need to feel whatever you're feeling, it's okay. I'm not here to judge. I'm just here."

But I don't cry. I just let Lawson hold me. Help me. *Heal me.* Just like he did when I broke down in here before.

I didn't know it then, but that was the moment I fell for him, when he didn't even bat an eye at my crying and just held me. When he didn't judge. When he was simply there for me, like he is right now, like I know he will be no matter what.

This man will do anything for me: buy me ice cream in the middle of the day, hold me when I break down, call me out when I'm being too bratty, worship my body and make me feel like the most beautiful woman on the planet, and take care of me even when I don't ask him to. Lucas Lawson loves me…and I'm going to let him.

After several minutes of us just holding on to one another, I pull back, looking up at him. Like so many times before, my heartrate picks up at the sight of him. Because of him. *For* him.

And I know…I know no matter what, no matter how scared I am, no matter how often I want to run away from whatever it is I'm feeling…I won't. Not when I have him looking at me the way he is.

"What?" he asks quietly, the corners of his lips twitching.

"You're totally going to pay for that man to move into an assisted living facility, aren't you?"

"What? I don't know what you're talking about." He scoffs, dragging me to him once more, burying his face in my neck like he's trying to hide from his good deed, but I know.

I know he's going to pay for it. He's going to take care of Walter, not because he feels like he has to, but because he genuinely wants to. Because his heart is just that big.

I was wrong about Lawson all those months ago. He's not just some playboy. He's not just some jock. He's more than that. He's good, and he's all mine.

"Lucas?"

"Yes?" he asks, pulling back.

"I love you."

He sighs, gathering me closer once again, resting his forehead against my own. "I wish we had a star right now."

"Why?"

"So I…"

"Yes?"

"So I could make a wish to make you mine forever," he whispers, almost like he's afraid to say it any louder for fear of scaring me off.

"Well, that'd be a silly waste of a wish."

"It would?"

"Yes, Lawson." I press my lips to his in a soft kiss. "I'm already yours."

"Really?"

I nod. "Forever."

Those damn blue-gray of his bore into me, looking for a sign of a lie, of me running, that I don't mean it, but I do. I mean it more than I've ever meant anything before. When he sees that, he slants his mouth over mine, kissing me softly and tenderly like we have all the time in the world, and I guess we do.

Because this? Lawson? It's real, and I'm not running away from it. Not this time. Feelings are normal, and I have big ones for him.

"Forever, Wednesday," he whispers against my lips. Then he starts our kiss over again.

Epilogue

LAWSON

"Daisy, no! Leave Duke alone."

She looks up at me with those eyes of hers I struggle to say no to, but I don't let her win this time. With a huff, she drops Duke's ear from between her teeth, snuggling back against her new baby brother who is already growing way too fast.

Last month, someone dropped off a puppy at the doors of the clinic, and after one look at the dog, we knew—he was ours. We took the little guy in and are now a bursting family of five with me, Rory, Hades, Daisy, and Duke.

It's the first time I've thought about moving out of my apartment since I got it. It's not that I don't love where I live, but it's getting kind of cramped with all the dog and cat toys lying around. Besides, I think getting a house just a little outside the city wouldn't be

so bad. That way, we could see the stars a bit clearer…
and maybe have a little more privacy on the balcony.

"Shit, man, those dogs are cute as hell." Fox tips his
beer back and takes a healthy swig. "I wish I could
have a dog, but my lease won't allow it."

"That should be a crime," I declare.

"Should it? Those things shed and cause chaos
wherever they go," says Keller, always the buzzkill.

"Do you like *anything*, Kells, or are you just here to
shit on everyone's good time?"

He shrugs, unbothered by the accusation.
"Someone's gotta bring a dose of reality to the
situation."

"Don't worry, it'll always be you." Locke pats him
on the back, earning himself a glare from the enforcer.

"Or you're just a big dick."

"Big dick with a big dick."

"Not what I heard."

"Aw, is your mom talking about me again, Lawsy?
Tell her I said hi." The asshole winks at me, and I push
off the counter, moving toward him.

Hutch sticks his arm out, stopping me. "Can we
not fight? Especially not in my brand-new house?
Auden will murder both of you if you damage
anything."

I clench my jaw, annoyed he's won this round, but
settle back against the counter.

"This really is a nice place," Fox says, looking around the expansive kitchen. It's bright and modern with a touch of vintage flair. It reminds me a lot of The Sinclair Hotels we stay at during the season. "Auden has a real eye for this shit."

"You don't build a billionaire-dollar company if you don't." Hutch grins, clearly proud of his girlfriend. They spent the summer building this place and just finished it up last week, and I have to admit I'm excited about it. Now we'll have a good meeting place for the Serpents Singles Club.

"Is this what she's working on now that she's sold her company? Residential stuff?"

"She hasn't decided for sure yet. Think she's just taking it a day at a time still after busting her ass for so many years. But she loved designing this, so who knows? Maybe it could turn into something for her."

"Think she could help us with a place?"

"Yeah, definitely. Are you moving?"

I shrug. "Thinking about it. Nothing official yet because I don't know what Rory would say, but with the dogs now, my apartment is getting a little full. Wasn't exactly planning on moving someone in when I got the place."

"But now you are because you're in looooove," Fox singsongs, then kisses the air.

Locke joins in too, and it takes Hutch all of three

seconds to start doing the same. The only one not poking fun at me is Keller, who is standing there with his arms crossed looking salty as usual, and Hayes is missing from our pre-season gathering.

"For the record, I think it's ridiculous you had us form this little club, then broke the damn rule," Keller gripes.

I shrug, because I don't care if this was my idea and I didn't follow through on it. I'd do it again and again if it meant having Rory. For her, I'd do anything.

I slide my eyes over to her. She's sitting in the living room with Auden and her best friend, Lilah. They're laughing about something. Rory's head is thrown back, and she looks as gorgeous as ever. Happy. Relaxed. If I wasn't worried she'd rip my nuts off, I'd march over there right this instant and press my mouth to hers, claiming her in front of the world.

After the season ended, I took Rory to meet my mother, and they hit it off just as I suspected they would. Then we spent the summer wrapped up in nothing but one another. If we weren't in bed laughing and lounging and making love, we were taking weekend trips to the cabin or down to Portland just to explore. We hiked, drove the Highway 101 Loop more times than I can count, took so many pictures I had to go out and buy a camera for our adventures, and simply had fun with each other. I wasn't on social media. Hell, I hardly even checked the group chat. Rory took up all my time, and I wouldn't have it any other way.

Besides, I needed the break after the disappointing end of last season. The Serpents lost the Wild Card spot by one game, and it was a brutal loss. I thought for sure we could do it with Coach Smith backing us, but we just couldn't make it happen.

Next year, though, we got this. I can feel it in my bones.

"Lawsy?"

"Hmm?" I ask, turning back to Fox. "What's up?"

"I said, how do you feel about the whole Hayes thing?"

"What Hayes thing?"

Fox's eyes widen. "You don't know?"

"Know what?" I look at my teammates, who are all wearing varying expressions of unease. "Oh shit. What happened?"

"He spent his summer in court."

My brows shoot up. "He did? Fuck. What'd the idiot do this time?"

Fox pulls out his phone and then shoves it in my face. On the screen is an image of Hayes, but that's not all.

There's a kid, a little girl with dark hair who looks to be about six or seven. Either she's doing a really good Keller impression or she's genuinely unhappy, because she isn't smiling. In fact, there's no light behind her big blue eyes at all.

"Who is that?"

Fox shrugs, tucking his phone back into his pocket. "Don't know her name yet, just that she's sticking around."

I whip my head back. "Sticking around? Is she…"

The goalie nods. "Yeah. Looks like the new kid isn't such a kid anymore. He's a dad."

Bonus Scene

LAWSON

"Fuck, baby. I wish you could see yourself right now." I press my thumb against the metal of the plug that's fit snuggly inside Rory's ass. "Can't wait to see this beautiful hole stretched around my cock."

"You won't if you don't hurry up," my girl says.

"So impatient," I murmur.

Her backtalk quickly turns to moans when I tap the metal once again.

"Holy fuck." She groans loudly. "I can feel that *everywhere*. Please, Lucas. Fuck me already."

I chuckle darkly, loving how vulnerable she is just a little too much.

It's not often I have the upper hand when it comes to Rory, but right now, with her ass in the air and a plug deep inside of her? I have the advantage.

She is entirely at my mercy, and I fucking love it.

If the way she's wiggling back toward me is any indication, she loves it too.

"Lawson…"

I lift my hand and land a hard blow to one of her cheeks.

She lets out a loud cry, but there's no pain in it. It's pure pleasure.

"What'd I tell you?"

"Lucas," she amends. "It's Lucas when you're inside me. But you're not inside me. You're—"

I use her distraction to my benefit and begin pulling the plug out.

She whimpers with need as I tug the metal free inch by inch. When it's finally loose, I don't waste a second, pressing my already lubed cock against her hole. The swollen head slips in with ease, and we both sigh.

With how my cock is sliding into her with such little resistance, I'd say she's perfectly prepared.

"Fuck, fuck, fuck, *fuck*," she chants as I watch her ass swallow my cock. Our silky gray sheets are fisted into her hands, and she's taking deep breaths, but she's doing good.

"That's it, baby," I tell her softly, massaging her cheeks that are red from my palms. "You're doing so fucking good. This ass was made for my cock, Rory. You feel incredible."

It's almost too good. I'm about five seconds away from spilling my load inside of her and have to do everything I can to not. We've been working toward this for too long, and there is no way it will be over in mere minutes because I can't control myself.

The last thing I expected tonight when I got home from losing our second game in a row was to find Rory bent over the kitchen counter wearing nothing but my jersey and the plug.

I didn't even bother taking off my shoes. I simply dropped to my knees behind her and showed her with my tongue how much I appreciated her, licking her cunt and her ass until she was begging for more. It was only then that I carried her to the bedroom, set her on the bed on all fours, and undressed so I could properly worship her.

That was half an hour ago.

Thirty minutes of pure fucking torture.

Now this on top of it? Her asshole squeezing my cock so fucking tight I think my dick could break off? Her moans filling the room? Her pleas and her eagerness?

If I were to blow my load right now, I'd say I have a good reason to.

"Is there more?"

Is there more? Is she serious?

"I'm halfway in."

"Oh, god. I can't, Lucas. I can't. I—"

I press into her again, and she lets out a loud groan when I bottom out inside of her ass.

"Holyshitohmygodyesfuckthatfeelssodamngood."

It might be twelve words, but it comes out as one, and I don't blame her one bit. I'm having a hard time keeping it together myself.

"Rory?"

"Hmm?"

"Are you okay?"

"*Yes.*" The single word isn't said…it's *breathed*, like she can barely remember how to push air out of her lungs.

"Talk to me," I instruct. "I need to know if this is okay."

"Okay? *Okay?*" She groans loudly. "God, Lucas, I've never felt so fucking full before. This is more than okay."

I grin. "Yeah?"

"Yes. Now, stop smirking at your accomplishments and fuck me."

I laugh, loving that even when she's completely exposed like this, she's still Rory.

"Oh my god, I can feel that too." She lets out a soft whine. "Move, Lawson. Please."

Unable to deny her or myself any longer, I heed her pleas and rock into her.

She's tight and slick and so, so, *so* fucking magnificent as I pick up my pace, her soft moans letting me know she's enjoying this as much as I am.

"So beautiful." I rut into her. "So tight. So fucking good. So… *mine.*" She releases a soft cry, and I smack at her ass once more. "Say it, Rory. Tell me."

"Yours, Lucas. This pussy is yours. This ass is yours. *I'm* yours."

"You're fucking right you are," I growl, slamming into her.

And she lets me, bucking against me like she can't get enough as I work her over, using her and loving every second of it.

"Please…" she begs softly, and I know what she's getting at.

She's close, and so am I. Hell, I've *been* close. But now my legs are shaking, and sweat is sliding down my back. I'm holding back so much it's almost starting to hurt.

I need to come soon.

"Touch your cunt, baby. Get there with me because I don't know how much longer I'm going to be able to hold on."

I don't even get the whole sentence out before her hand is between her legs and she's rubbing hurried circles over her clit.

Her teeth sink into her bottom lip, her head thrown back as she fingers herself, and I pound into her.

She's never been more beautiful, and that's saying something because I think Rory is *always* beautiful, even when she wakes with messy hair and drool dried to her face and morning breath that smells like she's been sucking on cheese all night long. She's still stunning even then.

It takes only five more strokes for us both before she's clenching around me, her orgasm rocking through her, and the moment her ass squeezes me, I'm done for, spilling into the condom in a way I never have before.

Euphoric.

It's the only word I can think of to describe the moment.

Just utter fucking euphoria.

Rory slumps forward, her breathing labored and her legs shaky as I slowly pull out of her. She winces, and so do I because I hate the idea of hurting her, but when I'm fully out, I don't miss the way she pushes back like she's already seeking me out again.

I leave the bed just long enough to dispose of the condom and set the plug in the bathroom so we can clean it later, then grab a wet washcloth for my girl.

When I return to the bed, I slide it over her backside, cleaning up the mess we've made, then toss it aside before wrapping her in my arms and tugging her close.

I kiss the back of her neck over and over as I run my hand over every inch of her that I can reach. She hums softly, loving the closeness.

I don't know how long we stay like that before she rolls over, facing me.

"Hi," I say once she's settled.

She giggles. "Hi."

I kiss her nose because I can't help myself. "How was your night?"

"Oh, you mean, how was it getting fucked in the ass? Splendid."

I laugh, shaking my head because *of course* she would be so direct. "You're something else, Wednesday."

"So I've heard." She rolls her eyes, then winces as she shifts around.

I frown. "Are you okay?"

"Yeah, just a little sore, is all."

"Your…"

"Ass? No. Well, at least not the part *you* think it is."

"The spankings?"

She nods. "But I like them, so don't you dare stop." She narrows her eyes on me, yet there's no playfulness behind the gesture. She means it.

"Yes, ma'am," I tell her, leaning forward to give the

tip of her nose another small kiss. "Spankings are staying."

"And the anal. I liked that too."

I laugh. "Noted. Butt stuff is strictly *on* the table, then."

"Hmm," she hums, letting her eyes drift shut, almost like she can't help it.

That's how we stay for far too long—Rory's eyes closed and me watching her.

"It's creepy when you watch me sleep."

"I don't do it that often," I argue.

She peels her eyes open. "Liar."

I don't even bother countering with a response. We both know it's pointless because we both know I *do* watch her often.

Can I be blamed when the moonlight is casting such shadows over her? When she looks so gorgeous? So content? It's impossible not to watch her.

Just like it's impossible not to love her.

It's been just under a year since that fateful Christmas Eve when I found Daisy, and not a moment has passed when I haven't thanked whatever entity I need to for the gift of stepping into Rory's clinic.

Not just because she lets me do all the dirty, dirty things to her I want.

No. It's far more than that.

It's *her*. The way she laughs. The way she smiles.

The way she rolls her eyes at me and the way she isn't afraid to call me out on whatever bullshit I'm spewing.

The way she *loves*.

Because for someone who was so scared to admit she loved me, she loves hard. Fiercely. And she doesn't let a day go by where she doesn't remind me of it, either.

"Are you going to sleep?"

"Hmm," she answers again, snuggling deeper against the pillow.

Oh, yeah, she's about out for sure.

I lean over, pressing my lips to hers, and despite how tired she clearly is, she kisses me back, even whining when I pull away.

I chuckle against her. "Good night, Rory."

"Night, Lucas. Thank you."

"For anal?"

She smiles. "And for loving me."

"It's easy. It's *me* who should be thanking *you* for loving me."

She wrinkles her nose, her eyes closing once more. "Yeah, you really should. You're pretty annoying."

"You love it when I'm annoying."

"I do," she mumbles, nearly asleep already. "I really, really do. Just...don't tell anyone. Feelings are gross."

I laugh. "Your secret is safe with me, Wednesday."

Then her soft snores fill the room, and I fall asleep with a smile, something that's becoming a regular occurrence.

And it's all because of Rory.

THE END

Other Titles by Teagan Hunter

SEATTLE SERPENTS SERIES

(steamy hockey romantic comedies)

Body Check

Face Off

Delayed Penalty

CAROLINA COMETS SERIES

(steamy hockey romantic comedies)

Puck Shy

Blind Pass

One-Timer

Sin Bin

Scoring Chance

Glove Save

ROOMMATE ROMPS SERIES

(romantic comedies)

Loathe Thy Neighbor

Want to be part of a fun reader group, gain access to exclusive content and giveaways, and get to know me more?

Join Teagan's Tidbits on Facebook

Stay on top of my new releases, cover reveals, sales, and more by visiting:

www.teaganhunterwrites.com

My husband, Henry. You're my number one cheerleader, and I couldn't imagine doing this crazy career without you by my side. Thank you for always being my sounding board. Always and forever.

Laurie. I'm not sure I'd be still be writing without you. Thanks for always giving me that extra push I need and for always, always, always having my back.

My editing team. Caitlin, Julia, Judy… You ladies are the BEST. I'm never letting you leave me.

Kim and Nina and the VPR team. Cannot stress enough how there is no way in hell I would be where I am now without your incredible guidance. Lucky doesn't even begin to cover it. Neither does thank you. I owe you BIG TIME.

Shannon, Katie, and Emily. These covers are EVERYTHING! Your talent astounds me. Thank you for making this series look so damn good!

Tidbits. You have my heart.

sMother. Thanks for always believing in me.

Hockey. I can't get enough of you. Thanks for always being there when I need a break. Sure, you make my heart race entirely too often, but it's the good kind. Usually.

You. I hope this book gave you a bit of escape we all deserve.

With love and unwavering gratitude,

Teagan

TEAGAN HUNTER writes steamy romantic comedies with lots of sarcasm and a side of heart. She loves pizza, hockey, and romance novels, though not in that order. When not writing, you can find her watching entirely too many hours of *Supernatural, One Tree Hill,* or *New Girl.* She's mildly obsessed with Halloween and prefers cooler weather. She married her high school sweetheart, and they currently live in the PNW.

www.teaganhunterwrites.com

9 781959 194712